OUR DANCING I

Lucy English was born in Sri Lanka and grew up in London. She studied English and American literature at the University of East Anglia and has an MA in Creative Writing from Bath Spa University. She works for a charity, is a performance poet and the mother of three children. Her earlier novels, *Selfish People* and *Children of Light*, are also published by Fourth Estate.

OUR DANCING DAYS

Lucy English

FOURTH ESTATE • *London*

First published in Great Britain in 2000 by
Fourth Estate Limited
6 Salem Road
London W2 4BU
www.4thestate.co.uk

1 3 5 7 9 10 8 6 4 2

'Each Moment' by the Incredible String Band. Words by Robin
Williamson. Reproduced by kind permission of IMP Ltd.
Lyrics from 'Astral Weeks' by Van Morrison.

A catalogue record for this book is available from the British Library.

ISBN 1-84115-241-2

Typeset by MATS, Southend-on-Sea, Essex
Printed in Great Britain by Biddles Ltd, Kings Lynn & Guildford

This was our dancing day
So even those with nothing to celebrate
Shook off their unfathomable gloom
And were lost with us in that meadow.

From 'Albion' in *Spirit Level*, a book of poems
by Andrew Bell

Chapter One

Bristol is built on several hills. In Totterdown there is a street that seems to cling to the steepest edge of one on a high embankment above Temple Meads Station. Tessa's studio was on the top floor of a house in this terrace. From here it wasn't difficult to entertain the idea that one was floating above the city like the hot-air balloons do on a fine day, but it also wasn't difficult to imagine the whole street of houses slipping over the embankment; the gardens already lay at perilous angles. It was with this feeling of landing in front of the 10.45 from platform 6 that caused Tessa to stop working and look out of her studio window.

The ten forty-five gathered speed and whirred past harmlessly, but Tessa still felt she had fallen beneath its wheels. She also knew why she felt like this. She had that morning received a letter from her ex. It had just stopped raining and there was a break in the clouds. Sunlight fell onto the other side of Bristol, emphasising the lumpy forms of the university building, the glass edges of the city office blocks, and, pointing up between, the spires of Christchurch and St Mary Redcliffe; Bristol's skyline was urban but not unpleasant. She could also see the parklands of Ashton Court and the gardens of Brandon Hill, for it was May and the trees were blossoming and fresh.

Smudgy sunlight on pinkish stone, pastel blue between moving clouds, it's definitely a watercolour, thought Tessa turning from her window and back to her art, but her canvas was dark and red and large with jagged forms like a gaping dragon or a charred accident.

She poked at her work with a brush dipped in vermilion, but only

1

not savage enough, it's blunted and dead.'

always had this effect on her. Tessa's walls

brooding canvases; she sold approximately

The rest of her work lay in folders, because

lustrator; watercolours of gardens, country scenes,

, for calendars, birthday cards and coffee-table books.

urray who owned the gallery in Bath where she had first

ited fourteen years ago and they had been lovers for eight of

em.

Murray Maclean now lived in Edinburgh reinventing his Scottish roots. He had opened another gallery there, mostly for young Scottish painters. He still had the gallery in Bath but he showed only an indifferent attitude towards it, like he showed towards other left-behind projects. And Tessa was another project, she knew that. His letter was like a public relations handout, with a list of all the artists who would be exhibiting that summer, what cafés he had visited and who would be coming up for the Festival. His letter was like him, smart and to the point. Murray was in his fifties now, tall and elegant with thick grey hair. At the end he said, 'If you're up for the Festival Claudia and I would love to see you, that is if she isn't too busy buying clothes at Baby Gap.'

Tessa stabbed at her painting again with red paint as thick as a placenta. Right from the start she had said to Murray, 'I don't want kids. Kids drive you mad.' They had stayed with that but when he turned fifty women of child-bearing age became more attractive. Claudia was twenty-nine and had just had his baby in March. He met her some months after he split up with Tessa but that didn't make it any better. 'We'll still be friends,' he said, but he meant, 'I'll still sell your paintings.'

The other letter she had received that morning was from her agents and in an hour's time she had an appointment to see them. Murray had introduced her to Wessex Artists so at least she could be grateful he had given her a living.

*

2

She left for her appointment on her bicycle and in her cycling gear. Her lodger in the basement, whom she had nothing to do with apart from collecting the rent, referred to her as 'that dyke'; but what did she know, she was a chirpy English student, what did she know about sharp-looking forty-six-year-olds?

Tessa was sleek and wiry. Her hair, if it had been long, would have been corkscrew curly but she kept it short. It was dark brown, nearly black and the strands of grey at the front she dyed bright red. She wore black or grey. Trousers never skirts. Boyish casual clothes and sometimes a red velvet scarf. Her appearance was clean-cut and unadorned. She looked like she would prefer a day's cycling to a morning in front of a mirror. She had the taut sun-touched skin of the very fit.

Some women might adopt the boyish look as a tease, 'Guess what, I'm a real girl underneath,' but with Tessa it was more complicated. Her appearance said, 'I'm a woman, but I'm independent,' or more usually, 'Clear off' – but Tessa was not a dyke.

Wessex Artists were on the eleventh floor of a block in the centre of Bristol. The view was panoramic. Tessa waited, watching squalling, reeling seagulls and rain clouds gathering. 'They're ready for you now,' said the secretary.

Coral and Pumpkin looked Tessa up and down. Pumpkin sniffed as if Tessa had arrived fresh from a pig farm.

'Do sit down,' she said.

They were misnamed. Coral was round and squashy in voluminous florals. She had fuzzy hair. It was Pumpkin who more resembled a calcinated sea-creature. They were at least ten years older than Tessa, preserved perpetually in a mould made sometime in the fifties. Nice gals. Pumpkin's suit was tweed-grey like her hair; she was small and neat.

'Did you read the letter?' Her voice reminded Tessa of metal tinging.

'Sure.' Tessa crossed her legs.

'Well, what did you think?' Pumpkin tapped her desk with a pen.

'It's OK.'

Pumpkin's tapping became louder, her mouth pursed.

'I don't know what you expect me to say,' said Tessa after a while; 'I'll do it, you know that.'

'Yes, yes, of course.' Coral was becoming agitated. 'It's just that,' she caught Pumpkin's eye, 'we had a little talk the other day, and eventually, after some time . . . it was a long talk, Tessa . . .'

Pumpkin glared. 'It's your attitude I'm worried about.'

Tessa laughed. 'Come on, Pumpkin. I'll do the work. What is it? Six Christmas cards, the suspension bridge at night, bunny rabbits?'

Pumpkin was silent. Coral fidgeted nervously, wobbling.

Pumpkin patted her skirt. 'You see, Tessa, you're good.' She paused.

'You're very good.' She picked up some papers for emphasis. 'You're in demand and yet . . .'

'Your watercolours are lovely, Tessa, so sensitive,' interrupted Coral, '. . . and yet, you treat it as though it were—'

'Rubbish?' suggested Tessa.

'Your other work won't sell, it won't ever sell.' Pumpkin's voice was steely. 'Especially now that Murray's in Scotland,' she added.

'I . . . don't . . . care,' said Tessa like a two-year-old. It was a manner guaranteed to irritate Pumpkin.

Pumpkin sat up straight and smoothed her skirt again. She threw Coral a look. 'Tell her about the assignment, then.'

'Oh, yes, well, it's really nice . . . last summer do you remember *The Historic Houses of Oxfordshire*? Well, of course you do.' She smiled, regarding Pumpkin with caution. 'They liked your work, said it really made the book . . . so this time they want . . .'

'Seven more books to make a series? Eight more? Fifty more?'

Pumpkin made a hissing sort of noise.

'Er, no, no, Tessa,' Coral said, 'just one more book actually.'

4

Her eyes were on Pumpkin. 'They would like you to do six out of fifteen, so you've got the lion's share. Pumpkin, she's got the lion's share, hasn't she . . . Pumpkin?'

'Yes,' said Pumpkin suddenly; 'six houses, three sketches of each, pencil and wash, there'll also be photographs, you know the format. So you'll do it?'

'Oh, Pumpkin, we didn't say where, did we? Oh, silly us. *The Historic Houses of Suffolk.*'

Tessa's face became uncertain. 'Suffolk?'

'Yes, you know, in the east, Ipswich, Norwich . . .'

'Norwich is in Norfolk, Coral.' Pumpkin took a sheet of paper out of a drawer. 'Choose the ones you want, there's a description of each, ring us tomorrow when you've decided.'

'I'll do it now,' said Tessa briskly; 'I know Suffolk.'

'Oh, do you?' Coral said. 'I went there for a holiday once, years ago, to a pretty place, it was, near the sea. Well, it was on the sea, actually, there was a lighthouse, I think.'

Tessa scanned the list without paying any attention to Coral. It was taking her a long time. Pumpkin looked at her watch.

'Suffolk's lovely,' continued Coral; 'Constable country. Well, I didn't actually go to that bit, but I've been told it's lovely. Where I went it was rather flat . . .'

Tessa handed the list back.

'We'll send you the brief,' said Pumpkin. 'Fleming Hall, Bedingfield; well, I thought you might choose that one. Hengrave, yes . . . Kentwell Hall and Long Melford – don't forget to see the church . . . Lavenham, well, there's plenty there . . . Heveningham . . . wasn't that bought by an Arab? . . . St John's Hall? Oh, I am surprised, Tessa, I thought you might have chosen Ickworth, or Alston Court, or Glenham. It's the smallest one, you know, of minor interest.'

'But it's terribly old,' said Coral; 'actually it's the oldest, isn't it?' She began to look through a folder.

'It's twelfth century,' said Tessa, 'but was enlarged in the fourteenth and then again to its present size in 1585. The windows of the great hall came from a nearby nunnery and are in two different styles, decorated and perpendicular.'

'Oh, I say!' said Coral.

Pumpkin studied the list. 'It doesn't say here about the windows. You know the place, then?'

Tessa stood up to go. 'Actually, I used to live there.'

She cycled back across Bristol in the rain and up the slow climb to Totterdown. She kicked open her front door and clattered the bicycle in the corridor. Why the bloody hell did I take that on? I don't want to go to Suffolk, and go to St John's. Shit! She was soaking wet, and as she threw her wet clothes across the bedroom was confronted with an image of herself first arriving in Bristol after hitching in the rain. She had left Suffolk with nothing, not even a rucksack. She pulled on dry clothes. She was so angry she was close to tears, but it was a long time since Tessa had wept.

I left it all, I left the whole damn lot!

Don had kept sending her things in parcels, and then the money, but she sent it all back. She had bought this house herself with the money she earned from painting and knew every inch of it intimately, since for the last eight years she had scraped and peeled it down to its bones. The house was hers, absolutely hers. Murray had never lived there. Nothing here is yours! She had given up sharing things.

She sat on her bed staring at another of her bleak canvases. Ring up those two bitches, tell them to stuff their assignment! But the hard forms of the painting gave her inspiration; ice and steel, rock and stone, bone. Stone blunts scissors, scissors cut . . . what's scaring you? she thought. It was not part of her present self to be emotional. Murray leaving, Claudia's baby, she had coped with that. It's a job. Paint the damn place then sod off. She thought how completely she had created her environment here, all hers, bare wood furniture, plain walls, cream, white. She knew everything in her house down to the furthest corner of the most

6

hidden cupboard and her mind scanned these places.

Then she remembered the box she had not sent back. It arrived unexpectedly long after the other parcels and she kept it in her last moment of sentimentality. Under the stairs, seven years ago. She searched it out and took it up to her studio, which was the place she felt most inviolate.

Dusty, a letter – 'Dear, dear Tessa, please keep these. One day I hope you will forgive us, Don.' Soppy. Rubbish. She screwed it up. The box was full of photographs. She tipped them on the floor, her life in one heap. There were she and Dee-Dee, spades in hand, smiling in front of the vegetable garden, long hair, wellies, Peruvian jumpers and floppy skirts, stupid clothes for gardening. Don in the orchard in his dressing gown with a basket of apples, smiling. The dressing gown was his coat . . . St John's in the snow and all of them outside, smiling. 'We are the smiling revolution.' A pile of happy people, summer fairs, winter bonfires.

It wasn't like that, thought Tessa . . . And here were she and Don again, in white because that was their wedding. Shit. And she and Dee-Dee swimming in the moat. Tessa felt herself slipping again down the embankment. There were older photographs too; Swinging London, she and Dee-Dee in mini skirts, and now one in black and white, two little girls in a suburban garden, Theresa and Deirdre, puffed sleeves, buckle shoes, arms round each other, smiling . . .

CHAPTER TWO

It was late August, the Saturday before the bank holiday. The weather throughout the summer had been indifferent, some might even have called it rotten, but Tessa did not care for sunshine for with it came droves of people, in summer clothes, soaking up the day like pink sponges, with noisy children, grandmothers, dogs and radios. And at the moment Tessa did not care for people.

She had now been in Suffolk for ten days. The rain had slowed her work, for although she preferred damp landscapes, it was more difficult to sketch satisfactorily under dripping trees. At Heveningham she tried for two hours to draw the ribbon wall, but spent most of the time in the orangery avoiding a thunderstorm.

She was in her hotel room in Bury St Edmunds surveying her work. She was quite pleased. They were rough sketches on rain-blotched paper, but she could see how they could progress. Remember, light on stone mullions, indigo shadows under cedar trees. She scribbled notes on the paper. Remember, wet skies, big clouds. The light, pale gold, could be pale green. Sienna-ripe wheat, barley's softer . . . Tessa had travelled right through Suffolk, from the rolling willow-banked fields of the Essex borders and the Stour valley to the bleaker wheatlands of what is called High Suffolk, which is almost a joke since nothing except church towers are really high in Suffolk, to outside Bury St Edmunds, the hedgeless fields, agribusiness wheat deserts, no weeds, no poppies, no cornflowers. But it's not got worse, thought Tessa, remembering exactly what it was like to be in the middle of a wheatfield, when the far end of it was ages away, and the trees by the ditches seemed tiny. And Tessa paused with this image of herself, 'walking away from the Hall', and as she saw herself becoming tiny in the distance, she felt uneasy and uncertain, for she had yet to go to St John's.

I'm slipping, she thought, and she was tired, for she had worked hard, concentrating on forms and colours and angles and light and the present, always the present, the now of the image in front of her, nothing at all to do with memories. And Tessa felt sad and vulnerable. Ring up P. and C., said one part of her; oh weak, weak, where's your steel? Where's your ice? said another. And she thought of her stark canvases, but they were miles away on the other side of England.

She wrote a postcard to Murray. 'Hope you enjoy the Festival. Couldn't make it this year. I'm on an assignment in Suffolk. Love to Claudia and the kid.' She had never told Murray much about Suffolk and what she did say was rather vague. Oh, I lived there in the seventies with some hippies. Her life before him held little interest for him. He was a man of the present. She licked the stamp. She had a picture of him in her mind at the opening of one of her exhibitions. Murray, in the centre of the room with a group of people around him. He was a tall man. He turned round suddenly to look for her and in that sweeping movement seemed to Tessa like a magician who could conjure up who he wanted, and make disappear who he didn't want. She decided she wouldn't write to him again.

She left her room and went to the abbey gardens; the hotel faced one of the old gatehouses. Bury St Edmunds was lively that Saturday; the market was on, the car parks were full, in the abbey gardens were people enjoying themselves in the manner Tessa found so repugnant. But now she was preoccupied.

The abbey, the burial place of St Edmund, had once been huge, the largest ecclesiastical building in Britain. Its size today would compare to a shopping complex, but there was virtually nothing left of it, eroded since the Reformation by weather, and also by townsfolk who used the place as a quarry; there were many houses in Bury built out of the abbey. Only a few portions of wall and excavated foundations remained. The lumps of stone, to Tessa, were baffling, a piece here, another bit at the far end of the gardens. A sign said 'The Dormitory' – did monks really sleep there? She couldn't imagine it – where? There wasn't anywhere. She stood in the nave by the high altar. Over her head should have been a vaulted roof but instead there was the Suffolk sky with hanging clouds moving slowly. It would have all vanished, thought Tessa, if someone hadn't preserved it. It was time for her to start working.

From Bury St Edmunds she drove east and north, for St John's was close to the Norfolk border. She had hitched up and down this road dozens of times but now the road was wider and faster, by-passing all the villages – the windmill at Stanton; Botesdale and Rickinghall Superior, so close to each other they were quite entangled; Walsham-le-Willows. She was watching the road signs. Harlesdon, with its wide, open street and Georgian houses. Ten miles to go. The road ran alongside the Waveney. Here she felt she must know every tree. Wortwell. It's a job, I'm on a job. Piccadilly Corner. Wasn't that where? . . . Six places, three sketches of each . . . Flixton, the old aerodrome, it's been ploughed up. Well, the pub's been tarted . . . Earsham . . . I waited for a lift there for three hours once. Then just before Bungay she turned off the main road with the lorries and holiday cars going to Lowestoft, into the lanes, into the area called the Saints, where there's a local saying that once you get into them you can't get out, and it seems true, for the roads meander irrationally and the signposts, if you can find them, are confusing. Left, St Margaret's, right St Margaret's. But Tessa was not lost. Here the countryside was open and the sky fell right down to the ground uninterrupted. The road swept round in a huge arc avoiding no apparent obstacle. This was the Saints. Left was St Margaret's, St Michael's, St James, St George, St Lawrence, the other St Margaret's; and right was St John's.

*

10

St John's was barely a hamlet, four cottages and a farm close to the church. Once over the bridge there was no more of it, a truly uneventful place. But across the fields was a group of tall trees which the eye was drawn to as the trees in this area were usually solitary; and as the road turned again the Hall could be seen. Tessa saw it now and felt again the impact, for although the Hall was neither huge nor grand it was imposing.

* * *

Three of them in a car, cruising round Fulham on a hot day.

'What shall we dooo?'

'Come on, Don, you're full of ideas.'

'. . . We could go somewhere.'

'Yeah, what a turn on.'

And then Don said, 'I've got a super idea' and Tessa and Dee-Dee fell about laughing. 'No, honestly, a really good idea . . . I've got a sort of cousin . . .'

'Wow.'

'He lives in the countryside, in an amazing place . . . stop laughing . . . right, you don't believe me, I'll take you there.'

'Don, Don, we believe you . . . mind that lorry! . . . Don, Don? Where are we going?'

'Suffolk.'

Three of them in a car all the way to Suffolk, and Tessa and Dee-Dee sang 'Magical Mystery Tour' and kept saying 'are we nearly there yet?' but as they got further and further from London the joke wore off. They drove for hours beyond Baldock, Royston and Newmarket, for this was when Suffolk was the sleepiest place on earth and nobody ever went there.

They turned the last bend and there was the Hall across the fields. There were more hedges then but it still stood out boldly. The sun shone on its church windows.

Dee-Dee scrambled next to Tessa to get a better look. 'Oh, oh, is this it?'

'Yes.'

'Does he live here by himself? Oh, Don, I'm not smart enough.'

'He won't mind.'

The drive was a mud track full of potholes. There was a collection of crumbling barns. The place seemed derelict. They drove into the courtyard, where weeds grew between brick paving under a huge chestnut tree. Three of them, in crumpled London clothes. Dee-Dee pulled her mini skirt straight, but Tessa just stared.

'What do you think?' said Don. There were weeds growing on the roof.

'It's wild,' said Tessa; 'it's like a dream . . .'

* * *

Tessa, in her cream Morris Traveller, turned into the courtyard. It was neatly gravelled, but the chestnut tree was as massive as ever. Its branches skimmed the roof of restored barns. In front of the house was an area of lawn.

She glanced at her brief. The owners were a Mr and Mrs B. Hallivand. Tessa had always used the side door by the kitchen but she supposed a Mr and Mrs B. Hallivand might not. The main door was in the porch, very like a church porch, two-storied with a tiny room above. Gargoyles gaped. The knocker was twisted brass, heavy. No answer. She knocked again and the noise echoed through the house. She tried the side door, no answer. Shit. She studied the brief. 'Copy of letter sent to Mr and Mrs' etc. 'Thank you for your co-operation in the production of *The Historic Houses of Suffolk*' (in red letters). 'This book will be a unique document examining the most beautiful and,' etc.

'Schedule of work. The artist, Ms Tessa Foolks' (spelt wrongly) 'will arrive at your home on Saturday 24th August at one-thirty promptly.' Typical Pumpkin. It was now one-twenty-five. Tessa waited and smoked a French cigarette, which was something she did in times of extreme stress. St John's was locked and silent.

12

Shit. Stupid rich bums, I should have phoned! She much preferred working at a house not privately owned; at least she could cold-shoulder inquisitors. 'Yes, thank you, it is very good and I've got one more hour to finish it.' You couldn't say that to an owner. They always hovered about making sure you included their favourite meconopsis, or got the patina exactly right on the hautboy. She waited and smoked another cigarette.

Damn you, she said, partly to the house, partly to the Hallivands and also partly to her invading memories, but she was holding them back, concentrating hard; this house, the present, this job. Except at that moment there was no job.

She stared at the house. The stonework had been recently cleaned and was buff-gold, the chimney stacks were straight, there were flower beds alongside the walls. Marguerites, artemesia, not bad choices, well weeded, probably had a gardener. To the left was a brick wall surrounding the orchard. The old apple trees leaning and twisted, they were still there, a good crop of apples coming, no vegetables, that was to be expected.

The grass was closely cut. On it were white metal chairs round a table, old ones, looked French. A striking herbaceous border ran down this side of the house; behind were espalier pear trees. The lawn fell down to the moat. From here it seemed as if the house were completely surrounded by water but in reality the moat was crescent-shaped, the furthest end of it under the tall trees in a dank wilderness. Between the moat and the Hall was a narrow strip of grass. Three doors opened out onto this. It was the most sheltered part of the garden, protected from the winds that always blew across Suffolk, straight from Russia. This narrow lawn led to another enclosed area. Tessa felt proud of the gardens. The Hallivands' beautiful borders would not exist had she not spent nearly ten years in her wellies, chopping, cutting and digging. Gardens were the one thing Tessa still let herself be emotional about and she was actually smiling as she approached the rose garden.

Old roses with trailing stems and heavy flowers, dark red petals

13

on the lawn. In June a deep musky scent only old roses have . . .

There was a door there now. Of course in August there would only be a few blooms, perhaps one or two on the Zépherine Drouhin . . .

There was concrete under her feet and what? . . . at first she couldn't take it in: there was a swimming pool . . .

'The peasants!' shrieked Tessa. She couldn't believe it, what about the Provence rose and the musk rose? The damask roses?

White concrete, flowers in tubs, a square of blue-bottomed swimming pool. Tessa felt sick. The Zépherine Drouhin still climbed the wall, but her garden, her special place, lying on the grass breathing in sweet rose air, her quartered roses of burgundy and darkest crimson, almost purple . . . There were glass doors and a patio with barbecue furniture. I'm going, she thought, but a car was coming.

A maroon Volvo estate turned into the courtyard. Tessa was storming across the orchard. The owner flounced towards her unstably on high heels. They met on the lawn in front of the house.

'I'm so sorry, didn't you get my message?'

'No.' Tessa was obviously furious.

'How dreadful, it's simply unforgivable.'

'Yes, it's unforgivable.' This digs up roses, thought Tessa. It was tall and glamorous, hair unnaturally strawberry-blonde and shiny. It smiled determinedly. 'You see, I had to go to Norwich, there was a snuff box in Elm Hill . . . Bernard's at an auction . . . I phoned the hotel . . . It's so awful when this happens, have you been here long?'

The owner wore silky peach and a face trying to be cheerful but visibly unsettled by Tessa, scowling, in black trousers and a tight T-shirt like a dark urban angel. But Tessa was less angry; she decided this person was not a malicious vandal, more an ignorant one with a high-gloss finish. It offered an elegant hand with pearly fingernails.

14

'How do you do, I'm Mirabelle Hallivand, and you must be the artist, Tessa Fooks.'

'Fulks, they always spell it wrong,' and she smiled.

Mirabelle laughed and threw her head back, showing perfect white teeth. 'Well, here we are . . . What a day . . . and the snuff box was a fake, I could tell at once . . . and you've been waiting, and the help's off . . .'

'I'd better start work,' said Tessa; 'I do have a schedule.'

'Of course, but please, do come in and let me make you some tea.'

What Tessa noticed first as they stepped inside was the familiar smell; wet stone, damp rush-matting and woodsmoke. She always supposed people gave houses their particular odours, but St John's seemed to have one of its own. The porch was not filled with gardening tools, flower pots and muddy boots; on the floor was an exquisite rug.

'This is the great hall,' said Mirabelle, opening a door in the panelling. There were tapestries on the wall. An ornate brass lantern hung from the rafters. 'Make yourself comfortable,' said Mirabelle, showing Tessa an enormous sofa.

There was a grand piano, Persian rugs on the stone floor and large Chinese vases. Mirabelle brought tea in fluted porcelain. She perched on an embroidered chair near the mouth of the huge fireplace.

'So, you're going to paint St John's.'

'Sketches, really, I finish them off later, they'll mostly be for page decorations. Has the photographer come?'

'Last week, he was most charming . . . It's nice to have company, it gets isolated here.' Mirabelle was extremely thin, like a whippet, and had a whippet's habit of trembling. 'Bernard has to go to auctions, you see, he's a dealer.'

'Got a shop, has he?'

Mirabelle laughed extravagantly. 'This is the shop. It's all

15

for sale!' Her gesture included the entire contents of the great hall. 'It's much nicer for clients to decide in a relaxed atmosphere.'

'Do people come out here?' Tessa was amazed.

A tremble ran down Mirabelle's arm into her teacup. 'We don't sell to the popular market, our clients are very discerning.'

Tessa quietly estimated the cost of the rug under her feet. To think they had slept on this floor huddled by the fire.

'I'll have to start work now,' she said.

'So you like painting houses?' said Mirabelle, keen to continue.

'I like painting gardens.'

'Well, we've got lots of those here,' she laughed.

Tessa put down her drink. 'I believe there's a rose garden here, with old roses. I was looking for it earlier . . . some rather rare roses, I thought,' and her brown eyes fixed on Mirabelle.

'Ah . . . well, yes, there was.' Mirabelle's bracelets jangled. 'I'm afraid there was a rather bad winter . . . well, in the end Bernard had the swimming pool.'

'What a shame, I love roses.' Tessa stood up and Mirabelle stood up too.

'It happened before . . . me . . . you see, I'm the second Mrs Hallivand.'

The light through the church windows struck her sideways, emphasising wrinkles under her make-up. In her youth she would have had petal-pink skin but she hadn't aged well.

She's as old as me, thought Tessa. 'I see,' she said. Mirabelle's eyes were the palest blue; curiously, the more uncertain they became the more she smiled.

'Well . . . well, I shan't keep you.'

'Yes, I'm better working uninterrupted.'

'I could show you the house, the photographer was very impressed.'

'Not today, I'm already late.'

'And if you wanted anything, you will ask, won't you?'

'Yes,' said Tessa opening the door. 'Thank you, Mrs Hallivand.'

'Oh, please, please, call me Mirabelle,' and a tremble ran right through her, clanking all her jewellery.

CHAPTER THREE

Tessa took her sketchbook to the far side of the moat, where the cornfield met the grounds of St John's. Here the Hall could be seen through the trees. This was the first glimpse one saw from the road, so it seemed the best place to start. Murray would be impressed by St John's, she thought, and this made her smile because he would never see it now and when they were together he had shown no interest in this section of her life. He loved gardens and it was gardens that had brought them together. Tessa had advised him about the tiny courtyard garden at the back of his gallery. The gardens of St John's would make him very quiet and put his head to one side, and say, as he did when he was interested in something, 'Hmm, possibilities . . .'

The Hallivands' improvements were not noticeable from this angle. Through the trees the Hall was as mysterious as it had ever been when weeds grew in the courtyard and the gardens were a knot of brambles and nettles. In the field the ripe wheat was prickly against Tessa's legs and she began to draw.

* * *

They stood staring at the house feeling out of place and uncomfortable. Don, whom nobody embarrassed, was at a loss for words. 'Er, um,' he said, and it had been his idea in the first place.

Then a door opened and a woman strode out, short, squarish, a broad face and black hair scraped into a bun. She marched towards them as if they were dirty geese. 'Shoo! Shoo! Off you go.'

Don ran up to her. 'Molly, it's me! Don't you remember? It's me!'

Molly was not impressed.

'Oh, Molly, it's me, I'm Donald, George's boy, George and Hetty, the Bells, you know; Miranda, Donald.' At each name he showed how high they used to be. 'Frances and little Marsha, she's twelve now . . .'

Molly threw up her hands. 'Donald! It is you, and you so grown, when I last saw you, you were . . .'

'A squirt, and I was always up the apple trees, and Miranda played the grand piano . . .'

'She had a lovely voice.'

'She's at the Royal Academy now, she is, she plays the cello too.'

'And Frances? Such a serious little thing, dark, not like you.'

'She's a scientist, she's brilliant, she's going to Cambridge.'

'And the baby?'

'Oh, Molly, you wouldn't recognise her, she's the beautiful one, blonde . . .'

'Like you.'

'Like Mummy. Well, Marsha's twelve, she's quite a lady,' and they both laughed.

Tessa and Dee-Dee were still standing by the car, Dee-Dee tugging her mini skirt. Don pulled Molly over to them.

'You must meet my friends! This is Tessa and Dee-Dee.'

Molly looked them up and down gravely. Tessa's mascara had smudged into her cheeks.

'Gosh! I don't know their surnames . . . I met them a week ago . . . they're at art school, London's great at the moment.'

'I'm Theresa Fulks and this is Deirdre Stallard,' said Tessa, feeling the whole situation needed clarifying. 'Don invited us to see his cousin.'

'Yes, yes, and how is Geoffrey, I'd heard he wasn't too—'

'He's bearing up very well,' said Molly stoically; 'rests a lot, we try and look after him.'

Tessa and Dee-Dee gazed at the overgrown garden and the sorry state of the barns. Molly was embarrassed. 'Charlie's back's

19

been bad, he can't do much now, and I can barely keep up, what with the cleaning and all.'

'Oh dear, Molly, I didn't realise, I should have written. Have you got a phone yet?'

'Oh, no, Mr Bell won't have it . . . shall I tell him you're here? He will be pleased, Donald.'

'We shouldn't have come,' Tessa whispered to Dee-Dee.

Molly led them through the porch and into the blackness of the Hall. It smelled of wet stone, damp rush-matting and woodsmoke. Dee held Tessa's hand. Molly opened the door in the panelling. Light through the high church windows streamed onto an old collection of broken furniture, stuffed animals under glass, piles of books, Indian dhurries and half-dead geraniums. The great hall was lofty and damp, there were broken window panes and on one of the rafters was a bird's nest. Beside the stone fireplace, in which a few logs smouldered on a heap of ashes, was an armchair, and in this slept an elderly man in a dressing gown. They moved closer and Tessa could see he wasn't really old but had the shrivelled yellowish appearance of the terminally ill. His dressing gown was brown checked wool, bought for someone once larger than he. His wrists were thin.

'Mr Bell, Mr Bell,' said Molly shaking him gently, 'there's somebody to see you.'

The sick man opened his eyes and smiled. He had a kind face, which even illness could not hide. 'Molly? Is it tea-time already?'

'No, Mr Bell, there's Donald to see you, come all the way from London.'

Don rushed over and shook his hand enthusiastically, but Tessa could see how upset he was, he had not expected to find his cousin so frail. 'Geoffrey, it's been ages.'

'Dear Donald, what a surprise. Let me see you, doesn't he look like George, Molly, a blonde George.'

'He's brought some friends, Mr Bell.' Molly pushed Dee-Dee and Tessa nearer.

'What modern ladies . . . and you too Donald, quite the thing, and such a shirt.'

'Oh, everybody in London wears this sort of stuff, Geoffrey.'

' "With it", that's what they say now, isn't it?' He held Don and Dee-Dee's hands. 'How splendid of you to come all this way, and such beautiful ladies . . .'

Dee-Dee's knees went pink.

'Molly, make some tea, bring out your best fruit cake. Donald, find some chairs, and let's celebrate.'

An hour or so later everybody was relaxed, laughing and stuffed with Molly's cakes. She kept running into the kitchen to make more sandwiches. 'There'll be no more food left at this rate, Mr Bell.'

'Never mind, Molly, tomorrow we'll get Ram's to deliver.'

Geoffrey insisted his guests be well fed. 'I like to see ladies with good appetites.' He offered Dee another slice of fruit cake. She was completely taken by him, he was absolutely charming. She gazed at him rapturously.

'What beautiful hair you have, my dear, like the ripest wheat in the afternoon sun . . .'

'Geoffrey, you are a one, you used to say things like that to my mother.'

'Quite right too, Hetty was a beauty, still is. Her and George, so romantic, they were. They still write . . . Young lady, boys these days are not romantic. Is Donald romantic?'

'Donald?' And they screamed with laughter.

'But tell me, George says you're "dropping out" of Oxford.'

'Yes, yes, I am, and I'm not going back . . . Oxford's dead, Geoffrey, everybody's so out of touch. I want to read about Ginsberg and Kerouac and Michael X, not dead people. It's all happening now, in people's houses, in pubs and on the street, Geoffrey. Art and literature isn't stuffed away in libraries, it's alive . . . Tessa and Dee-Dee, they're artists, they know, it's not just paint and paper, is it?'

'No.' Geoffrey was smiling knowingly.

'It's true, Geoffrey, it is. What do I get if I stay at Oxford, a degree, a piece of paper? I'll know all about Milton and Shakespeare and Donne, oh they're OK, but what about Bob Dylan . . . it's poetry, it is . . . don't laugh, Geoffrey . . . it's got meaning and rhythm and most of all it's got life . . . I don't want a job and work from nine to five, I want to . . . Be . . . Read Thoreau, Geoffrey, and Tolstoy and Gandhi, and William Morris and Steiner and Huxley, they got it right . . . oh yes, and Jesus . . .'

Geoffrey was laughing. 'And Jesus . . . what it is to be young!'

Don's face was pink, but he wasn't embarrassed; he was never embarrassed. Tessa and Dee-Dee exchanged glances. Don was the most un-hip creature on earth but he could be pretty inspiring.

Geoffrey was quiet. He poked the dying fire with his walking stick.

'We were all young, George, Hetty, and I, we all awaited the imminent transformation of the world . . .'

Molly hovered behind them. 'Don't let them tire you, Mr Bell.'

'Molly, you take good care of me.'

'Are you tired?' asked Don. 'Shall I show the girls the rest of the house, I know they'll love it.'

'It's not like it was, my boy.'

'We don't mind, do we, it's years since I was here.'

'This is the kitchen,' said Don. China sink, one table, pots and pans hanging from the beams. 'Hetty said it was impossibly archaic. We used to come here every summer. This is the breakfast room.' An Aga, a long table, a sofa under a window which looked out over the moat. A stone floor. 'The dairy's in there, nobody uses it now. You see, it was a farm here before Geoffrey.' Up winding stairs. 'That's Molly's room, it's private.' Another bedroom. 'This is the solar.' A pile of old furniture covered with

22

dust sheets, a huge bed, carved. 'I think Geoffrey sleeps downstairs now . . .' More bedrooms, more stairs, Dee-Dee and Tessa were quite lost. 'I always slept in here, it's called the chapel because it's above the porch. In winter there's ice on the inside walls, can you imagine? We only came here once in the winter, though . . . This room's above the hall, my sisters slept in here.' The ceiling had fallen in, there was more unused furniture. Don examined some. 'I think it's his mother's, my great-aunt, it all came here when she died. Oh look, the hat stand, I do remember that . . .' Up more stairs, down more stairs, narrow corridors, everywhere damp and dusty and crumbling. Don looked out of a window at the courtyard. 'I love this place,' he said thoughtfully.

'What will happen when Geoffrey . . .' Dee-Dee couldn't bear to think of him dying.

'I suppose it'll be sold. George said it should have been sold years ago. Geoffrey could never really manage it. When we used to come down George used to help, but . . . I don't know, Geoffrey wasn't well, we grew up, Hetty and George, they're getting old too . . . I like Geoffrey, I wish I'd seen more of him now . . .'

'It's so sad,' said Dee-Dee and a tear ran down her face.

Three of them in a car all the way back to London and Dee-Dee sobbed copiously because Geoffrey was going to die. He had bravely walked to the door to see them off, leaning on a stick and helped by Molly, and that was Tessa's last memory of him, a sick gentleman in a dressing gown.

'Bye-bye, Don old boy, come again soon.'

'I will, Geoffrey, I promise, I'll come and see you.'

'Goodbye, ladies, so pleased to have met you. Goodbye, goodbye,' leaning on Molly and waving his stick until they were all out of sight.

Some weeks later, Don was with Tessa. She was painting a mural in a friend's flat in Fulham. She was covered in paint and the walls and the floor were covered in it too, but it was cool, it was OK.

'. . . And that's the sea, where all living things come from, and these are the molluscs and the reptiles and the whole of evolution,' said Tessa, splash. 'And at the top is man in the clouds, and the sun is Ra the sun god giving out light and inspiration.' Splash, a shower of yellow droplets splattered Don.

'I'm going to see Geoffrey again,' he said.

'Good, I am pleased . . .' Splash, red paint.

'But I can't take you this time, I'm afraid, you see Hetty wants me to persuade him to go to a hospice.'

Tessa stopped. 'That's heavy.'

'Isn't it, but the doctors say if he doesn't he'll die in three months, if he goes to a hospice he might . . .'

'Linger for years . . . Shit, Don, Geoffrey's pure, he's real, it makes me sick when people want to destroy that.' She splashed black paint angrily. 'Why can't people do what they want? Do you think he wants to linger in a fucking-stupid-full-of-morons-hospice?'

Donald laughed. 'No, he doesn't, he's very single-minded.'

'Shit! That's too much black, it doesn't look inspirational any more.'

Don wasn't listening. He wiped the paint off his shirt. 'I like Geoffrey,' he said.

It was September, a year since they'd visited St John's. Geoffrey was still there, dying, but comforted by his life's clutter, Molly and Don, who visited him frequently. Tessa and Dee-Dee were established in London. They called themselves artists but didn't really paint much; they never stayed in one place long enough. They had moved twelve times since the previous spring. They worked evenings in a dismal Greek restaurant off the Charing Cross Road, but this too was temporary. They changed jobs as frequently as their addresses. When they'd first met Don that summer they had been ingénue suburban art-school students, but they were now real hippies, much to the bewilderment and disgust of their parents.

24

Dee-Dee and Tessa's families had known each other for years but since their daughters' abandonment of all that was proper and respectable a certain coolness had developed between the Fulks and the Stallards, one silently blaming the other. 'If it wasn't for their daughter and her ways . . .' But to Tessa and Dee-Dee their parents were uptight, straight and uncool. What did they know?

Dee had grown her hair long. It was ginger-blonde and crinkly, like a Pre-Raphaelite maiden. She wore round-rimmed sunglasses day and night, dressed in purple with a purple crocheted pull-on hat, and moved in a mist of patchouli. She was always in love, and the latest was called Jeremy. He played the flute, often, and had wild curly hair. He looked like a dissipated cherub and he was only sixteen. They stayed in bed most of the day.

Tessa was leaner, dark and frizzy-haired, which made her look Caribbean, another source of irritation to her parents; in crimson crushed velvet, with her tarot cards and brown gypsy eyes, her intense murals and love of things Eastern, she was known as a freaky lady.

They lived in King's Cross in the basement of a partially demolished house. Tessa had painted all the walls yellow to cheer it up, but it was so damp she preferred to go out. Her ambition, if it could be called that, was to live in Notting Hill. Don, of course, lived in Notting Hill. His flat was the top floor of a house overlooking a square. He lived in some style. Tessa and Dee-Dee owned virtually nothing – their clothes, some records – but possessions seemed to cling to Don like burrs on a tweed skirt. 'Doing his own thing' was working as a porter in Bonham's, but he also had the knack of finding pieces of junk in Portobello that later turned out to be valuable. His flat was a cave of Indian paintings, hookahs from Morocco (bought last summer), Turkish rugs (the spring before), seventeen different types of tea and seventeen tea-pots, books everywhere and on the ceiling one of Tessa's murals, 'The awakening of Consciousness'. It was here she spent most her time.

It was Tuesday but it could have been any day of the week, and what time it was was unclear; Don's four clocks bonged hours and half-hours intermittently. Outside, yellowing leaves fell in the square. It was misty. Tessa and Dee-Dee were lying on the floor listening to *Astral Weeks*. The music was dreamy and melodic, Van Morrison's peculiarly nasal voice felt right for their mood. Don's room was autumnal too, brown, yellow and crimson. They were sad. Geoffrey had finally died, Don was at the solicitor's with his father, the will was being read.

'The Hall will be sold. Who will buy it?' asked Dee-Dee on the goatskin rug.

'Somebody,' said Tessa.

They were smoking dope and were very stoned. Curiously the smell of hashish reminded her of the musty smell at St John's. Dee-Dee started crying again, she had been doing this on and off since they first heard and that was a week ago.

'Another time another place . . .' sang Van Morrison.

'Death's not a bum trip,' said Tessa; 'it's just moving from one thing to another like . . .' but she couldn't think what it was like.

'We could have gone to the funeral,' said Dee-Dee.

'Funerals are for family, anyway we only met him once.'

Then Donald burst in. Tessa and Dee-Dee were stretched out on the floor; the atmosphere in the room was definitely comfortable, but Don jumped over both of them and ran to the kitchen.

'God, I need a drink.'

'Don, cool it, what's happened?'

He sat on the floor and poured himself a cup of whisky.

'What is it, have you been busted?'

He looked at their serious faces and began to laugh. 'Geoffrey's left me St John's.'

'Far out!'

'He has, all of it, the whole bloody place, birds' nests and all!'

'Oh, Don!' said Tessa and Dee-Dee in unison.

He poured himself another cup of whisky.

26

'What are you going to do?' said Dee-Dee, all anxious.

'Do? I'm going to live there.'

'That's wild,' said Tessa.

'Like Geoffrey . . . and there's money, too, that furniture of his, it's valuable, it's not rubbish . . . and the paintings . . . Hetty and George got the best things, two Stanhope Forbes and a Morrisot, we thought they were sold years ago . . .'

'Oh, Don, what are you going to do?' said Dee-Dee again.

'Anything, anything I like . . .' and his face took on a familiar far-away look.

CHAPTER FOUR

So, Don went to Suffolk and Tessa and Dee moved into his flat. It was a satisfactory arrangement, for Notting Hill was the centre of the underground universe. Here were crash-pads for drop-outs, the Electric cinema and a macrobiotic restaurant. Here were happenings, music everywhere and enough marijuana to ensure everybody was stoned. Life at the flat was unscheduled, unrestricted. They woke and slept as they pleased and there were always people, thumping bongos, strumming guitars, dancing, reading poetry and smoking dope. To Tessa and Dee-Dee this was freedom.

Don led a nomadic life between London and Suffolk. He bought a van to ferry Geoffrey's furniture to sell in auctions. He was trying to raise money to restore St John's. The builders had started re-roofing, re-plumbing. What he was going to do with the place was a source of endless discussion; a hospice for the dying? 'but Geoffrey wouldn't have liked that'; a museum of Eastern Art? That idea lasted two days; a free school 'where children learned through their own experiences in the here and now and adults could change their perceptions of reality . . .' But somehow anything to do with schools meant regulations and planning permission. The idea that was most consistent was to 'fill the Hall with interesting people all sharing and co-operating . . .', but St John's was only slightly more than a ruin.

The following August, Tessa, Dee-Dee, Jeremy and a person called Edgar Bukowski from New Orleans all attended the Festival of Communes at the Roundhouse. This was 'a big informal information-exchanging and food-sharing meal and meeting for Communes and people interested in Communes plus (perhaps) chanting and other signs of togetherness plus (perhaps) Quintessence and Third Ear Band'. In long dresses, loons, beads and bare feet, they danced, drummed and laughed, experiencing togetherness and being and felt it was as important as Woodstock. Don was there too, conspicuous with schoolboy hair and brown polished shoes, talking avidly to long-haired anarchists, but his communal ideas were hardly being clarified.

The sixties were over. Hendrix was dead, Janis Joplin was dead, the Beatles had split up, the Isle of Wight was a muddy memory. Uncertainty and doubt were creeping into the earthly paradise. Tessa and Dee-Dee in Don's flat were restless. Previously their constant moving had satisfied a need for change, a feeling that if they stopped long enough to accumulate possessions and familiarity with a place then they would be settling down, or, worse still, be straight. They feared acutely normality as displayed by their parents' uneventful lives in deepest Middlesex. But in the year that the old money was abandoned and in came tinny decimalisation, they began to wonder, 'What now?'

Dee-Dee, Jeremy, his flute and an alarmingly small amount of money hitch-hiked to India to find the truth. They went after an all-night party on a damp November morning. Tessa stayed behind. She felt there was nothing she could find in India she couldn't find in Notting Hill; after all, India, the Taj Mahal and everything were just places. The real truth was inside. Her restlessness was spiritual; she became inert. The crashers at Don's flat were inert too. They lay on the floor to music, usually stoned or, more usually, tripping. Edgar Bukowski was now a permanent resident. He was a chunky six-foot with long lank hair in a ponytail. He claimed to have met Bob Dylan in a jazz bar in New Orleans. He said, 'Hey, Bob, I love you,' and Bob said, 'Man, that's cool.' It may not have been true but it gave Edgar Bukowski kudos. He and Tessa were lovers. There were other people who were Tessa's lovers, both men and women, but during that winter

Edgar had precedence. Together they blacked out all daylight in the flat, consulted the tarot, read Alistair Crowley, listened to the Doors and Captain Beefheart, and embarked on an inward journey to darkest parts. Here, the Queen of Swords was a fiery red and sliced the air with her weapon, the unforgiving chariot crushed them underfoot and the dogs of hell bayed to the moon as crayfish crawled out of a primeval slime. The walls of Don's flat shook, grey-faced half-dead once-people moaned, Edgar's face crawled like the crayfish and they made love, but it wasn't love but something like hate, deadly and punishing.

A spring morning; Tessa pulled away the black cloth over the bathroom window. She had just been sick. The light came in cold and slicing. She didn't know what day it was. Avoiding her reflection she stumbled back to where six or seven people were on the floor. There was no sound, the air was foetid. She pulled away the black cloth from all the windows but even harsh daylight couldn't wake them. Then someone rolled over snored.

Angry, she began to kick them.

'Hey, man, wha's happening?'

Other people woke. 'Cool it, what's the problem?'

'Get up! Get up! Get up!'

'Heavy games, lady.'

'Cool it.'

'It's a raid,' shrieked Tessa.

At these words there was instant panic. They scrambled for the door, falling over each other. 'Beat it, it's the Fuzz,' and they crashed down the stairs and into the street.

Tessa watched from the window and laughed. They ran down the road like surprised rats, not even noticing a complete absence of policemen.

Now she was alone. Edgar was not there. She vaguely remembered he had gone at some point in the night, but she didn't care. She locked the door, which was something that had never been done before.

Feeling sick again, she hauled herself to bed. 'Oh shit . . . oh Christ . . . oh God . . . oh Jesus . . .'

Some days passed. There was a knocking at the door. Tessa thought it must be Edgar and stayed put under the grimy sheets. She blocked her ears. Edgar was six foot plus, he could kick down any door. She waited.

But it couldn't have been Edgar; the noise was weak, almost scratching, like a wounded animal that had crawled home.

'Tessy, Tessy, where are you, where are you? Let me in, Tessy, please let me in.'

Tessa sat up. It was Dee-Dee.

There was much hugging and tears. 'I thought you'd gone away, Tessy, I really did.'

'Here I am, sort of . . . did you go to India?'

'Yeah.'

'Wow, and was it amazing?'

'I don't know . . . I suppose it was . . . it was weird . . .'

'Where's Jeremy?'

'He's in Goa playing the flute.'

Dee-Dee was very thin. Her eyes looked huge, like a lemur's.

'I had enough, I thought I'd come back . . .' She began to cry. 'Tessy, it was awful, it was worse than a bad trip, and we had no money, we had to beg, but there's so many beggars . . . and I got sick, I don't know, I ate dahl off a stall . . . I got sick in Afghanistan too, but that wasn't too bad . . . Afghanistan's great, the people are tribal and the women wear veils and you never see them . . . and the deserts . . . I mean I saw a real camel and a mirage. I did.'

She blew her nose on her skirt.

'But India was so full and they're all dying, even the babies.' And she dissolved into sobs.

'So you didn't find a guru, then,' said Tessa after a while.

'Everyone in India's a guru.' Dee-Dee was hardly ever bitter. 'We were supposed to be going to an ashram near Poona but I

31

wanted to lie down all the time and then we went to Goa. I was pretty flipped out by Goa. It was like paradise, and we got sort of stuck . . . then I was in hospital, and when I came out I just couldn't get into it any more . . . Jeremy kept phoning his mum to send him more money, but I didn't want to do that, I'd rather beg . . . so I went to Delhi and met some Australians.'

'Did you see the Taj Mahal?'

'The Australians took me, they had a minibus, and the Taj was really magical and special, I wanted to stay. We waited for the moon to rise, and we saw a deserted palace called Fatehpur Sikri . . . Then the Australians took me to Kabul, they were called Rod and Mike, they were great . . .' She sighed. 'They wanted to see the inner land and the great statues but I wanted to get home. I met a lorry driver called Dick and he was going to Manchester so I took a lift.'

'And here you are.'

'I've just come back from Manchester. We were in a hotel. He wanted me to stay, but he was married, Tessy, he had kids, and, I mean, he was sweet and all that, but he was so straight . . .'

She lay on the bed. 'I'm so tired, I want to stop moving.'

She gazed at Tessa's painting on the ceiling, 'The Awakening of Consciousness', much obscured by smoke and dirt. 'What about you?'

Tessa came and lay next to her. 'I don't know,' she sighed too; 'I just kicked everybody out and locked the door. I'm sick of hash and acid and junk . . . and people dossing . . . and Edgar . . . he's heavy, he's on junk, anyway, I suspect he's trying to score . . .'

'What shall we do, Tessy?'

'I don't know, I don't know any more.

They might have slept for a whole day or it might have been two. When Tessa woke it was very early morning and the sun was beautiful and the birds were singing, and she felt clear and pure.

'Wake up, Dee-Dee, wake up.'

'Tessy, what is it?'

'Listen, wake up you mug, I know what we must do, I've just realised . . . we must live here and make it beautiful, like when Don was here. I'll paint it and we can get pretty things.'

'Oh, Tessy!'

'And flowers and everything. We'll clean it and it'll be ours and we won't have dossers . . .'

'Oh, Tessy.' Dee-Dee had started to cry.

'There won't be any Edgars or Jeremys laying heavy trips on us, it'll be our space, we'll do what we like.'

'I could do knitting . . .'

'And I'll paint, and we'll cook real food, not rubbish, and get strong and powerful . . . We'll do it now, come on Dee, we'll get some food now.'

And they bought six croissants and took them to the park and ate them by the boating pond, shivering in the spring sunlight, and Dee-Dee puked hers up but it didn't matter, and back at the flat they began to clean and clear it, and Tessa sold all her hash and they bought paint and bleach and washing powder, and they scrubbed and scrubbed and Dee-Dee cooked a big pot of stew, and after two weeks she wasn't being sick any more, and Tessa made bread and Dee-Dee started to knit a stripy jumper.

After two months the flat was how they wanted and Dee was becoming pink again. In the evenings they listened to early Incredible String Band and wept buckets and Nick Drake and wept buckets, and *Astral Weeks* and Al Stewart and Donovan and Bob Dylan and all the songs of the innocence and peace they loved and wanted to re-create.

It was early afternoon. Tessa and Dee-Dee were not doing much but they were happy. It was May. Dee had picked a branch of cherry blossom from the square and put it in a jug on the kitchen table. Then Don arrived.

'Well, this is very different,' he said, looking round.

'Don, I haven't seen you for ages.'

'I was up before Christmas.'

'Were you?'

'I think you were tripping . . . actually I think everybody was tripping . . .'

'Dee-Dee's here, she went to India and back.'

Dee rushed up and kissed him. 'Don, is the countryside beautiful? India was awful and I got sick, and Jeremy's still there, and Edgar left and never came back, and Tessa makes bread now . . .'

'Tell us about the Hall, Don.'

Don laughed and sat down. 'Oh, it's still a wreck, but I love it, Tess, it's going to be amazing. I sleep in the hall by the fire and read Geoffrey's books and I watched the spring coming in and now summer's coming, there's martins under the eaves and a kingfisher in the moat, and five ducklings. There's just me, Molly's Charlie's not well now, so they moved to a council house in St Lawrence.'

Don was wearing a pair of Geoffrey's tweed trousers held up with braces. His hair was longer but he looked different from anybody else they knew. His face was fresh and healthy. Dee got bread and honey and they ate thick slices.

'Are you down in London to sell something?' asked Tessa.

'No, I've come to see you.' He smiled. 'The flat looks good . . .'

Tessa and Dee had hung old lace at the windows, 'The Awakening of Consciousness' was painted over white, pretty china from the antique market stood on the kitchen shelves. Dee-Dee and Tessa wore thirties print dresses and coloured scarves.

Don nodded. There was something on his mind. Any minute now he was going to say 'I've got a really good idea,' but he didn't, he finished his bread and honey. 'So, Edgar's gone. I didn't really like him.'

'He was weird, smack wasted him.'

'Hmmm.'

Dee put on a record, *I Looked Up* by the Incredible String Band. Tessa rolled a joint. They sat on the floor.

. . . Each moment is different from another, each moment is different it's now, ow, ow . . .

'I've been thinking,' began Don, and Dee-Dee and Tessa glanced at each other, 'About St John's. I can't live there always on my own, sometimes I think I'd like to, but there's money . . . one needs money. Geoffrey couldn't do it and he had more money than I, and anyway, it's selfish, isn't it? I feel I want to share St John's because it's so wonderful, but then there's another question, with whom? I'd like to start a community, there's some already in Norfolk and Suffolk and they seem to be going fine. I went to see one and asked them "How do you know who the right people are?" and they said "You soon find out." But I don't want to make mistakes. St John's is special, it's got something, I suppose one calls it History. It would be a waste if unappreciative people lived there . . . There's enough land, it's got to be cleared, of course, but that could be done . . . What I've seen, the most successful communities are where people work hard, like Findhorn and monasteries. I've just been to stay at Downside, being Catholic does have advantages . . . the ritual, the prayer, the work, the belief keeps them going . . . but what's our creed, "The road of Excess leads to the palace of Wisdom" . . . do we still believe that? Must we still base our identity on intensified experiences, tune in, turn on, drop out, wait for the next high? You see, I've been finding this out. The days and the seasons have their own rhythms, in the countryside one really notices it. In the town, OK . . . it's a fine day. It's sunny; it's not, it's raining, but since I've been at St John's each day is different.'

Each moment is different from another, each moment is different it's now, ow, ow . . .

'Yes, that's it. The leaves open in the spring, slowly each day, every minute there's a change. When the snowdrops came out I cried, I did, it wasn't sentimental, it was joyful. Winter's dead, spring's here! I never felt that in London . . . It's medieval. Ancient people lived much closer to nature. The winter must have been long, long and dark, then the spring and summer. Wonderful! You don't shiver any more . . . God, I was cold this winter, I was bloody freezing . . . but now, the hawthorn's in blossom and the elder.'

He looked at the bough of cherry in the jug. ' . . . and here I am in London.' He smoked the joint.

'I get fed up with London,' said Tessa. 'Parties and people talking, doing the same things, smoking dope, getting laid . . .'

'But we've made it nice here,' said Dee-Dee.

When you find out who you are, beautiful beyond your dreams . . .

They were silent. The record came to an end. Don's face took on a distant look, reminding Tessa of a soldier on a war memorial.

'Listen,' he said, and they listened, to the electric hum of the fridge, the cars on Holland Park Avenue, an aeroplane, people outside . . .

'What I hear at St John's is timeless, it's been heard since forever; wind, lapwings, ducks on the moat. Must I be the only person to hear it? . . . Come back with me, we'll be the beginning, we'll find more people. "Why may we not have our Heaven here and Heaven hereafter too?" Why not?'

They had not expected this at all.

'Yes, you two, you're prefect, I can see it . . . it'll be hard work, but you don't mind about that . . .'

They stared at him.

'We'll clear the land and grow vegetables. There's two acres, we could be eating our own food.'

'Oh,' said Dee-Dee.

'Come on then.' He stood up.

'Now?'

'Yes. Why not? I've got the van outside. All this—' he glanced around '—Bring it. It's yours, isn't it?' he began to unplug the record player.

Dee-Dee and Tessa in the middle of the room faced each other. Dee-Dee was becoming tearful. 'Tessy, what shall we do?'

But Tessa was certain. 'We'll go.'

It wasn't until they arrived at St John's in the dark that they realised the enormity of their decision. Only the great hall was inhabitable; the rest of the house was a pile of furniture and rubble. On everything was a layer of white plaster dust. There was no electricity.

Dee-Dee and Tessa stood in the damp gloom of the great hall. Don, with a torch, sought out kindling to make a fire. In front of the fireplace was a large mattress and blankets. Tessa and Dee-Dee sank onto these.

'I'll light the Aga,' said Don. 'It takes a bit of time, but then we can have hot water. How about some food, are you hungry?' Tessa and Dee-Dee's faces were blank. Don sat next to them. 'Well, it is primitive, but you get used to it.' The fire was beginning to burn and smoke. 'It does that,' said Don, poking it. Tessa and Dee-Dee coughed. Wind blew down the chimney. Tessa thought of their comfortable flat in Notting Hill, now packed in Don's van. She felt too tired to move. Don went to the kitchen to coax the Aga. They wrapped themselves in blankets and gazed into the smoke.

'Oh, Tessy,' whispered Dee-Dee.

'It'll be fine,' said Tessa, not sounding very sure.

Don came back with bread and soup. 'It's nettle gruel, I picked them yesterday.' He lit a large candle and placed it by the fire. There were no spoons so they drank straight from the bowls. It was lukewarm.

'This is our first meal here,' he said solemnly. 'It's a celebration, we have begun a new existence. It's not going to be easy. We have chosen to live in this ancient and wonderful house. We have given up comforts . . . At the moment what we see is the ashes, but we will be like the phoenix and rise out of the ashes.' He paused. 'Do you believe in God?'

'No,' said Tessa.

'I'm not sure,' said Dee-Dee.

'Nor am I,' said Don, 'but I think we need a prayer; prayer's very strengthening.'

'We could pray to the spirit of the house,' suggested Tessa, feeling very much that St John's was a living being they were going to capture.

'Yes, that's it.' Don was very excited. 'Let's join hands, then . . . and close our eyes . . . how shall I start?'

They sat in a tight circle. The fire crackled. 'St John's, you have seen many people . . . um . . . look down on us now and have mercy . . . we have not come to destroy but to rebuild . . . we want to see you filled again with a working community as it was . . . oh, gosh . . . ages ago . . . St John's, have mercy on us and give us strength, you were built by men, but have outlasted men, you have stood through storms and wars. Help us to achieve our purpose, to become a centre of inspiration.'

Tessa listened, to the wind in the chimney, the fire, the silence of a country night. She opened her eyes. Dee-Dee and Don were smiling at her. 'Phew,' said Don, and wrapped himself in the blanket too.

'That was beautiful,' said Dee-Dee, all dreamy.

'This soup is disgusting,' said Tessa, and they all laughed.

'Where shall we sleep?' asked Dee-Dee after some time. The fire was nearly out.

'Oh,' and Don was only slightly embarrassed; 'I thought perhaps you could sleep here with me . . .'

* * *

Tessa put down her pencil. She had finished. Then what

happened, she thought as she picked up her things. Dirty hippies have a sex orgy. But as she walked back to St John's she was angry. It hadn't been like that, it hadn't been sordid, it had been beautiful and special . . . she opened her car door and Mirabelle came running out of the house.

'Have you finished? Do have some more tea.'

'I have to go.'

'How's it coming on?'

'Oh . . . fine . . . it hasn't changed much,' said Tessa, off guard.

'Changed? Then you've been here before?'

'Oh . . . only once . . . years ago . . . in the seventies.'

'Then you must have known the . . . previous occupants?'

'No . . . not really, friends of friends, you know.'

'Bernard said they left the place in a terrible state. And that little girl . . .' She quivered. Tessa said nothing. There was an embarrassed silence.

'Well, well . . . they knew all about vegetables and flowers and things, so Bernard says . . . are you sure you won't have more tea?'

'I'll be back tomorrow at nine-thirty,' said Tessa, and left.

CHAPTER FIVE

Tessa woke in her hotel room in Bury St Edmunds. She had been dreaming about Dee-Dee. Whenever she dreamt about Murray or Don she woke feeling angry, but a dream about Dee-Dee always left her sad. She had close female friends now; Fiona, who worked in the gallery in Bath, and Bunty who she went cycling with, but nobody was as close as Dee-Dee had been.

As far back as she could remember Dee-Dee was there. She came to play every other Saturday. Tessa was an only child. Her parents felt she needed 'company'. Her dream was vague but what remained was a picture of Dee-Dee, crinkly gingery hair, wide blue eyes, pink cheeks and freckles, the little girl and the adult fused into one. She wondered, but only briefly, what Dee looked like now. With this thought she got out of bed and drew the curtains.

It was sunny, a good day for sketching. She wished bitterly she was back in her house. The hotel room with apricot sheets and curtains depressed her; there was nothing here she could use to strengthen herself. She ran a bath. At least the bathroom was stark and white. It was only seven o'clock.

* * *

Two girls in the garden with all the dolls. They were playing hairdresser's, Dee-Dee's favourite game, or rather she was playing and Tessa was watching.

'. . . And this one's called Dibby and she has beautiful yellow hair and I'm going to plait it and put blue ribbons on, and this one's called Dobby and she has beautiful black hair and I'm going to make it all curly . . .'

40

She stopped in the middle of her monologue.

'Tessy, will we always be friends?'

'Yes,' said Tessa; she couldn't imagine it any different.

Dee-Dee began to brush the doll's hair vigorously. 'You're full of tangles, you're quite matty . . . Tessy, will we be friends even when we're married?' getting married was Dee-Dee's other favourite game.

'Yes,' said Tessa, turning one of the dolls upside-down.

'You mustn't do that, she's having a perm . . . Tessy, when people are married they don't have friends . . .'

Tessa looked at her seriously. Dee-Dee had rosy cheeks and ribbons. She was pretty, Tessa wasn't. Her parents called her 'peaky'. 'Why not?' she said.

'They just don't. My mummy's got no friends at all, and my daddy . . .'

Tessa thought, it was true, her parents didn't have any friends either. The only person who ever came to stay was Auntie and she was horrible.

'You see,' said Dee-Dee, 'when people get married and grown up they go and live in houses and they . . . don't . . . have . . . friends.' She threw the doll across the lawn. 'You're too bad, you're too fidgety!'

'Why can't we still be friends?' said Tessa.

'Because we can't, it's not allowed.' Dee-Dee was cross. She went all pink when she was cross.

Tessa thought again. She thought of next door and across the road and all of Lime Avenue and down to the shops and back. People in houses with babies and dogs and gardens. It made her cross too. She jumped up.

'I want to be friends for ever.'

'Well, we can't!'

'Why can't we?'

'We just can't.' Dee-Dee had started to cry. Any minute now Tessa's mother would run out and ask what on earth was going on.

41

Tessa sat down. 'Dee-Dee,' she said, 'why can't we be different . . .'

* * *

Tessa moved her feet in the bath water. Ripples ran up her body. She moved her feet again and more ripples ran over her. She was lean and muscular. She used her body as a means of transport. These days she rarely connected it with pleasure.

* * *

Dee-Dee woke in the middle of their first night at St John's.

'Tessy, where's the loo? I can't remember, I'm dying for a piss.'

'Oh, Dee . . . it's on the other side and up some stairs.'

'That's miles away . . . I can't find the torch . . . Tessy, there might be spiders . . .'

'Shhhhh.' But Don was fast asleep. They looked at him. He was lying on his back, both arms stretched out.

'He's exhausted,' said Tessa, and they giggled.

'Oh Tessy, don't, I'll wet myself.'

'You'll have to go outside.'

'Somebody might see me.'

'Dee-Dee you are a dope, we're in the middle of nowhere.'

'Will you come with me?'

'If I must.'

Wrapped up in one blanket, they stepped into the night.

'Oh, look! Wow!' The sky was filled with stars. There was a thin new moon and the constellations were clear, each star a pinprick of brilliance. The Milky Way reeled over the Hall.

'It's trippy!' said Dee-Dee, breathless. 'Oh, I must have this piss.'

'Now I want to go too.'

They squatted by the wall. Their two streams of urine merged into one and ran gurgling down a drain. They stayed there gazing at the heavens.

'I got used to squatting in India,' said Dee-Dee. 'Everybody

42

squats . . . the stars there were . . . cosmic. Jeremy tried to tell me the names but I've forgotten.'

'I used to have a book about stars, that one like a W is Cassiopeia and that's Taurus the bull, and that's Hercules . . .'

'I can't see it.'

'In the book there were pictures, it made it clearer.'

They held hands under the blanket.

'Don's lovely, isn't he?' said Dee after a while.

'Yes.'

'Do you think it will be like this every night?'

'Why not?' and they laughed nervously.

'Are you in love with him?' asked Dee-Dee.

'I don't know, really . . . but I like him . . . are you?'

'I don't think so, but he's special, you know.'

'Well, we'll share him then.'

'Until?'

'Until what?'

Then a shooting star skidded across the sky and disappeared behind the barns.

'Ohhhh!' exclaimed Dee-Dee.

'It's a sign,' said Tessa.

* * *

Tessa drove to St John's. It was a clear Sunday morning. There was much less traffic than the day before. The fields and villages flashed past without interruption. No shoppers, no energetic families. People were still in bed or reading the papers at breakfast. Yawning, stretching. Only much later would start the rush to the sea.

A sunny day, slow-moving puffy clouds, hardly a breeze. It was going to be hot. Farmers were deciding to start the harvest. Combines heaved down the narrow roads of the Saints, their drivers shut away in airless glass. Modern harvesting is dusty, noisy, unpleasant. But around St John's the fields were quiet; after

43

all, it had been an unpredictable summer. The wheat was golden, its grains plump and ripe. It was doomed.

Mirabelle was dressed and immaculate. She looked like she had been up for hours and her manner was just as brightly brittle. Tessa felt over-casual in old jeans and a white shirt. Mirabelle was in dusky pink with matching shoes and nails. Her lips were also pink. They framed her smiling teeth.

'What a lovely day . . . I do love the sun . . . do you want coffee?'

'Later perhaps.'

'At eleven? Yes? I'll bring it to you. Will you be in the same place?'

'No . . .' Tessa frowned at the Hall. The sun glinted on the church windows. St John's appeared bold, defiant almost. 'Does the walled garden still exist?'

'The parterre?'

'You could call it that . . . I'll start there, it's an interesting foreground.'

'Bernard says the design is Tudor . . .' she paused. 'I'm afraid you might not see Bernard, he's gone to Belgium. He's after a clock . . . this is always happening. I hoped he'd be back for the holiday, but . . . well, there it is.' She shook as if struck by a cold wind. 'I might go out later . . . I think the gardener's in, but he won't disturb you.'

The walled garden was set some distance from the house on the other side of the barns. It was the old kitchen garden and even in Geoffrey's day Molly's ageing Charlie cultivated it, and it had not succumbed to the brambles and nettles that took over the rest of the grounds. It was the first section of St John's they tackled. Later, when other land was cleared, they laid out the walled garden as a Tudor knot, with herbs, salad crops and soft fruit, bordered by low box hedges. It was still how Tessa remembered it except the grass paths had been replaced by sterile gravel. There was a statue in the centre, a marble Victorian lady pretending to be Greek. Tessa sat by her, and looked towards the Hall, framed by the arch in the wall.

* * *

That first summer, when Adam and his two Eves lived in Paradise. They knew little about gardening. Don sold his van to buy tools and they sowed beans too early and peas too late. Consequently they lived off bread and cheese and apples. But it was summer and it was glorious. They swam in the moat, sunbathed nude, walked everywhere and discovered empty churches and cautious farmers. They carried bagfuls of shopping three miles. They had bonfires every night, burning away dregs of years left behind by Geoffrey. They hacked at brambles, burnt those too, and in the walled garden dug up weeds and also things they had just planted.

By the fire in the great hall in the evenings Don read Huxley's *Island*.

'Listen to this. He says here that everybody in Pala has to dig for two hours a day. Well, he's right, isn't he, digging's so . . . physical, isn't it? Digging's the only work one should be doing, not sitting at a desk, where does that get you? It makes you senile.'

'I'm knackered,' said Tessa.

'Of course you are, but don't you see it's doing you good. Winstanley had something to say about it, now where's Winstanley?'

Wherever Don was there was always a book. The great hall was filling up with dusty tomes rescued from other parts of the house. Winstanley was underneath *Paradise Lost*.

'Listen to this . . . Tessa? Dee-Dee? Is she asleep? This is about the diggers: "Let everyone that intends to live in peace get themselves with diligent labour to till, digge and plow the common and barren land to get their bread with righteous moderate working among all moderate minded people. This prevents the evil of idleness." Isn't that right? Have you ever worked so hard? And weren't we idle before, bumming around?'

Tessa lay down. Dee-Dee was breathing regularly and gently; it was soporific. Tessa felt as if every muscle in her body had been stretched, but she liked this new feeling. I am strong, she thought. She was much stronger than Dee-Dee and probably more than Don.

'. . . To get their bread with righteous moderate working . . .'

They bought their bread in Bungay.

* * *

Through the doorway into the walled garden came the gardener; balding, red-faced, old cardigan, cord trousers, cap. Standard rustic. He was pushing a wheelbarrow. He looked like a Hoskin. Molly's Charlie was a Hoskin.

'Morning,' he said. He looked at her strangely, but then most people looked at her like that. Perhaps it was the flashes of red in her hair like the crest of a strange bird of paradise. 'Ah, ha.' He put down his wheelbarrow.

'The garden's lovely.'

'Flowers! You can't eat they.'

'I wanted to say your Savoys are splendid.'

'Not a bad crop,' he nodded critically. 'I eats most of it myself. Er and 'im, what they don't eat I gets and 'im 'e's never here and 'er, she don't eat.'

'Bit of a waste of time, then?'

'I think 'er freezer's full, I think 'er's got ten freezers . . . work on a Sunday, too. I got to keep it smart, some high-faluting type's getting it put in a book.'

Tessa smiled. 'That's me, I'm doing sketches.'

He snorted. 'I hope they pays you.'

'And I hope they pay you.'

'Oh, they do that. I said to 'im, there's work for six here and 'ee said, I'll pay for six . . . did you ever? Now, when them hippies were here, you heard about that?'

'Yes.'

He laughed. 'Those girls in their noddy nothings, and the lads. I hid behind a bush once, see.'

46

Tessa said nothing.

'Now, Charlie Hoskins, he were my cousin and he said to me, "Now Bob, you wouldn't believe what they gets up to."' He picked up the wheelbarrow. 'But I tell you, they didn't put nothing in the freezer. They grew it and they et it, now that's right, isn't it?'

Tessa resumed her work. She didn't believe for a moment Bob had hid behind a bush. She was sure that story was circulated by anyone who visited the local pubs. She well knew they had been objects of amusement. They were tolerated and later even liked, but the Hoskins, the Becks, the Palmers, and others who were the inhabitants of the Saints, could never understand why Don and his friends chose to live unheated, with dirty clothes and bare feet.

Don was respected in a strange sort of way. He was 'gentry', one of them, moneyed and mad. 'Old man Bell', as Geoffrey was known, was revered. 'In Old man Bell's day', that golden age, pre-war, pre-tourist, pre-European Community, when the pubs were smoky, with rickety chairs and lino floors, and the men played cribbage.

* * *

They discovered one of these pubs in a village called St James, which had even fewer houses than St John's. The George was shabby. The bar was the size of a small sitting room. There was one table, some benches and a fire, even though it was July. They went there to find something to eat.

'Do you serve food?' asked Don.

The landlord, thin and wrinkled, stared. His mother, small and very fat, stared too. Two men in caps by the fire started laughing.

'What you want, then, chicken in a basket? Fish in a basket? Turkey in a basket? Nelson, get 'em roast beef in a basket.'

'No food,' said the landlord.

'We've walked miles,' said Tessa.

'There's no food.'

47

'But there's beer,' yelled the men.

In the end Nelson's mother made sandwiches, curled white bread and spam. They drank so much they could hardly stand.

'This place is amazing,' said Don. The beer was amazing too. The notorious George, open all day and most of the night. Don went back frequently.

It was late September. The harvest was over, the straw and stubble had been burnt, the fields were being ploughed. It occurred to Don, Tessa and Dee-Dee, like it occurred to the grasshopper in the story, that winter was coming and they were unprepared. Their only successful crop was spinach, and one can eat enough spinach. Don's daily reading was *The Cultivation of Vegetables and Flowers*, printed in about 1888, but it was getting colder and working outside was not appealing. Inside was colder too. They moved their bed from the great hall to the solar. Don had kept Geoffrey's carved bed. At night they wore thick socks and wool vests. They kept the Aga burning constantly.

'The winter's going to be fantastic,' said Don; 'wait until it snows, it's like the snow palace in *Dr Zhivago*.'

But Tessa and Dee-Dee were not so sure.

They were chopping wood. This was a daily pastime. Tessa was insistent they should have enough fuel for the winter, but how much was enough? Dee-Dee was hopeless at chopping. Every time she hit the wood, she either dropped the axe or hit cross-grain and the axe got stuck. She was almost in tears.

'Tessy, I can't do it, I can't.'

'Look, Dee, it's like this: swing, let it fall.' The block split neatly in two.

They were in the orchard. One of the old apple trees was being sacrificed. It only had four apples. The other trees gave so many they were sick of the sight of them.

'Try again.'

'Oh, Tessy, I'm useless, I can't do it.'

48

'You have to do it.' Tessa chopped angrily. 'Do you want to freeze? We won't have enough wood. Where's Don? I can't do this all myself.'

'He's gone to the George.'

'Shit! He's never around when he's needed, what's he doing at the George?' She hacked at a knotty section of the trunk. Splinters of wood flew in all directions.

'Tessy, be careful.' But Tessa was furious.

Dee-Dee collected the pieces in a fire basket and heaved it towards the house. 'I'll make you some herb tea . . .'

'I (chop) don't (chop) want any fucking herb tea!'

Her axe stuck in the apple trunk. She sat down. Chopping had kept her warm but now she realised how chill the wind was so she put on her coat. There were a few apples still on the trees and plenty brown and mushy on the grass. So many had been wasted. She was hungry, but not for apples.

Getting the shopping in an autumn wind was a terrible chore. They had run out of bread again, and cheese and potatoes.

'Shit! Shit! Shit! We're so dumb!' She could dig and chop but she couldn't plan. Don had all the plans in the world but he was at the George. Dee-Dee could cook and that was about it. The three sillies, thought Tessa, and looked across the ploughed field towards the village and the church tower. The sky was grey with low clouds. Two people were coming up the road. They stopped by the drive discussing something, then began to walk towards the Hall. One of them was Don. The other man was taller. He wore boots and a workman's jacket. Don, next to him, was excited, waving his arms and jumping in the curious way he had. Tessa frowned. Another electrician, or plumber probably; St John's innards were still archaic. But they didn't come up to the house; they went into the walled garden. He's met him in the pub, thought Tessa suspiciously. She gave the axe a last heave and it came free. With this in her hand she went to meet them.

They were in the middle of the walled garden talking. The man bent down in mid-sentence and picked up a clod of earth. He examined it, letting it run between his fingers. His voice was not Suffolk drawl, nor standard English, nor any accent Tessa could place. He sounded faintly Scottish.

'. . . You're doing it all wrong . . . you'll get club root if you don't rotate your brassicas . . . and eel worm in the potatoes. I'd recommend a four-year rotation on four plots, perennials and a fruit plot, that should do it. There's only three of you, you'll have plenty . . . What's this?'

'It's a potato,' said Don.

'What, on limed ground? . . . My God . . . and what happened to the beans and peas?'

'Um . . . they didn't grow.'

'When did you plant?'

'I think it was July . . .'

'My God.' He stalked round the garden like a man asked to sift through refuse because a valuable jewel had been lost there. '. . . It's not irretrievable, needs working . . . dried out, though . . .'

'It was a hot summer.'

'Hasn't been looked after properly for years . . .'

'Hi,' said Tessa, swinging her axe. He looked her up and down with one sharp glance. He had thick curly black hair, tanned skin and alarmingly blue eyes. He rubbed his beard.

'This is Tessa,' said Don. 'She lives here. This is Jack, he's—'

'Look,' said Jack, 'I'll tell you the best thing to do. First, manure heavily, sow potatoes, when they're lifted, lime, and the next year, peas and beans. After that get your brassicas in. The following spring, onions, tomatoes, radishes, could have marrows, then your root crops, but not turnips or swedes as they might get club root, after that it's spuds and you're back to the beginning again.'

'Of course,' said Don; 'could you write all this down . . .'

'You can do it on the four plots and have soft fruit, but I'd start soon if I were you, get it mucked. Potatoes go in in February. What other land have you got?' and he stamped off to look.

'Who was that?' asked Tessa.

50

'What? Oh, he's Jack.'

'He's vile.'

Don laughed. 'No, he's not vile, he's an expert.'

'How do you know?'

'When I went to the communes I heard him mentioned. He's against using chemicals. When there was a problem they said, "Let's ask Jack." And here he is, Tessa. I met him in the pub.'

'In the George? He's having you on.'

'No, it's him, he came up for Barsham Fair, which was amazing and we didn't go to it.'

'We didn't know about it.'

'There's lots of people doing what we're doing, and they all met there. Jack's been staying up since, he's been sorting people out, he says they all come to the countryside and don't know how to use a spade.'

'Don, he's horrible . . . You've asked him to stay, haven't you?'

'Well, of course, he's going to sort us out, Tessa. Next year we'll be eating our own potatoes and cabbages and peas, we could even grow asparagus . . .'

Dee came running into the walled garden. 'Oh, there you are, I'm so scared, there's a man with a big black beard. I looked out of the window and there he was, I think he's a gypsy, what shall we do?'

Tessa swung her axe high in the air.

'Oh no!' screamed Dee-Dee.

'He's called Jack,' said Tessa. 'He's Don's gardening expert and he's come to stay.'

CHAPTER SIX

They never worked so hard as they did that autumn. Under Jack's instructions the whole of the walled garden was re-dug. A cartload of manure arrived and the smell from the oozing organic heap seemed to fill every part of the garden and house. There was little point in washing; every morning they stumbled back to shift more barrow-loads of ordure. Every morning Dee-Dee was in tears, but Jack was unsympathetic. The worst part was that he worked harder than anybody. He obviously enjoyed physical exertion. After a day's work, when Don, Dee-Dee and Tessa could only hobble back to slump by the Aga, Jack would begin to chop wood, or rebuild a crumbling wall.

'He's so strong,' said Dee-Dee in awe, staring at him through the breakfast-room window. The only words she ever said to him were 'Yes, Jack.'

Don stared too. Jack's physical prowess had a hypnotic effect on him. When he was with Jack, he nodded and jumped, his eyes excited. Like what? thought Tessa; a dog with its master. It was only she who felt mutinous.

Mucky autumn slid towards winter. They sowed winter beans and peas, they planted gooseberries, raspberries and blackcurrants, they built a greenhouse against the far side of the garden wall, compost heaps were established. If they had had enough energy to reflect, they would have seen that the garden was turning into an ordered food-producing unit. The frosts came, the ground hardened, and Jack turned his attention to re-wiring the Hall, but he did this half-heartedly; the entrails of a house, it seemed, were not as fascinating to him as Nature's crusty skin.

Jack had established himself in the attic room. He did not mind that it was freezing up there; in fact he flaunted his tolerance of the cold by boasting he wore nothing in bed, when the others shivered nightly in woolly underthings. However, nobody checked whether Jack was as hardy as he claimed. Nobody dared go into his room. What Jack got up to when he closed the attic door was unknown. He demanded long periods of complete solitude. He said he was meditating using techniques taught to him by a Buddhist monk in India.

The darker winter evenings saw Jack off to the George, with Don in tow, whatever the weather, and Tessa and Dee-Dee in aprons cooking food for them when they returned. Dee was happy with this arrangement, but inside Tessa smouldered feelings of resentment and injustice; but these were not expressed. Don was so obviously infatuated and Dee-Dee's reactions she couldn't quite gauge. It occurred to Tessa that she sometimes didn't understand Dee-Dee. Since Jack's arrival she was different; the way she stared at him when he spoke to her, which wasn't often, made Tessa wonder. Dee-Dee, Don and herself still all slept together in the solar, but sleeping was all they got up to these days, bundled in clothes, dog-tired.

They were making bread by candlelight; the electricity was still erratic. Jack and Don were at the George, it was evening. Christmas was in a few weeks. Tessa had written three letters to her parents basically saying the same: 'Yes, I'm fine; no, I'm not starving; no, I'm not coming back for Christmas.' Every year, without fail, her parents started, usually at the beginning of November. 'We're getting old, you're our only child . . . you shouldn't be so selfish . . . why haven't you got a proper job . . . you're wasting your life . . . we need you . . .' For some reason Tessa was more annoyed about their behaviour than in previous years. She slammed the dough on the table. Dee-Dee was stoking the Aga. Her parents did not wave the flag of duty as often as Tessa's; besides, she had two nice sisters married to two nice men, cooking them meals in nice houses.

'The oven won't be hot enough, I'm sure,' said Dee-Dee exasperated.

'Sod it! Can't we bake the damn stuff tomorrow?'

'But Tessy, they'll be back at eleven.'

'Christ, Dee, what are we? What's our purpose in life, feeding men?'

'Tessy, they'll be hungry.'

'Sod them, I'm knackered, I'm going to bed . . . Anyway, Jack's always bloody hungry, he's a pig.'

Dee looked at her. 'That's unfair, he works hard, he has to eat a lot.'

'And we have to cook it. We work bloody hard too, you know.'

Dee-Dee was not often angry. 'You're so unfair, where would we be without Jack? He works harder than all of us, he's done everything, he got us the manure and there's a turkey for Christmas.'

'Good old Jack.'

'Tessy, I don't understand you, he's done so much.'

'And all for nothing, all for a bit of attic floor to meditate on. Whatever did we do without him. In fact, in a couple of months we won't be able to do anything at all, we'll have to ask him if we want to breathe. No, we'll have to ask Don to ask him because Jack won't talk to us.'

'Tessy!'

'Well, it's true, isn't it, when did he ever talk to you? I mean really talk, not just say, "Perhaps we can get the brassicas down in the spring." '

'He's busy . . .'

'He talks to Don.'

'Of course he does, Don has plans, they're sorting things out . . .'

'And what about us!' shrieked Tessa. 'Don't we count, don't we have plans? This is our place.'

54

Dee-Dee sat down at the table. Tessa felt if she continued Dee-Dee would burst into tears and she didn't want that.

'Why can't we all be happy?' said Dee-Dee after a while. 'I didn't know you didn't like Jack.'

'I hate him, he makes me feel inferior. He makes everybody inferior. He's unreal.'

'Oh, Tessy, he's a bit blunt, he's got a rough manner. Perhaps he's like that because he's shy.'

'You would say that,' and Tessa laughed.

Dee-Dee went quite pink. Tessa waited for her to say more, but Dee-Dee glanced at the Aga. 'Oh no, look, the oven's ready. We've got to put the bread in now.'

After the baking, Tessa went alone to bed, but, shivering under the blankets, she only half-slept. Dee-Dee waited up for the men. They came back stamping and laughing. There were other voices. They had probably met friends in the pub; Jack knew everybody.

'Wow, bread, I'm starving.' That was Don.

Jack would be tapping the loaves to see if they were done. He and his friends could devour four loaves in one sitting. Tessa listened.

'Now, the proper way to make bread . . .' began Jack. Tessa turned over irritably.

'Yes, Jack,' said Dee-Dee.

'. . . And if you add rye flour that of course improves the texture . . .' And only later, when Dee-Dee and Don climbed under the sheets too, both of them warm, smelling of yeast, honey and beer, saying, 'Shh, shh, you'll wake her.' Did Tessa finally slip away into dreamless sleep.

She did not challenge Dee-Dee again. Whatever she thought about Jack, she had to admit that throughout the winter they had enough food, they had enough fuel and this was directly due to him. He knew everybody, it seemed, from the most remote hippie in West Wales, to the farmer in St Margaret's. A spare bit of this, a bag of that, a van for a week, a goat for a month. In the George, spinach was swapped for potatoes and ducks for chickens. Tessa and Dee-Dee baked bread, pies, cakes, biscuits, to feed a stream of people who had 'just popped round to see Jack'.

Don loved it. 'Dee, this is Herbie, he's a botanist; Tessa, this is Woody, he's a carpenter . . .'

Jack, it was discovered, played the guitar and the mandolin and on Saturday evenings other musicians gathered in the great hall. Jigs and reels, ballads and shanties drifted across the fields. It seemed as if the house itself were dancing.

There were more people coming to Suffolk and Norfolk now, leaving grimy London to rent tumbledown farmhouses and cheap cottages. An influx of long-haired, floppy clothed, befuddled idealists, all harbouring the harmless intention of 'discovering Nature'.

'It's happening, it's happening,' said Don. 'The old order is breaking down. Us, everybody out here, we're going to be the new society.' And he said this when they were all stoned blotto and the music in the great hall was going on past midnight, and Jack had just scored four sacks of flour and Dee-Dee's treacle tart tasted just amazing, and everybody believed him . . .

Spring brought cold winds, rain and more hard work. Jack's list of things to be done was endless. He had established a growing schedule for the next four years and that was only a start. Between him and Don they had plans to cultivate land to feed six people, have goats and a cow, bees, chickens and ducks, but for the moment the main concern was to sow the spring vegetables.

As the months progressed, a new pattern of labour arose. Don became the contact man. He spent a great deal of time, under Jack's instructions, visiting, talking, buying and selling. He did all this without transport, so it was really a remarkable feat. He was away most days. Dee-Dee was cook, because she liked it, because she was pleasant to visitors, unlike Tessa, and she also hated gardening. She was never out of an apron. She washed all the clothes too, by hand, but this was such a chore they tended to wear things until they were unbearably filthy.

This left Jack and Tessa to manage the gardens. Her dislike for him submerged under more important considerations about where to site the cloches, and when to prune the gooseberries.

Jack's knowledge of the habits of peas and beans and cauliflowers and curly kale and artichokes was formidable. There was no point arguing with him. There was no point in saying. 'Why grow marrows, none of us like marrow,' or 'Can't we put the radishes over there?' Jack's decisions were final, ultimate; he had the authority of a demi-god.

Tessa clearing the land behind the barns, digging up the bramble roots; Jack on the roof inspecting the tiles; Don with four people who knew about barns; Dee-Dee banging saucepans, 'Dinner's ready, Dinner's ready!' – there was a pattern to life, a structure. In the breakfast room, all around the big table, Dee-Dee bringing in a huge pan of soup. Jack and Don hotly discussing the merits of growing a green manure crop, and Tessa by the Aga warming her feet, watching, the steam from the soup curling upwards in the candlelight, Dee-Dee's forehead damp from cooking, Jack's hands on the table, mud-stained, hairy, tanned, and Don's next to them, long-fingered and bony. A pattern of life. Jack in the attic doing whatever he did up there, Dee-Dee, Tessa and Don all in the big bed . . .

Don was reading aloud Hopkins poems, Dee on one side of him and Tessa on the other.

'That was beautiful,' said Dee-Dee, sighing.

'I'll blow the candle out now,' said Don. The weather was warmer, they didn't wear so many clothes in bed now.

'Night-night, Tess, Night-night, Dee,' said Don.

Tessa stared at the ceiling. There was a plaster pattern of a circle within a circle connected by radiating lines, with lumpy bosses at intersections. She was falling asleep. Don was snoring.

'Tessy?'

'Hmmm?'

'Are you awake, Tessy?'

'Yeah?'

'I want to talk to you.'

'Sure.'

'Do you think Don will hear?'

Don snored loudly. He was a heavy sleeper.

'What is it?' said Tessa.

'I've been thinking,' said Dee-Dee and she sat up. 'I've liked sharing this room, but I want my own room now. Do you think Don will mind?'

'Why should he?'

'. . . I mean, it's not so cold now, and summer's coming and it was nice at first, oh it was. Tessy, I want my own bed.'

Tessa propped herself on the pillows. She was very tired. 'It sounds fine to me.'

'Oh, I am glad you said that, I've been thinking about it a lot . . . I'll have the room above the dairy . . . but if Don minded I wouldn't do it.'

Don snored again.

'I don't think he'll even notice,' said Tessa.

Dee said nothing and Tessa closed her eyes. She was just on the verge of sleep when Dee said, 'He always liked you best.' And there might have been a hiccup in her voice but Tessa was too tired to even answer.

Dee-Dee's move to the room above the dairy, Molly's old room, was undramatic. She put up flowery curtains and laid out bits of pretty china. It was reminiscent of their old flat in Notting Hill. She had a knack of making places comfortable, a few jugs of flowers, a pile of patchwork cushions; her room was the most homely spot in the whole house. It became a place for her and Tessa to meet away from cooking smells and drying shirts. There was no animosity between them; it seemed to be accepted that gradually Tessa had become something of Don's and Dee-Dee hadn't.

Tessa was never sure of her relationship with Don. He never said, 'I love you, I think you're wonderful,' but 'I say, don't you think it would be amazing if we could build a bake house?' Don needed an audience and at night, now that Dee-Dee wasn't there and Jack was in the impenetrable attic, it was Tessa who became that.

Spring came and summer came, the vegetables grew and they ate delicious beans, new potatoes and lettuces. Dee-Dee and Tessa had been at the Hall a year. They knew they had done the right thing. The blossom on the fruit trees, the white hawthorn hedges, the ducklings in the moat all confirmed it. It had been cold, yes, wet pretty often, grubby and disorganised, but one can suffer anything in the garden of Eden.

With the warmer weather, Jack was off. There was a string of people from Newcastle on Tyne to Newcastle Emlyn who were 'useful contacts'. He persuaded Don to buy him a truck, which wasn't difficult as Don would have given him anything. Jack's absence did not mean they were thrown into ignorant chaos because he left detailed instructions.

Tessa was now chief gardener. Don helped erratically, and Dee only when she absolutely had to, but Tessa was in the garden all day, every day. The land behind the barns was cleared and planted with fruit trees, the walled garden was bursting with vegetables faster than they could eat them. It was Tessa who now read *The Cultivation of Vegetables and Flowers*. Jack, the expert, could talk for hours about what strain of carrots to grow, the methods, the techniques, but Tessa was an amateur. It was still new enough for her to be thrilled when leaves could be seen above the soil, to water them, to nurture them. Watching the marrows plump and swell, digging up white bare new potatoes, and the worms that wriggled under the clods. Even in the rain Tessa was out there, in the greenhouse, checking for leaks, weeding along the root crops on wooden planks, taking in the smell of the wet soil, earthy and rich.

A hot week in July: Tessa was tanned deep brown, Dee-Dee was golden and freckled, and even Don was sun-tinged. A summer evening; he and Tessa were in bed. The windows of the solar were open and she could see the slowly darkening sky. They had been making love and Tessa felt settled, complete, like a perfect 'O'.

In bed, in the evenings, was the only time they were together alone and during these times Tessa could almost feel that they were a couple rather than two people put together for convenience. Don talked to her in a low fast voice about gardens and vegetables, as if he were telling her some great confidence and she was the only person who was allowed to hear it.

But now he was peaceful, unusually. Downstairs in the breakfast room beneath them someone was playing an Irish whistle. Its tinny sound was lilting and melodic.

'Well, well,' said Don.

'OK?' asked Tessa.

'Oh? . . . fine . . . yes,' and he smiled. When Don smiled he looked even more like a character out of *Boys' Own*. His teeth were white and regular. 'You know . . . I think we should get married . . .'

'When, now?'

'No, in the autumn, at harvest, I think that would be right . . . everybody could come, it would be like a fair . . . people could stay . . . the Norfolk communes, I'll ask them . . .'

'Do I have a say in this?'

'What? Oh, of course, you think it's a good idea, don't you?'

They did get married, in October, which was when they had the most vegetables. Dee-Dee was ecstatic. She made Tessa a dress out of lace curtains, she cooked mountains of food. Don went to

Barsham Fair solely to invite people; the entire alternative population of England was expected. Jack came back; he had been in Wales and met someone near Carmarthen who told him. He gave Don two crates of parsnip wine as a present.

Don persuaded the vicar to marry them in St John's church. It rained the whole day. Don insisted on walking from the Hall to the church and by the time Tessa stood in front of the altar her dress was sopping and muddy. She wore gumboots. Dee-Dee and Jack were witnesses. Jack had brushed his hair down flat; he looked like Jesus. Dee-Dee cried. Tessa's unfortunate parents arrived. Her mother, in an ugly hat and Crimplene, shuffled into the cold church. If it were any consolation their daughter was marrying an aristocrat, but Hetty and George were unlike any aristocrats Tessa's parents had even seen. Hetty, with her hair in plaits, wore a faded dirndl skirt; George had the pink pure skin of those brought up on boiled fish and in chilly houses. His tweed suit had leather patches on the sleeves. Don's sisters were there, beautiful in a strange large-eyed languid way.

'We are gathered here today . . .' said the vicar, looking baffled at the bedraggled pair.

'. . . I will,' said Don.

'. . . I will,' said Tessa.

The party went on for the whole weekend. Tessa's parents had brief words with Hetty and George over some elderflower fizz, then went, leaving their mad daughter to the unholy revels. The folk music was in full swing in the great hall, women were dancing, hair and dresses swirling. There were jugglers tossing apples, bananas, plates; Jack was pouring parsnip wine into any available receptacle; Don's sisters wandered like lost souls; Hetty found a beautiful young man with auburn hair down past his shoulders.

'I see, and you're a carpet salesman?'

'Well, I got these rugs from Kashmir . . .'

'Oh, I love Kashmir, let me give you my number in London, perhaps we could meet sometime . . .'

61

Jack was telling George about his proposals for St John's. 'Four years, four years and this will be the organic growing centre of the east . . . Now, about my plans for converting the barns . . .'

'Of course, dear old Geoffrey used to have such plans . . .'

'Try this plum wine, it has an amazing texture.'

'Don, well, it's quite a gathering.'

'It's wonderful, isn't it. This is the new world you're looking at.' Herbie, the botanist, handed George a joint.

'I haven't had any of this stuff since Peshawar 'forty-nine. It's better in a hookah . . . did I ever tell you about the month I spent with the Pathans?'

Dee-Dee and Tessa were dancing to the fiddle music, diddle-dee, doodle-dee, diddle-dee, dee. Tessa's dress was ripped, but she didn't care. Miranda, Frances and the ballerina-like Marsha were being whirled by German anarchists from Lodden. The music went faster and faster.

'Tessy, I'm so happy!' said Dee-Dee, quite dizzy.

'Yes, I'm happy too.'

'Where's Don?'

'Oh, I don't know, he could be anywhere.'

Sunday evening and it was still raining. Most people had drifted off back to their cottages and farmhouses. Those in caravans and trucks were still there, extending as long as possible the comforts offered by St John's. Hetty and George and Don's sisters were going. 'Come and see us again.'

'We will, Don.'

'George, are you sure you can drive?'

'No I'm not. Frances can drive. Where is Frances?'

'Jack's explaining crop rotation to her.'

'Explaining crop rotation! She's a biologist,' said Tessa.

'She won't mind.'

'Where's Marsha? Here she is, and Frances too, now where's Miranda?'

'Oh Daddy, fascinating, I just met someone who makes rebecks . . .'

They left. 'I like your family,' said Tessa to Don. Married life so far meant exchanging the briefest of comments.

'Yes . . . yes . . . I like them too.'

'They seemed to have enjoyed themselves.'

'Oh, they always do . . . Tess, listen, there's somebody here who knows about bees. I think he's called Wally. I must find him . . .'

He left her standing there. Tessa felt some expectation, some hope drop into her boots. Last night, just before he fell straight asleep, he said, 'We could have bees . . .' Not the most romantic of phrases for a honeymoon night. The wedding hasn't changed anything, she thought, and she watched him talking earnestly to Wally. But something about Don's energy moved her. This enthusiasm was pure and unaffected. He saw her and waved and smiled, a quick flash radiant smile like sunlight.

No, I don't want him to change, thought Tessa. Being married to Don was to be part of that celebration of life.

She wandered to the orchard. There were ten or so people dancing under the apple trees in the rain. There was no music, only that which could be heard from the Hall. Dee was there, water dripping from her hair, the others Tessa didn't know. Their faces were serious, solemn almost. They were weaving in and out of the trees, dodging windfallen fruit on the grass.

Tessa looked across the moat to the tower of St John's church. It was from here last year she had watched Jack stride up the drive to rearrange them all. The sky, low with rain, seemed to touch the ploughed fields, but Tessa didn't feel gloomy. What she felt was entirely new, like being on the edge of something, like opening a door and stepping into a different world. What now, she thought, in her torn muddy curtain dress, in her boots and stripy socks.

Dee-Dee saw her and beckoned her over, silently, as if she too felt something momentous had happened. Tessa took her hand and together they joined the circle of noiseless dancers.

63

Chapter Seven

First the winds in the autumn. Digging in the walled garden. Sheltered, but not so sheltered that the wind wasn't physical force. Bringing home cabbages, Brussels sprouts, parsnips, turnips. Boots doubled with mud, like walking with concrete feet. In the porch, the spades and forks and hoes. Across the stone flags in socks. Past the great hall, too draughty to sit in. In there were boxes of apples, their cidery rotting smell adding to the damp odours. Winter fuel was stored in heaps against the wall. A few relics from a summer; a jug of dead flowers and empty wine bottles.

The corridor to the breakfast room was dark and there was a row of candles along the big table. The windows were steamy. Stew with dumplings was cooking on the Aga. Wind rattled the windows, blew through all the cracks in the door, boomed down the chimney. The breakfast room, the heart of the house. Tessa put the box of vegetables on the table.

Then the rain. Lying in bed listening in the early dark morning, the rain hammering on the solar window, Tessa felt relieved, perhaps, but also frustrated; there was so much to do and none of it would get done. The gutter was blocked. A jet of water spurted onto the courtyard. And the rain meant baking, but that was frustrating too, for the Aga was slow and the dough wouldn't rise and the whole of the breakfast room oozed damp. Dee-Dee's hair was tied up all anyhow. Jack and Don were off to talk bees with Wally.

Tessa thumped the dough. The table shook and the candles wobbled, and Dee-Dee looked uneasy and scared.

* * *

Sitting on Mirabelle's French chairs in an August orchard, she drew the flowers in the borders. Yellow marigolds, hollyhocks, marguerites, but she was thinking of snow. Snow that fell quietly in the night and she only knew it was there by the unusual stillness of the morning, the windows laced with intricate ferny frost patterns.

* * *

She blew on the frost and scraped with her finger, shivering on the floor boards in her socks and pyjamas. Outside was all white and the truck had a drift of snow against it. It was almost covered. The snow was clean. There were no footsteps yet.

Quietly she dressed and woke up Dee-Dee. Don was still dead to the world.

'It's been snowing. Let's go out.'

'Is it early?'

'The sun's up.'

Outside, the sun was red and heavy. There was no wind; everything was still and frozen. The snow, powdery, crumpled under their feet. Theirs were the first human footsteps. Tracks of little birds dotted the courtyard. In the orchard were the paw-prints of, possibly, a hare. They walked silently. For as far as they could see the fields were white and, as the sun rose further, dazzling. The moat was frozen. Tessa kicked the ice with her boot. It made a hollow sound.

'Is it safe?' asked Dee-Dee.

'I think it's quite thick.'

'Shall we go on it?'

They eased themselves down. The ice creaked. 'Oh Tessy!'

'It's fine.' Tessa jumped, laughing. 'God, it must be two foot deep!' and they slid about giggling and throwing snowballs until their feet and hands were too cold to feel any more.

An upstairs window opened and it was Jack.

'Come outside, it's wonderful!' yelled Tessa.

'Get off that ice, you stupid women.'

'Jack, it's really solid.'

'Get off it at once, if you fall in you'll last minutes. It must be minus four.'

'Oh Christ!' Tessa hurled a snowball at him, but he was too high up. He slammed the window shut.

'He's right,' said Dee apologetically, banging the snow off her gloves.

'Jack is always right.' Tessa stormed to the walled garden and sulked inside the greenhouse until she was as cold as the Brussels sprout stumps in the snow.

Back at the Hall Dee-Dee was making porridge and Don was burning the toast.

'Oh Tessy, you must be frozen!'

'There you are,' said Don; 'Jack's going to show us Arctic survival techniques.'

* * *

Tessa in Mirabelle's orchard drawing the flowers. For her, growing onions, leeks and cabbages hadn't been enough. She wanted St John's to be beautiful.

She realised this in the spring when the snowdrops came up and the banks of the moat were white with them. Don cried when the snowdrops came up, so he said, and she felt like that too. Dee-Dee wanted to pick bunches for the house but Tessa said, 'No, leave them, they look better where they are.' The first flowers. Winter was over.

Jack and Don were discussing the spring planting. This year would see the first crop of asparagus.

'I think there should be more flowers,' said Tessa by the Aga, and Jack and Don looked up, surprised, as if she had said, 'I think we should get an elephant.'

Jack rubbed his beard. This habit annoyed Tessa; it meant he disagreed with her. 'Flowers would not be profitable, we'd need greenhouses.'

66

'Profit? What are you, a capitalist?'

'Unfortunately, we need money to survive, vegetables we can sell . . .'

'I think he's right, Tess,' said Don, wanting to avoid argument. Tessa scowled furiously.

'Of course, we do have a manpower problem. Our resources are stretched.' Jack was being forcibly calm. He turned his back on Tessa. 'I think we should try an earlier ripening strain of raspberries; summers are dry here . . .'

Dee came in with a cake. She saw at once that Tessa was angry. 'Oh dear,' she said. 'Would anyone like some?'

'Sod you!' shouted Tessa, but not to Dee-Dee. 'Can't I grow flowers if I want to? Not to sell, you burk, but to look at.'

'Yes, I would like some,' said Jack.

'Christ, you won't even listen to me!'

'We are short of money, we are short of resources.' Jack spoke softly but with an air of finality.

'I'm the resource, I'm out there in the bloody garden, don't I have a choice what to do with my time?'

'This is almost good,' said Jack with his mouth full; 'however, a fruit cake should be more moist.' Crumbs fell onto his beard. Tessa felt she had never hated anyone so much.

'You two, you plan and decide, but I do the work.'

'Tess, we all work,' said Don, 'in our own ways.' He cut himself a piece of cake. Tessa's moods did not upset him.

'Oh dear,' sighed Dee-Dee.

'Listen!' shouted Tessa. 'It won't cost money, it won't cost time. Of course what we eat is a priority, but if you,' and she pointed accusingly at Jack, 'can scrounge wood and old nails all for bloody nothing, then I can scrounge flowers, especially as you reckon they're so worthless. I'll look after the sodding vegetables, there's no question I won't, all I'm asking for is a bit of crappy land to plant flowers. You can always close your eyes when you pass them.'

Jack stood up. He was extremely angry.

'This is a scrummy cake, Dee,' said Don.

'We have no plans for the borders along the house . . . as yet,' said Jack.

'Hmm, yes, flowers would look good there,' said Don.

'And what about the bit of garden with the old rose bushes, I've heard you say it would take too much work to cultivate.' Tessa stood up too.

'I did say that,' said Jack, and left.

There was an uneasy silence.

'Well, that's all settled then,' said Don, but one glance at Tessa could tell that it wasn't. 'Wally and Sue've moved into Hare Cottage at Redlesham. I thought I might go round there . . .'

Jack was outside chopping wood audibly.

'Er, yes . . . he might want to go as well . . .'

Tessa and Dee-Dee in the breakfast room listened as Don tried to start the truck. Jack was giving sharp instructions. Eventually it choked awake and they heard it rattle and bump out of the courtyard. Dee-Dee cut Tessa a very large piece of cake.

'Here,' she said. Tessa was silent, but victorious.

Tessa's father used to show dahlias and her memory of growing flowers was connected with the fussy business of staking, slug pellets and storing tubers in boxes over the winter. Her ideal garden was wild and rambling. There was order enough in the vegetable plots, weedless rows of onions and neatly spaced fat cabbages. However, apart from dahlias she could only recognise a handful of garden plants.

'How about herbs?' said Dee-Dee. 'They'd be great for cooking.'

Jack made notes on how much time Tessa 'wasted'.

'I remember what the gardens were like when we first used to come here,' said Don; 'there were tall purple things, and white flowers with scented leaves and Miranda used to make scent out of rose petals and vinegar . . .' All this was very unhelpful.

'Herbs have to be near the house,' said Tessa. She and Dee were in the great hall. It was April. The mice had eaten all the apples, there had been a leak in the roof, the Hall was in a wretched state.

'Here's a book on gardens,' said Dee-Dee, wiping off a thin film of furry mould. They were cleaning the place up.

'We could plant the herbs by the dairy where the rose bushes are,' said Tessa.

'I thought they were brambles.'

'No, I think they're a sort of wild rose.' She was trying to make a fire, unsuccessfully; the smoke wouldn't go up the chimney. 'There must be a bird's nest up there.' She peered up into the blackness. It was raining and water dropped onto her face. 'It's leaking again, I thought Jack had fixed the flashing.'

'Here's another book,' said Dee-Dee. 'It's called *The History of Gardens*, it's got nice pictures.'

Tessa poked a broom handle up the chimney. 'Are there many gardening books?' She left the fire and joined Dee-Dee sorting. They found an encyclopedia of garden plants and various tattered paperbacks. The encyclopedia was damp but had hundreds of coloured photographs. They sat on the floor. 'Dahlias, daphnes, delphiniums.'

'I like those. My grandmother grew those,' said Dee-Dee.

' "*Delphinium elatum*. Pyrenees to Siberia. Height three to five foot," ' read Tessa. ' "This hardy erect perennial has deeply cut and toothed palmate leaves." What does that mean? "Derived from crosses with *Delphinium grandiflorum* . . . cuttings should be taken close to the rootstock and inserted in equal parts (by volume) peat and sand, in a cold frame." '

'Do you understand all that?' asked Dee-Dee.

'Sort of, it's like vegetables really, there's a cold frame by the greenhouse.'

'Jack'll go barmy if you use it.'

Tessa shrugged her shoulders. 'I could probably start things off in here, it's cold enough.' Something fell down the chimney and landed with a wet thud in the fire.

'Uggh!' said Dee. 'What was that?'

'Probably a bird.'

'I don't think I want to look.' Whatever it was the smoke began to seep upwards. The thing crackled.

Tessa flicked through the book. 'Euphorbia, genista, helianthus, ionopsidium, I've never heard of half of these.'

'Are you going to grow them all?'

'I don't know, I'll have to read the book first.'

'Tessy, it's massive, it'll take you all year.'

'There are things growing here. I'll identify them when they come up . . . it's got a section on roses, that'll be useful . . .'

Dee-Dee was getting bored. She began to sweep the floor. A large spider scuttled from under the sofa. Dee thumped it with the broom; she hated spiders.

' "Old roses . . ." ' read Tessa, as if reading a book of spells, '"hardy shrubs, of open and lax habit . . . a precise classification is difficult . . ." '

Hot weather: they threw open the windows that overlooked the moat, sat on the grass on the sheltered side, and watched martins swooping from the eaves. Jack and Don were out, like primitive hunters, except it was not meat they were after but tyres, panes of glass and elderflower wine.

Without Jack to supervise, Tessa could do what she pleased and this meant restoring the rose garden. It was her task, her obsession. The rose bushes, unlike modern roses, were straggling and floppy and the stems trailed. In a way they were ugly, if one expected roses to be highly coloured and pert. But in June the tightly packed flowers were wonderfully fragrant, shaded from the palest pinks to the darkest crimsons, for old roses are never orange or vibrant scarlet.

The previous year there had been few blooms, but Tessa cut away suckers and dead stems, she pinned the climber back to the wall, she cut the grass till it was almost like a lawn, she read everything she could about roses.

Dee-Dee was baking bread. She brought the loaves outside to

cool. Her face was hot from cooking. The door to the dairy was open. In there, on the shelves, were stocks of jam and pickled onions, bottles of wine and cheese wrapped in paper. Tessa was sitting by the wall. She had cut a bunch of roses and was trying to identify them, comparing them to pictures in a book. 'Look, Dee, this one's called Charles de Mills, it's a gallica, the stems are stiffer.'

'Does it smell?'

'Not much. Try this one, it's a Mme. Isaac Pereire. It's supposed to be the most fragrant rose. If it's on a wall it can reach fifteen foot.'

'Oh, it's beautiful, it's like perfume. Tell me them all, Tessy, you're so clever.'

'I'm not really. Some only flower in June and July like the damasks, but the bourbons go on until autumn. The bourbons are floppy and so are the damasks, but they've got downy leaves. The gallicas are more like wild roses, and this is a moss rose, the stems are bristly. I think it's a Henri Martin . . . this one's a damask and it's bi-coloured and so is this one, it's called *Rosa gallica*. That's a Boule de Neige, the one on the wall's a Zépherine Drouhin . . .'

'I love the names, they're so pretty.'

'How about Baroness Rothschild, Mme. de la Roche-Lambert, Lavender Lassie, Duc de Fitzjames?'

'Are they really old, have they been here for hundreds of years?' Dee-Dee lay back on the grass and looked at the sky.

'Probably Victorian.'

'You know, you almost know as much as Jack now . . .'

'Oh Dee!' Tessa shut the book. 'Jack doesn't give a toss, he'd dig the whole lot up and grow rhubarb.'

'I didn't mean . . .' said Dee-Dee. She picked up the flowers carefully with a cloth. 'I'll put them in water or they'll wilt.'

Tessa inspected the bushes for greenfly. The glorious blooms wafted scent invitingly. She reached out to cup one and as she did so her hand jagged along a thorn.

CHAPTER EIGHT

Tessa took her sketchpad and walked by the moat to the rose garden that wasn't there any more. The ugliness of the swimming pool was still hurtful.

The concrete perimeter was hedged with conifers. An unsuitable choice, thought Tessa; they could have planted beech, hornbeam, hawthorn or even rugosa roses.

The conifers were a uniform flat green, almost unnatural. The patio doors opened and out stepped Mirabelle.

'There you are! I was going to bring you coffee, wasn't I?'

'It doesn't matter.'

'But look at the time! It's nearly two and you've had no lunch ... oh please!' She gestured to a sun-bed. Tessa sat on it awkwardly. She was not used to lounging by swimming pools. Although there was a breeze the sun was undeniably hot.

Mirabelle flitted restlessly. 'I do apologise, you must think me a terrible hostess . . . Three clients were after the same work, a Helen Allingham . . . I've been on the phone all morning . . . and I can't locate Bernard, it's most trying, his secretary's not at home, she always knows where he is . . . Lunch? I must make you lunch . . . Salad? Would that do? And pâté? It's from Bungay, it's very good.'

The patio doors led to what had been the dairy and was now a kitchen with a huge oak table, a stone floor and unused-looking copper pots and pans.

Mirabelle prepared the food. 'Of course, you could swim. The pool's not heated, Bernard says it's too expensive, so I never do, but it's so hot, isn't it?'

'I haven't brought anything,' said Tessa.

72

'There's a spare costume in the changing hut . . . Oh do, I like to see the pool used . . . It's pink. I bought it in France but I never liked it.'

Tessa changed into Mirabelle's swimsuit. She didn't feel ashamed to wear such an expensive rag and she didn't mind that Mirabelle looked her up and down as she walked to the pool. In a swimming costume you could see how athletic she was. She hadn't shaved her legs, though. Perhaps Mirabelle found that distasteful.

She dived into the water. It was cold enough to make her gasp; only a few inches on the surface were warm. She swam several lengths. They used to swim in the moat, which was murky and weed trailed their feet. After a hot spell the water was like green soup and noisy with flies. Mirabelle's pool was glass-clear and chlorinated.

'Your lunch is ready!'

Tessa heaved herself out of the water and shook herself like a dog. She was quite unlike a bathing beauty. Mirabelle handed her a towel, presumably to cover herself, but instead Tessa slung it over her shoulders. She sat at the table on the patio. Mirabelle brought an elaborate salad, like a work of art, with sorrel leaves and shreds of parmesan. There was one place set. She watched Tessa eat as though eating were a habit alien to her. Tessa bit off a large chunk of bread smeared liberally with pâté. She picked up a sorrel leaf with her fingers and ate that too. Mirabelle shuddered.

Tessa devoured the salad. Swimming had made her hungry.

'We could have wine,' suggested Mirabelle.

'I don't drink.'

'Not at all?'

'Never.'

'Er . . . religious reasons?'

Tessa laughed. 'I like to be sober these days.'

*

73

The phone bleeped and Mirabelle ran to answer it. Tessa smoked a French cigarette and studied her sketches. Mirabelle came back with coffee in gold cups, and eclairs. These she did eat. Holding them delicately, she wiped the cream off her lips with her little finger. 'Can I see?' she asked, picking up the sketches. She studied them with a serious face. 'They're very good,' she said at last.

'Yes, I know.' Tessa took the last eclair and ate it in two mouthfuls.

They sat for a while in silence. Mirabelle toyed with a pair of sunglasses, putting them off and on.

'You don't really like it here, do you?' said Tessa.

Mirabelle turned towards her, hidden behind dark lenses. 'No, I don't think I do . . .' She smiled. 'When I first met Bernard, I was living in Putney . . . oh, we used to see all the shows . . . and eat out . . . that was a long time ago.' She laughed and threw back her head. 'Oh . . . he was getting a divorce and his wife was here . . . she liked it . . . she had a horse and three dogs . . . she lives in Norfolk now. I see her sometimes . . . but Bernard didn't want to be part of the county set, they're all so terribly dull. He's very cultured. His wife married a farmer in the end . . . and I . . . I used to be his secretary . . .' She took off her sunglasses and frowned. Something had just occurred to her.

'Children?' asked Tessa.

'Oh, me? No, I didn't have any . . . and, well, it never really happened . . . Bernard's got three sons, they're grown up.' She shuddered. 'And you . . . children?'

'No,' said Tessa.

'Well, well.' Mirabelle was taut like a piece of stretched paper. 'Anyway, I don't think this place likes children.' She laughed nervously.

'What makes you say that?' Tessa leaned forward. Behind Mirabelle rose the solid wall of St John's.

'I was thinking of that little girl, did you hear about it?'

'Oh, yes.' The phone sounded again in the kitchen.

74

'I'll see you later, yes?' said Mirabelle, hurrying.

'I finish at four.'

For some reason Tessa didn't want to listen to Mirabelle's telephone conversation. She dressed back into her clothes and went to the side of the house overlooking the moat. Here, on the doorstep, by a clump of artemesia, she could see the hamlet of St John's, but she didn't draw this, or the tangled banks of the moat, she began to sketch the rose garden as she remembered it.

* * *

Their third summer at St John's. Like it or hate it, it was their home. They couldn't imagine living anywhere else. In the rose garden Tessa planted lavender and rosemary. Other herbs grew in tubs by the dairy wall.

Early morning, and the grass was still wet with dew. Tessa was awake and sitting on the dairy doorstep. It was the last weekend of August. Dee came and joined her. She had made a pot of rose-hip tea. She poured the pink liquid into a cracked flowery cup.

'It's a lovely day.'

'Yes, it is,' said Tessa, smiling at the sun.

'You will come with us, won't you?'

'I'm not sure yet.' Jack and Don were already at Barsham, setting up. They were very much involved with the fairs and somehow this single fact made Tessa uncertain.

'Last year it was great, it was.'

Wally and Sue were coming later to give them a lift. 'Later' meant any time over the next two days.

'It's not like the Isle of Wight, Tessy, or Hyde Park . . . it's wonderful.'

'That's all anybody says about Barsham, "It's wonderful." '

Then up the drive came Wally's ambulance. It was half-past eight in the morning. Wally never got out of bed until lunchtime. They ran to meet him.

'What happened? Is it the baby?' In the car were Sue, Wally and their four children.

'We've been to Barsham. We've been up all night!'

Sue was breastfeeding their two-year old. The other children leapt out of the car and disappeared, yelling, into the garden.

'Hey, they're wild!' laughed Wally.

They had breakfast in the rose garden. Wally rolled joints, Sue knitted. Tansy, the two-year-old, unwound a ball of wool around the rose bushes. 'Yeah, like a maze, Tanse!' laughed Wally. He was long and lanky. His hair was long too. He was clean-shaven and looked young but withered. His teeth were blackened. Now he smoked only dope, constantly.

Sue was extremely beautiful, a Botticelli Venus, long blonde hair, not crinkly-golden like Dee's but straight and pale. She too was always stoned, and pregnant; number five was expected on the winter solstice.

Willow, the eldest, was seven. 'Sue, Josh and Jesse are playing football with a cabbage, Tansy has found a wasp and I'm sure it will sting her, can I have a drink? Josh has hit Jesse with a stick, when are we going? I liked the fireworks, will there be any more? Josh has hit Tansy and she's crying . . .'

'Wow, she so together!' laughed Wally. The twins were screaming.

'Darlings, petals, what is it?' said Sue.

'Josh is hitting me!'

'Jesse's broke a window!'

'Cool it, cool it,' laughed Wally. 'Aggression's only for politicians, yeah?'

Tansy stumped across to her mother. She was dumpy and dirty. She clambered onto Sue's lap and tugged her mother's breasts. 'Baby, darling,' murmured Sue. The child drank and eventually fell asleep. Sue, with one breast dangling, continued to knit.

Sometime in the afternoon they decided to go. The children were eventually packed into the ambulance.

'Oh, do come,' pleaded Dee-Dee. Tessa looked cautiously at the grubby, wailing gang.

'I'll sit with them, I'll tell them a story,' said Dee. 'I love children.'

Tessa squeezed next to Sue. Wally had rolled a joint for the journey . . .

There was a collection of vans, Morris Travellers, painted trucks and rusty cars. People in costumes, kings, queens, beggars – it was difficult to tell. Skinny lurchers prowled, wild tangled-haired children in jumble-sale clothes ran in packs like the dogs. Jugglers, maypole-dancers, stilt-walkers. People everywhere, sitting in groups drinking beer from plastic cups, or wandering about dazed and smiling. Jack by the beer tent, stripped to the waist; Jack by the maypole playing the mandolin. Dozens of Jacks, with bushy hair and black beards, blonde beards, ginger beards. Women like Dee and Tessa, in patched faded skirts and scarves, or wildly exotic in Rajasthani dresses. In the heat several were almost nude; a girl with dark hair plaited with ribbons wore silk camiknickers, a man in an Afghani-type head-dress wore a loin cloth. Tanned bodies, the young, the beautiful, the not-so-young and the blatantly revolting . . .

There were stalls, higgledy-piggledy and colourful, tied up with string, selling Indian jewellery, wholefood snacks, decorated belts, herbs and tarot readings. From the tall rickety structures of the domes and warrens flags flapped. Dee-Dee and Tessa sat down. What was immediately apparent and also unusual was that everybody was smiling – even the local people, noticeable in ordinary clothes, shoulder to shoulder with medieval peasants complete with a stick-on plague.

'Look at that' – a fire-eater. 'Come and see' – a Zodiac dance. Near Dee and Tessa a group of ruralists played folk music and behind them, with rolled up sleeves, an ancient codger tapped spoons, but he wasn't out of place. A plump woman in a sleeveless summer frock, a handbag on one arm, clapped in time. A girl in a kaftan started dancing . . .

Sue and Wally met up with some people they knew from Cornwall, and there was Don selling vegetables. 'Fresh fruit, garden fresh!' the sign over his stall read. 'Don's amazing organic produce.'

'Oh, wow, there you are! Isn't it wonderful? Did you see the gypsy caravans? Jack knows them from Wales. I found the most fascinating chap who told me about carrots. I wish you'd met him, Tess, he said you have to grow them in barrels . . . Look, there's Herbie and Trish . . . look after the stall, I'll just go and see them.'

He went for two hours, but it didn't matter. Above them flags flapped against the sky. It was hot and the lettuces were wilting. A dog pissed on the stall. Children ran off with some tomatoes. The couple selling bangles next to them rolled a joint. 'Organic? What's that?' asked a freckled-faced Beccles woman.

The afternoon became evening and bonfires started up. The stars came out, as did the bongo drums. Curry smells wafted. It was going to be a warm night. They went to find Jack. In a group were about fifteen caravans, from the most elaborate and beautifully painted to ones that were just trucks and tarpaulin. Piebald horses grazed nearby. And there was Jack, playing the guitar. He nodded when he saw them. His friends were older people, dark-skinned like himself. Perhaps they were real Romanies. A woman in headscarf and apron offered tea in tin mugs. 'Jack's friends, friends of ours.'

The fireworks began, but Tessa and Dee-Dee dozed by the campfire, on one side of them a snoring brindled lurcher, on the other Tansy. Dee-Dee patted her sticky hair.

'It's a pity there aren't any children at St John's,' said Dee-Dee dreamily. Other small children could be heard wailing; the older ones full of manic energy charged about.

'Do you think you'll have babies?' asked Dee-Dee.

Tessa on her back counted the stars. 'Oh probably . . . some-time . . .'

'And what does Don say?'

Don was accompanying Jack on the frying pan. 'I don't know, he's never really mentioned it.' She turned over and looked at him. From all over the fair could be heard drumming. Everything that made a noise was being thumped. The sound was unearthly but also celebratory. This is the new society, right here, thought Tessa. But a new society had to expand. She sat up and shook the debris from the fire out of her hair. Dee next to her was a picture, a perfect Madonna, golden and tranquil. Its ironic, thought Tessa. She had Don, but producing babies, for her, was a necessary chore. To Dee-Dee it was bliss, it was heaven. An apron tied round a fat belly, moving from the cooking pot to the nappy tub. Yet Dee-Dee, at the end of a potholed lane, had nobody.

Don and Jack stood up. Near the maypole people were dancing and singing; drunk, most probably, but not offensive. Their manner was spontaneous. 'Look at that!' said Don. 'That's it, that's what living should be like. Don't you think we're better than the dead souls in the ordinary world?' Tessa smiled. She felt that too. Jack stretched and yawned. He knew he was better than anybody.

'Dee?' began Tessa, but Dee-Dee was not listening, and now she wasn't gazing admiringly at sleeping Tansy, but across the glowing bonfire, at Jack.

CHAPTER NINE

Dee-Dee had a crush on Jack. She gave him the largest slices of pie, the first cut of newly baked bread. She washed and mended his sweaty shirts, she listened to anything he said as if uttered by an angel. Tessa put down her pencil. Dee's face was as real as it had been by the Barsham bonfires, tranquil, loving, smitten. Oh Dee, thought Tessa, what a goose, but lovingly. Only Dee-Dee could have fallen for somebody so arrogant. Jack didn't need women. He tolerated them when they were there, but his position as hero, provider, authority on all living things, was daily reinforced by men. Nobody could compete with him, for Jack's sole aim, it seemed, was to be the best. His wanderings through the alternative colonies of England weren't to find friendship but to gather knowledge, to gain status. Tessa felt genuinely sorry for Dee-Dee, her loving cooking, her sewing, her caring, it was hardly noticed – perhaps a grunt or a nod from Jack.

And just as her love for her friend could come to her unchanged across the years when there had been greater upheavals than concreting rose gardens, so her feelings towards Jack were unchanged too. And as she looked across the sunny fields to St John's hamlet, her dislike, her disgust, were as overwhelming as if a storm cloud had rolled across the sky and she was hearing thunder.

* * *

'It's four o'clock,' said Mirabelle. 'Oh? . . . oh.' Tessa blinked in the sun.

'I have to go out . . . something's cropped up.' Mirabelle smiled, but she was visibly worried.

'Well, I've finished.'

'I was thinking,' said Mirabelle, stroking her jewellery, 'about your work and how much I would like it . . . and Bernard too.' At his name she stopped and checked herself. 'It would be nice if you could sketch the inside of the house.'

'It's not on the schedule,' said Tessa.

'Yes, yes, I realise that, but I meant in addition. I would pay you, of course.'

'You'll have to contact my agents.' Tessa stood up.

Mirabelle's eyes were the palest palest blue, almost transparent. She smiled, forcibly; she was, after all, a business woman.

'Would that be really necessary?'

Tessa thought of Pumpkin's disapproval and laughed. 'A private arrangement?'

'Something like that . . . I thought, the rooms downstairs and some of the bedrooms.'

'Watercolours?'

'Oh yes.'

'Four paintings. I'll do more sketches, you can choose.'

'When could you start?'

'Well, I could start now.'

'Oh, I have to go out,' she quivered.

'Does it matter? Will you be long? I'll be about three hours.'

'You've been working all day.'

'I prefer it that way. It's settled then?'

'Yes, it's settled,' said Mirabelle.

Both of them looked across the moat. The breeze ruffled Mirabelle's pleats. The martins were flying lower now, wheeling in circles above the Hall. It was a sight so familiar to Tessa she felt she had never been away.

'You know, there's a saying, "Once you get into the Saints you can never get out." Do you think it's spiritual or physical?'

'I hope it's neither.' And the expression on Mirabelle's face was not so much worry as terror.

*

Mirabelle left in a flurry. The answerphone was on. Tessa was alone. She envied Don his months spent here; she never had more than a day before the place was full again with angst and people's egos bumping.

The walls of the house were thick. Few noises from outside penetrated. Inside, the silence was thick too, each footstep, each rustle of clothing was like a drum banged.

There was still an Aga in the breakfast room, but this one was new and shining, oil-fired. The Hallivands didn't have to stoke and poke it. A dark oak table rested in the middle of the room. On this were flowers arranged in vases and large cheese dishes. This was the oldest part of the house. The two windows were gothic and hewn out of the walls. On the sills, more china. It didn't seem to be a room that was much used, perhaps only for dinner parties. From the beams hung dried flowers, the sort one buys in decor shops, not the sort one picks from the garden. A new table, a new kitchen. In a way these seemed superficial, as moveable as paintings on a wall. St John's, from Geoffrey's old-fashioned discomfort and their muddle, to the Hallivands' antique furniture; their dairy now a kitchen, their kitchen now a corridor, and, before Geoffrey, the function of the rooms altering and altering again, back through extensions and raisings of ceilings and building and re-building. Yet somehow the original house remained.

She remembered her first night at St John's, feeling she was going to capture it, but how optimistic and naive that had been; they were the ones who were captured, dominated by the demands of such an ancient entity – 'the spirit of a place' – but for Tessa, alone, without Mirabelle to distract her, St John's was a spirit.

She drew a quick sketch of the breakfast room. She could draw four sketches in forty minutes, but Mirabelle needn't know that. She went upstairs. Dee-Dee's room was a pretty bedroom with

82

pale curtains and sprigged wallpaper in blue and yellow. The afternoon light was warm. From here was the best view of the rose garden. In early summer evenings the scent from the roses wafted upwards. Now, of course, it overlooked the swimming pool. The other side of the room faced the courtyard. Tessa felt this room was unused; there were no personal belongings, pots of make-up, paper tissues, little photographs. It was a show bedroom. Dee had filled the window sills with geraniums; now there were only printed flowers on the wallpaper. She shut the door.

Further up the stairs was the attic, Jack's room. This too, although tasteful, also lacked anything living. Cupboards had been built under the eaves, but the room was like a magazine example: 'What to do with all that wasted space'. The cupboards were empty.

Dee's room, Jack's room – there was not much of her in these places, even though she spent hours with Dee on the patchwork cushions, listening to her soothing chatter. Dee's presence was calming, like a warm blanket, but Tessa felt most herself only when alone. Sharp and stern, ice, steel, bone, she felt like that now. She went to the solar, her bedroom, hers and Don's. Don had never cossetted or comforted her.

The solar had heavy carved furniture, and the bed, though cleaned and restored, was recognisable. Don must have sold it to the Hallivands. The room was dark red and green, not gloomy because the windows were huge, but sombre and masculine. It reminded Tessa of Murray's house in Bath. There was something about it barring any decorative touches. Something about it barring anything emotional. She opened the wardrobe. In it were rows of suits and silk dresses in plastic covers. So this was the Hallivands' bedroom. On a chest of drawers was a silver brush and comb, but these were for display, not practical. One window overlooked the courtyard, the other the moat. She sat on this

83

window sill; it was low enough and wide enough. The curtains were heavy crimson velvet.

* * *

They were poor. The garden produced food for them, Jack scrounged extras for them, but there was no money. Don's inheritance was almost spent. He had been generous and Dee and Tessa knew it. He had only asked for dedication, but this couldn't pay for paint and wood and plaster. St John's continually crumbled. 'The money problem' was much discussed.

'We are not going to use the State, we are separate from the State, we are our own State.' This was Don's argument. 'It would be a failure if we signed on, it would be saying, "We can't manage, we need Big Brother to look after us." '

It was winter. There was always a crisis in the winter.

'Jack agrees with me, don't you?'

Jack nodded.

'Oh Christ, look at your bank statement, we can't even order seeds for the spring.'

'I'm sure I could arrange something,' said Jack, not looking at Tessa.

'And what if the truck breaks down?'

'I'm sure that could be arranged too.'

'You're so bloody certain, aren't you . . . and what if you break down?'

Jack laughed, a cynical snort. He always laughed like that.

'You're not immortal, you might get ill.'

'You're being ridiculous.'

'Tessy, Jack doesn't get ill, does he?' But Dee's comments only made Tessa more angry.

'Sod it! We're supposed to be a community, working together, but when it comes down to it, we're wasters who've spent Don's money and rely on scrounging.'

'That isn't fair,' said Don.

'We're broke and it's winter, look at us, just look at us, do we

84

seem inspiring?' They hadn't bought any new clothes for three years. It was fashionable to be scruffy, but they had long gone beyond the limits of fashion. Don wrapped his dressing gown around him. It was Geoffrey's and he was proud of it. Tessa and Dee-Dee were almost completely clad in patches and darns, and any bit of Jack that wasn't muddy was black with oil. Dee-Dee began to laugh.

'We shouldn't be judged on externals, it's our spiritual existence that's important,' said Don, but he did look so ridiculous. Tessa began to laugh too.

Jack wiped his greasy hand on his jeans. 'As I see it, I think it would be ideologically sound for one of us to take on a job for the good of the community.'

'Where, in the chicken factory?' said Tessa. 'I can't, I'm up to here in the garden.' She was still laughing.

'Oh, I see your point,' said Don, 'but it couldn't be any job, it would have to be compatible with our principles, like . . . We could sell more vegetables, the Barsham stall went well.'

Jack said nothing. It was obvious he was not prepared to be employed.

'And I could work,' said Dee-Dee, though nobody paid much attention to her.

Tessa and Don in bed in the solar. It was early evening, but bed was the warmest place to be. Hail rattled the windows. Don was drawing plans. He was excited about selling vegetables. He had talked about nothing else for a week.

'Look, if we cultivate the land on the other side of the orchard we can grow so much more. It's good land, Jack's already checked it and it's nearer the house. That would be easier, wouldn't it?' And Don had drawn a pattern, a circle within a circle.

'It's the ceiling,' said Tessa.

'Yes, yes, but it's also a garden, read this.' He dropped *The History of Gardens* into her lap. 'It's a Tudor knot, it's brilliant, it's a way of setting out a kitchen garden. The lines are hedges, in between are, well, lettuces, carrots, tomatoes . . .'

'We grow tomatoes in the greenhouse.'

'Oh, do we? And potatoes, and asparagus . . . what do you think?'

'Don. It's a lot of work, we can't sell stuff and change the garden about at the same time.'

'But the land by the orchard! It can be done, Jack thinks it's a good idea.'

'I don't know why you're even bothering to ask me.'

'Tess, we're all part of it, you see, you have to agree, because, well, you're the gardener.'

Tessa turned the plan round and round. 'What are the hedges?'

'Box.'

'That's expensive.' She frowned.

'You see, Tess, I could have a stall, and people could come here to buy. A knot garden would be an attraction, and there could be flowers. We could have trellises with roses and honeysuckle and everything, it would be amazing, wouldn't it?'

'I don't think it's going to solve things.'

'Oh yes, and Dee-Dee's going to get a job.'

'What? She never said anything.'

'Well, she doesn't know yet. A friend of Sue's friend who knows someone in Norwich says they need a cook in the wholefood café. Dee's a great cook, I'll take her there tomorrow.'

'Don, what if she doesn't want to do it?'

'Of course she will, I'll persuade her.'

Dee-Dee was delighted. To cook and get paid for it! Don convinced her in seconds. She looked so proud and flattered Tessa didn't have the heart to put up objections.

She got the job, Don made sure of that. She worked three days a week and he took her in in the truck. Soon he was friends with everyone in the café and everyone at the wholefood suppliers. At St John's the kitchen shelves bent with the weight of grains and beans.

* * *

86

Tessa, on the window sill, looked at the room she shared with Don, and for the first time in eighteen years she missed him. He never walked into a room but burst in, and she looked at the door as she had done so many times, expecting him to dash up and bounce onto the bed next to her. 'Fabulous, amazing, listen to this!' With his short hair and unfashionable clothes, his pockets full of string and conkers and bits of paper, Don the eternal schoolboy. And at night, Don sitting up in bed reading Blake or Walt Whitman by candlelight, and Tessa staring at the pattern of the ceiling and the flickerings across it, wondering if he realised she was there at all. Then he would put down his book and smile at her, and Don's smiles were so infectious, for he was never cynical or malicious.

'OK, Tess?'

'Fine, Don.' And she was.

* * *

Off the solar was a small room. They called it the panelled room. The Hallivands used it as a dressing room, but for Tessa it was her room, her little bit of private space. The Hallivands had a large wardrobe in here and not much else. Tessa used to have a table, a bookcase and a narrow bed. She stood by the window. Her table had been under it, looking out over the courtyard, but for Tessa this was the place where she looked inward. She painted in here, read books, or sat on the bed and listened; Jack and Don in the breakfast room, Dee-Dee clattering pans, a window creaking, and sometimes the flat silence of an empty house.

Tessa felt sad. When she used to sit here it was chosen solitude, now her aloneness was unrelieved.

'I think I'll go to my room,' and Don would look up from his book.

'Oh, yes, of course,' as if it were natural she should be by herself, and it didn't occur to her perhaps she was abandoning him, perhaps he might wake up in the big carved bed and feel lonely, that her insistence on more and longer periods on her own, which to her were vital, were necessary, where she could be calm and ordered and fully herself, might seem to Don like a drifting apart.

CHAPTER TEN

With Dee-Dee cooking in Norwich and Don off selling vegetables, Tessa and Jack were left to work the gardens. Despite her dislike of him, they worked well. The work was absorbing and as complete as a meditation. The vegetables grew on the land by the orchard. The parterre slowly, slowly took shape. Tessa was busy with the hoe, the spade, with mud on her boots, her hands and her face, coaxing the soil to grow what they wanted, not nettles, or dandelions. Jack could heave wheelbarrows, could dig trenches, and Tessa spotted aphids and pinched buds.

But when work was over he looked her up and down suspiciously, and she, defiant, said nothing. If it rained, and there wasn't much to do, not even in the greenhouse, she sat in her room and painted, which felt like meeting a dear friend after some years' absence. She drew the great hall and the church windows, and all of them at the breakfast table, and her in the rose garden, and flowers from life and the view from her window. What Jack did in these times she didn't care about at all. He never bothered her.

In these quiet hours before Don and Dee-Dee came back she felt as if nothing else mattered except the sternness inside her and she was like marble and she was like ice and as old as St John's itself and older even. There was only her and the world, and her paintings were not so much done by her as through her, for the world and herself were the same substance.

Dee-Dee and Tessa were in the walled garden. Tessa was hoeing the beds. The box hedges were growing well. It was April. The sky was as blue as a thrush's egg.

'You must come to Norwich,' said Dee-Dee.

'There's a lot of work here,' said Tessa. The wind was keen, Dee's hair kept blowing into her face. Tessa wore a stripy hat.

'Come when I'm not working, we could see the cathedral.'

Tessa stretched herself and smiled. 'Try to come Friday, Saturday maybe . . .'

'Would you have to sneak away like a secret boyfriend?'

'I don't have to sneak. What's the cathedral like?'

'Oh Tessy, it's wonderful.'

'We'll go then, I like stone things.'

'Don can give us a lift.'

Tessa leant on her hoe. 'No, let's go on our own. Don will get us to meet "fascinating people", we won't see anything.'

'Just you and me, like the old days?'

'Yes, like the old days.'

They went on Friday on the early bus. Norwich was busy and at first Tessa felt bewildered. She felt removed from ordinary people and ordinary pastimes, like a tourist stepped off a boat in a foreign port. Dee was the guide. 'Oh, we don't want to see this bit, it's all modern, the old part is on the other side of the market. That's the council building.' It stood high behind the market square. Red brick, massive, brutally post-war modern, it seemed to be frowning at the stalls beneath it. The market teamed. They didn't go in.

'Don says most of the vegetables come up from London, now isn't that crazy? It's really hard to get a stall, there's a terrible waiting list.'

In the older part the streets were narrow and cobbled. Norwich still had the air of a provincial town, not of a smart go-ahead city. There was something old-fashioned about the place. It might almost be called a backwater. On Elm Hill the old wych elm dominated the street. The houses were medieval black and white, their roofs uneven. It was quiet here, a well-preserved, quaint spot. Antique and gift shops prevailed. They looked at window displays listlessly. They had no money to buy expensive gew-gaws.

'I like the run-down bits best,' said Dee-Dee. Two smart women with headscarves and matching dachshunds passed by tutting to each other. Tessa remembered she hadn't washed for days.

'Let's go to the cathedral,' she said.

The cathedral was vast and bare with high Norman arches and a vaulted roof. They stared at the painted bosses until their necks ached.

Dee-Dee got the giggles. 'Tessy, you look so silly, stop it.'

'I can't, my head's stuck.' She bumped into a pillar. 'Oh shit!' People stared at them.

'Shh, we'll get thrown out!' Dee-Dee dragged her into the cloisters. 'The monks used to walk round here and say their prayers,' she said knowledgeably. 'Jack told me that. He said when he stayed in a monastery you could hear them chanting first thing in the morning.'

The carved bosses were here, too; they examined each one solemnly. Saints, angels, biblical scenes, and strange beasts that seemed to have nothing to do with the Bible or what Tessa could remember of it. The cloisters were quiet and damp.

'I wonder what medieval people were like,' said Dee-Dee, staring at a group of grinning gargoyles; 'they really believed in God, didn't they, I mean, they did all this for God.' The idea made her pensive.

'I suspect if they weren't barons and living in castles, they worked bloody hard, they dug and planted things, and watched them grow and ate them, and got freezing in the winter and loved the summer.'

'A bit like us,' said Dee-Dee

Spaced out by so much history they sat on the stone seats and counted their money.

'We could have chips and go to a park,' said Dee, but clouds were gathering. 'We could have lunch at the café . . .' Dee always referred to it as 'the café'. 'There's aubergine bake with a crusty

top, and rhubarb crumble and there's seven sorts of herb tea . . .
if we shared the crumble, Tessy . . .'

'What about the bus?'

'We could hitch. I'd love to take you there. Jude might be
working today, she makes baked apples with cinnamon and
cream.' On the cloister lawn rain was starting to fall. Tessa
counted their money again. She divided it into three piles. Two of
these she put in her pocket and gave the other to Dee-Dee. There
was about £1.50. Dee's face fell, but Tessa laughed and patted her
pocket. 'I hate chips,' she said.

The Sunshine Café was above the wholefood shop. It was a
modern building and not particularly attractive, but upstairs the
café was nearly all windows. It was on a corner and faced two
streets in the old city. It was a good place to sit and watch people.
As they opened the door there was a warming smell of baking
bread and coffee.

The man in the wholefood shop waved at them. 'Hi, Dee!'

'Hi, Richard!'

He was bagging up kidney beans. The wall up the stairs was one
large notice board: 'Friends of Western Buddhists – meeting',
'Learn acupuncture', 'Discover the full potential of the real you',
'Gentle vegetarian, Cancer, Male, seeks nurturing environment'.
The café was not busy. It was past two o'clock. They sat by the
windows on pine benches and watched the rainy streets. Above
their heads dangled a plant in a macramé holder.

'Hi, Dee.'

'Jude. Is there anything left? We're so late.'

Jude had an alert open face and short hennaed hair. She sat next
to them. 'God, it was busy today: Friday is always terrible, we're
nearly right out.' She smiled. 'But for you, dear Dee, you can have
the last bit of aubergine bake, there's enough for two.'

'We've got money, we're going to hitch back.'

'It's on the house, don't tell anyone.'

*

'She's so kind,' said Dee when Jude was in the kitchen. 'I see her on Tuesdays. The other days Tony is here. He owns it. He's more particular, but he's OK. Don and him get on like—'

'Hippies at a fair?' and they both laughed. They ate their way through the bake and the apples with cream and a chocolate slice, and Dee was giggly and bouncy in a way Tessa had not seen since they lived in Notting Hill and she used to bring back pretty bits of junk from Portobello. We might still be there, thought Tessa.

Dee-Dee was telling tales about the regulars. 'There's a man in a hat and a coat, he never takes them off, Jude calls him "the flasher", but I think he's a professor or something and he only has mint tea and there's a woman who's quite batty and says she's an actress and she knew Dame Flora Robson, well perhaps she did, and then there's the lot from the Norfolk communes, and the ones from Stiffkey come in a horse and cart and that's miles. They park it out there right on the road and buy sacks of flour and things . . . Jack knows them . . .'

Tessa sipped her coffee. There was a silly song going round her head: 'Something's lost and something's gained from living each new day.' All the worries about blackfly and leaf-curl, and her paintings and her distrust of Jack and feeling unsure about Don . . . She suddenly felt if she were never to go back to St John's she wouldn't mind, but would leave it as an unconcluded episode in her life, which was full of unconcluded episodes anyway. And strangely she thought of the jug of cherry blossom Dee-Dee put on the table in their old flat in Notting Hill, and how the jug was blue like the sky and the blossom was pale pink and the tablecloth was embroidered with pansies . . .

Dee was smiling. She had her misty Madonna look.

'We must come out together more often,' said Tessa.

'Oh, yes!' and Dee looked so happy she might float away.

Into the café came a woman with a child of about three, and Tessa only noticed them because the child was screaming. The woman slumped on a bench. She was fat and shapeless in a plastic mac. She looked old, old. The child lay on the floor and kicked.

93

'If you're good, I'll buy you a cake, a nice chocolate one and some apple juice, and look, here's the book we got . . .' She had a worn-out, patient voice.

'It's horrible, I hate it.'

'Shh, darling, I'll get you a cake, be a good girl now . . .'

Dee-Dee watched them with loving concern. 'She comes here a lot.'

The little girl was now sitting up. She emptied the sugar bowl on the table.

'Oh, darling, don't do that!'

'I want to, I'm making patterns.'

Tessa and Dee sat uncomfortably through the next episode. The woman ordered a cake and the child insisted she didn't want it, then changed her mind, then wanted a drink, which started off milk and became apple juice, then crumbled the cake up, then knocked the drink over.

'Dear dear,' said Dee-Dee.

The child began to wail. 'I'll mop it up, darling, it wasn't your fault, we'll get you another drink, have a piece of cake . . .'

Eventually the child stopped crying and became absorbed in mixing salt with the sugar. The woman ate her own cake and the rest of the child's, quickly and compulsively, not as if she enjoyed it. For a moment she glanced towards Tessa and Dee-Dee, but her face was not looking for kindness or tolerance but offered apologies. She wasn't old at all, but her way of moving was that of a person three times her age. Overweight, weary, she had given up.

Tessa was about to say, 'Well, let's go then,' but Dee-Dee was drawn towards them.

'Hello,' she said. 'I've seen you before, I work here, I'm Dee-Dee and this is Tessa, we're in Norwich for the day. Did you get caught in the rain? It's coming down quite hard now.'

The woman stared. She obviously wasn't used to people talking to her.

'Children hate the rain, don't they,' said Dee-Dee.

The child looked up from her game. 'I like it.'

'Yes, yes,' said the woman; 'she just wanted to jump in puddles, that's why she was crying, but where we live it's a bit difficult to dry clothes.' She talked rapidly. 'We're in one room, it's a shared house really, but the other people are students and they seem to sleep in the day and go out at night and we do it all the other way round, don't we?' The little girl ignored her. 'We go out a lot, to parks.'

'I hate parks.'

'Yes you do, darling, but not all of them, you like the one with the ducks. Don't you remember when we fed them currant buns.'

'I want a currant bun.'

'I don't think they've got any.' The child screwed her face up.

'We've got lots of ducks,' said Dee-Dee, 'and baby ones. We live in a house that's got a moat, which is like a river and there are twelve baby ducks and there's a heron, isn't there, Tessy?'

'We have to get our bus soon.'

But Dee was off. She began telling the whole story of how they first came to St John's and what they were doing and who lived there. The child listened fascinated. So did the woman. Tessa studied them. The mother was lumpy with flat brown lank hair. She had brown sad eyes in a face where all the features were either too small or too large. Her complexion was florid and spotty. But her child looked like a china doll. Her hair was thick and dark with auburn lights and her eyes, although the same shade of brown as her mother's, were lively, with long dark lashes. She was slim with delicate fingers.

'Isn't she beautiful!' said Tessa suddenly and surprised herself for saying it.

'Oh, she is!' And the mother smiled for the first time. 'I call her Beauty, she's my little Beauty.'

Dee-Dee was now saying '. . . and perhaps one day you and your mummy can come and see us in our big house and you can see the ducklings.'

'I want to go now!'

'Yes, but you have to go home now, and so do we, but I work here so I'll see you again.' She patted the little girl's hand. Dee-Dee had gone quite pink. She turned to the mother. 'You will come and see us, won't you, you could stay the night.'

'Dee, we'll miss our bus.'

'Oh yes, of course, I'll see you next week then, I'm in on Tuesday. What's your name? I didn't ask.'

'I'm Helen Clark.'

They did come to stay. Don and Dee went to fetch them in the truck. Tessa made sure she had plenty to do in the garden, but she couldn't avoid having lunch. Dee had gone to such trouble. She had made quiche, and rhubarb crumble. The child ate nothing, threw all her food on the floor, ran round the table, kicked Jack, pulled Dee's hair, and when she was bored by this sang at the top of her voice.

'I'm ever so worried about her,' said Helen.

'I would be,' said Tessa.

'She won't eat. I make her all sorts of things, I don't know what she lives off.'

'Tra la la la la.'

'She looks well enough,' said Tessa.

'Just biscuits, it's all she'll eat, there's no nourishment in biscuits.'

'It must be awful,' said Dee-Dee sympathetically.

'I want to see the ducklings!' shouted Beauty.

'Not yet, darling.'

'Now, now! I want to see them now!' She threw herself on the floor. Helen hauled her into the garden mumbling excuses. There was a heavy silence around the breakfast-room table. Jack ate a third helping of rhubarb crumble. Don brushed away some of the crumbs. Helen could be heard in the garden. 'No, no, darling, don't throw stones at them!' Jack frowned.

'It's not easy for her,' said Dee-Dee; 'she lives in a terrible place. I was so shocked when I saw it. It's not suitable for a child at all, is it Don?'

'It's a squat.'

'No, she rents it, she does, the landlord is awful, he won't do a thing, the loo doesn't work, there's water all over the kitchen. Helen's so depressed, but she can't find anywhere else.'

Helen came back. Beauty was smeared with mud and smiling. 'I hit one, with a big stone!'

'Oh, darling, it wasn't a very big stone, it was only stunned for a moment.'

Jack leapt up and the look in his eyes made even Tessa shudder.

'Whoops,' said Don. 'He's very particular about wildlife.'

Tessa escaped to the garden, but Helen and Beauty were staying the night. By the evening even Dee-Dee looked raddled. Beauty refused to go to bed; she was obviously tired and when cossetted by Helen her eyes closed.

'She's scared of the dark,' explained Helen. 'At home I have to stay with her until she's asleep.' Jack and Don disappeared to the George. The three women sat miserably in the breakfast room. Perhaps Dee was the most miserable; her lovely idea had soured. Eventually Helen carried a protesting half-asleep child upstairs.

'It's such a shame,' said Dee-Dee, and Tessa was inclined to agree with her.

In the morning Don took them back to Norwich but their presence lingered. Something about Beauty's wailing in the middle of the night had affected them all. Tessa wanted to consign them back to whatever mess they had come from and forget all about them, but Dee-Dee couldn't do that. Besides, she saw them frequently in Norwich. Their abject misery, their helplessness, was asking to be relieved. It was just a question of who was going to make the first move.

'The ceiling's fallen in in their bedroom,' said Dee-Dee. Every time she came back from the café there was another disaster of Helen's to relate. 'It happened in the night and Beauty's so freaked out she hasn't slept for days.'

Don sighed. Jack said nothing. He rubbed his beard.

'She should get out of that place,' said Tessa, and in saying it she knew she was stepping on new ground.

'Where could she go? I've asked all over. The Norfolk communes? But everybody's reluctant; Beauty's very difficult.'

'What about Beauty's dad?' said Tessa.

'She got drunk at a party,' said Dee-Dee. 'I did ask her, but, well, I don't think she really knows who he is.'

They were quiet for a moment thinking of the image of a senseless Helen being taken advantage of by several drunken lads. It wasn't a pleasant picture.

'Council house?' suggested Don.

'There's a waiting list and Helen's in such a state she can't get anything together.'

The inevitable outcome of this conversation felt like falling towards a black pit.

Don sighed deeply. He wrapped his dressing gown about him. 'Beauty is difficult, that's true, I'm no expert in child psychology but I suspect she's difficult because she's unhappy and her mother's unhappy and if they weren't so unhappy then Helen wouldn't be so . . . um . . . and Beauty might . . . why don't they come here?'

It was the bottom of the pit.

'She would never have asked us, I know she wouldn't,' said Dee-Dee.

'But it has to be unanimous,' said Don. 'If one of us is against it, it won't work . . . Tess?'

'I'm not sure, I need a bit of time. Ask the others.'

'Dee? You're sure, aren't you?'

'She'd want to help!' exclaimed Dee-Dee; 'she wouldn't just live off us. We must give her a chance. We've got the space, there's enough food. Oh, Jack, you must say yes.' It was the most she'd ever said to him.

He looked her up and down dismissively and she blushed all over. 'What can she do?'

'She could cook, oh she could! Now I'm in Norwich and you and Tess are in the garden. She could manage the house, it would suit us all.'

'I'm for it,' said Don. 'We mustn't leave her to the clutches of the State. This is an excellent place for children. I had a super time here when I was young . . .'

Jack was still frowning.

'Tessy, Jack, you must say yes, you must!' Dee-Dee was close to tears.

'It'll be awful,' said Tessa.

'We mustn't let that cloud our decision, we mustn't be selfish,' said Don. 'We've lived like lords here.' And Tessa knew that, after all, it was his place. If anything was to make her decide it was his generosity.

'OK, yes,' she said.

'Oh Tessy, I knew you would!'

This still left Jack.

'Three against one, I'm outnumbered.'

'No, Jack, it has to be unanimous. If you say no, it's off. You pulled us out of the mud, your position here is vital, you're probably the most important member of this community.'

It was a genuine admission from Don, not meant as an empty compliment, but Jack basked in the glory of it. He smiled, a lopsided smirk that made Tessa want to empty a bucket of slops over him.

'Let's give it until next March,' he yawned. 'We should know whether or not she's useful by then.'

CHAPTER ELEVEN

Dee cleared the room above the hall to make a space for Helen and Beauty. It was a large room, the width of the great hall itself. She scrubbed and cleaned, put up curtains, but her efforts could not hide the gloom hanging over everybody. The imminent arrival of Helen and Beauty was like waiting for Judgement Day. Dee tried desperately to be cheerful but Don was distracted. Jack and he were caught up with the organisation for the Bungay May Fair, an old horse fair resurrected. The event promised to be more chaotic than Barsham. Travellers of all kinds were already descending upon sleepy Bungay. The petty-crime rate soared.

Jack showed no emotion about the two events. The great organiser could not tolerate chaos, and Tessa decided she couldn't stand it either. For years, in London, she had lived unstructured, in a lazy dope haze, but she felt now the patterns they had developed at St John's were important. Each season brought its rigours, and she followed these ardently. Early summer meant planting runner beans, peas and radishes. There were cabbages to thin out, asparagus to harvest, onions and parsnips to weed.

During the weeks leading up to Helen's arrival she was busy. With the weather fair, the may blossom coming out and bluebells almost open under the trees at the far end of the moat, she found it more pleasurable to be in the garden. The harder she worked the more she was sure that Helen's arrival must not interrupt the growing life. After all, the vegetables were their currency. Their existence at St John's depended on them.

Helen arrived in Don's truck on the day before the May parade. The truck was to be used as a float and Don was in a state of heightened agitation. He hoped to use the parade to advertise St John's. And here they all were.

Helen clambered down from the truck. She stood in the courtyard, bewildered. Don began to carry boxes of what looked like rubbish into the porch. Beauty was wailing, but then Tessa had expected that.

'You can have the whole of the room above the hall, Helen, I've cleared it, there's no more junk in there . . .'

'Shall I take these up?' asked Don.

Helen didn't answer. She looked like somebody who had stopped making decisions a long time ago. She held onto Beauty, who was struggling and screaming, 'I want my dolly!'

'You threw it out of the window,' said Dee-Dee.

'I want it, I want it!'

Dee-Dee began to explain that dollies thrown out of truck windows were extremely difficult to find. Tessa helped carry the boxes.

'Her landlord kicked up a stink,' said Don on the stairs; 'apparently she hasn't paid any rent for months.'

'Oh Christ! What happened?'

'Well . . .'

'You paid it, didn't you?'

'He was threatening all sorts of legal action . . . and physical violence.' Don shuddered; he hated confrontations. He put the box down in Helen's room.

'Was it a lot?' Tessa dropped her box heavily. The sides split. It was full of dirty clothes. 'She should have said.'

'Don't take it out on her, Tessa.'

Jack came up the stairs with a trunk. He looked sideways at Tessa and Don. Beauty in the courtyard was shrieking, 'I want to go home! I want to go home!'

'Jack, don't,' and Don's face was so full of anguish Tessa wanted to hug him, but not with Jack there.

'We've got to see Steve about the floats.' Jack put the trunk down and made it seem as light as an eggbox.

'Sure,' Don sighed. 'You know three children were killed at Appleby last year.'

'It's not going to be the same. If this is properly organised it will be interesting, but it won't be liked Appleby,' and then Jack began one of his tales of how he had met up with Tad the harness-maker and gone with him to Appleby. ' . . . Tad might be coming, I heard from Jock in Redlesham.'

'Oh, amazing!' Don was cheered by this and they talked about all the craftsmen from the most unlikely places who were coming. Tessa felt entirely excluded. She carried up the rest of the boxes. There weren't many. All Helen seemed to own were some old clothes, some torn books and a few broken toys for Beauty.

Dee brought Helen up to the room. Beauty was still in the garden.

' . . . I got the curtains from a jumble in Norwich . . . the room's so big you could even have an armchair . . . it's the best view from here.'

Helen squinted at her things on the floor.

'Don't worry, I'll help you unpack.' Dee was being irritatingly cheerful.

Don and Jack were on the other side of the room. 'Really? Is he coming too? What, all the way from Devizes?'

'I'm expecting about twenty from the West Country.'

'And is Herbie going to show Betsy?'

'She's a fine lurcher.'

'Which bed would you like, Helen?' asked Dee-Dee. 'I thought perhaps this one, the other's slightly smaller, that could be Beauty's.'

Helen was not listening. She was looking out of the window anxiously. Tessa looked too. Beauty was picking flowers, roots and all.

The truck broke down on May Day so Don's float never happened and he had spent hours painting an elaborate sign. They walked into Bungay to watch the parade. There was an enormous maypole pulled by Suffolk punches, Buffalo Bill's show-wagon, a Chinese rickshaw and a scrap cart piled up with daffodils, but the residents of St John's were not feeling festive. Beauty had screamed all night. Don kept saying 'We must get the truck fixed before the fair,' and Dee-Dee kept saying 'I'm sure everything will be fine,' and Tessa was as spiky as a harrow.

The parade was a fortnight before the Bungay May Fair and during that time the tension at St John's was like a cable about to snap. Helen wandered in a sad lost state as her daughter caused havoc. Jack was supposed to be fixing the truck but most of the time was over at Mettingham with the travellers. Don and he had what was nearly a row, which left Don with such feelings of remorse he was unbearable to be with. Tessa hid herself in the most remote part of the garden and only appeared at mealtimes.

The Barsham fairs were friendly, muddled and all about what people thought a fair should be like; an idealised concept of freedom. They were so magical because, as Tessa and probably everybody else knew, they just couldn't last. All that wonderful sharing and good feeling, 'if only life were like this'. But it wasn't and it never would be. The Bungay May Fair had in it the seeds of Barsham for, on the face of it, it was a pretty crazy thing to attempt, a horse fair after half a century, but it also contained the seeds of a very different culture, and Tessa noticed this the moment the truck spluttered up the track to Mettingham Castle.

They were all there; the Suffolk hippies, the Norfolk communes, the raggle-taggle children, the Bungay locals, but here too were real horse people, with neck scarves and shifty eyes, who could assess the value of a horse at a glance, whose dogs slunk several paces behind them, tails between their legs. The horses were being auctioned, 'three-fifty guineas, four hundred, four-fifty, a fine Arab . . .' and the bidding was fierce.

The talk was all horses and harnesses: 'That britchin, he won't hold . . .' Alongside the herb-stalls and Indian jewellery stalls were saddle-makers and farriers. Small children rode alarmingly huge horses but they looked like they had been doing it since the day they were born. Jack was there and the ease with which he moved amongst the travellers made Tessa wonder. He was not one of them, he was too familiar; they eyed each other cautiously, but he was accepted. He was patting the back of a piebald pony, held by a man who came up to his chest, talking knowledgeably of its various attributes.

Who is Jack? thought Tessa, looking to Don for an answer, but Don was so delighted to see him again and eager to patch up any disagreements.

Jack led Don off into the male world of horses and lurchers and Tessa stayed with Dee-Dee and Helen. Beauty was unusually silenced by the visual impact around her, her mouth wide open. Can-can dancers whirled and flashed their legs in flurries of black lace; little girls in frocks danced faultlessly round a fifty-foot maypole. It was not clear which group were supposed to be the symbols of fertility. The May sun shone in the sky and a sharp breeze ruffled horses' manes and women's hair.

They were staying the night. Jack arranged that, with the travellers they had met at Barsham. The woman wore the same headscarf. The gypsy caravans lined up could strike nostalgia in even the most hard-hearted, but Tessa was not excited or hopeful as she had been by the Barsham bonfires. Beauty got lost for the hundredth time and Dee and Helen went searching for her. Tessa remained with the woman and her tea in tin mugs. Jack and Don met Tad and they were still talking horses.

'It's nice here,' said the woman; she was a creature of few words. 'It's nice to be out after the winter.'

'Where were you for the winter?'

'We've got a bungalow near Fishguard, nice place.' She wiped a plate on her apron. 'Nice and clean.'

Tessa and Dee-Dee went to the ceilidh, if only to get away from Beauty, who was now being cossetted by at least a dozen women all offering conflicting advice. 'Poor mite, she's cold', 'Camomile tea's very soothing', 'My second never went down well', 'Look, her feet are quite blue', 'Auntie Lisa's brought you a little puppy to see.'

'Take your partners!' yelled the caller and Dee was grabbed by a hairy man. 'Dosey Do! Gentleman's star!' Bodies whirled. Dee-Dee exclaimed 'Oh! Oh!' but she was enjoying herself. Tessa stood alone; nobody grabbed her. And there was Jack, swinging the women until they squealed, smiling like a demon. 'Grand chain!' Out of the corner of his eye he saw Tessa and swung towards her, but she saw him coming and dashed out of the tent into the black sleepless night.

Sunday was the day of the races. All around were excited horses held by people whose ability to control them was doubtful. Someone's old nag who never did more than chew buttercups was now hoofing the ground and snorting. Lurchers and other cross-breeds snapped and growled. The horse traders looked on knowingly, strangely smart in their shabby suits and caps.

'And they're off!' The bare-back riders galloped away, a jumble of different-sized horses, long-haired men, and gypsy boys who looked like they would never fall. The horses thundered past, children were grabbed, the dogs barked louder, and where was Beauty?

Helen pushed through the people calling for her, but so many names were being called, 'Come on, Dusty!', 'Come on, Starlight!' 'Beauty! Beauty!', just another horse's name.

'She was right by me,' wept Helen; 'Don said three children were killed at Appleby.'

'She's all right, I'm sure,' said Tessa, but she wasn't. She pulled Helen out of the crowd.

'Come on, Primrose!' 'Come on, Dolphin!'

'Beauty! Beauty!'

Dee-Dee came running. 'What's happened?'

'She's got lost again.'

'Oh, how awful! I nearly got trampled.' A pony had bolted and three bare-footed men were running after it. Some distance away was a policeman looking conspicuous and edgy. Tessa ran up to him.

'Lost your horse, miss?'

'No, a little girl, aged three, dark hair . . .'

'Why you lot can't hang on to them I don't know.'

Dee came up with Helen sobbing. 'We can't find her little girl, we're ever so worried.'

'Not another one?'

'It's the same one,' said Tessa.

The crowds were cheering the winner. 'What a day,' said the policeman. 'Look, I'll keep an eye out, any I find they're in the tent, there's about twenty already. What's this one called?'

'Beauty,' said Helen.

The policeman didn't raise an eyebrow; he had heard strange names all morning.

They found Beauty over by the gypsy caravans, completely unharmed, covered in dirt and being fed biscuits by Jack's friends. Tessa persuaded Don to take them back to St John's.

'But there's another dance tonight,' said Don.

'You go to it, we've all had enough.'

St John's was blissfully peaceful. Helen and Beauty went to bed. They were exhausted. Tessa and Dee sat in Dee-Dee's room doing nothing but being quiet and the afternoon sun sliced in through the geraniums.

That night in her bed in the panelled room, Tessa listened to the comforting sounds of a sleeping house, far away from the clamour of humanity at the fair. Silence, she loved silence, but a thought slid by as she drifted into sleep: with Beauty and Helen living there, St John's would never be silent.

*

She was woken the next morning by Helen shouting 'Beauty! Beauty!' She heaved herself out of bed to look. Outside in the courtyard Beauty in her nightdress was running and laughing. Chasing her, out of breath, lumbered Helen. 'Come and get dressed!'

Beauty's laughter was high-pitched, almost a squeal, and persistent as she ran into the orchard. Every day is going to be like this, thought Tessa, leaning her head on the window pane.

* * *

There was a noise outside and Tessa looked up. Mirabelle's car stopped with a squeal of brakes. She ran across the courtyard and into the house, slamming the door.

Chapter Twelve

Tessa had breakfast in her hotel bedroom on Bank Holiday Monday, sliced-bread toast and gelatinous marmalade. But what concerned her was the day ahead. Yesterday Mirabelle had run into the house in tears. Tessa felt that whatever tragedy was unfolding itself in Mirabelle's life was somehow linked to her own. Her coffee was bitter and lukewarm.

Shit. She felt like she had felt after her wedding, dancing in the rain, something, something was going to happen, opening a new door, but this time she was dreading it. Ice, steel, bone, there wasn't much of that left. Stone. Yesterday she knew Mirabelle was crying for she could hear her, but she had not gone down. She stayed alone in the panelled room, her old room, as if the sight of someone in tears would be too much. Only when the house was silent did she collect her paintings and descend.

The staircase handrail was worn smooth, the newel posts were carved and knobbly. Mirabelle was standing in the corridor like a lost person.

'I'm going now,' said Tessa.

'Oh,' and Mirabelle turned round. She did not acknowledge her misery; instead she smiled. 'Well . . . Well, what a day.'

'A bad one, was it?'

Mirabelle twitched. 'Can't be helped.' She smoothed her immaculate hair. Her appearance did not suggest disorder. 'You've finished?'

Tessa hesitated. 'There's some rooms I haven't done yet . . . the great hall.'

'Oh, but you must!'

'I could come tomorrow, if I worked until two. It is the bank holiday.'

'I've nothing planned,' said Mirabelle quickly.

Half-past nine in the Saints and already it was hot. Clouds of dust from the combines rose from the fields near St John's, although the land immediately adjacent was still untouched, a last island of wheat. After the harvest the fields would be shorn and bare and St John's would seem more separate in its oasis.

Mirabelle wore pink figured silk. She looked like a rose, except roses are fresh and youthful. 'Coffee by the pool?' she asked, pleased Tessa had relieved her isolation.

Tessa, in navy shorts and a black T-shirt, looked sporty and ready for action. 'I'd like that,' she said.

Mirabelle fussed with coffee cups and percolators and little cakes and Tessa watched the approaching combines.

Mirabelle sat down. 'I'm afraid I have to go away this morning.' She was upset, but not, Tessa thought, devastated. In a way, she was more composed that she had ever seen her.

'The help will lock up at two.'

Tessa sipped her coffee. It smelled and tasted delicious. 'I won't see you then.'

Mirabelle peeled the paper off a cake. She had long thin fingers. Her nails were still pearly. 'No.'

'A holiday?'

Mirabelle tensed. She swallowed the cake as if it were a mouthful of sand. 'Bernard . . . ' she said with difficulty, 'is in Switzerland with his secretary.'

'Not Brussels.'

'It was a lie,' said Mirabelle, and then quietly, 'everything was a lie.'

They sat in silence under the great stone walls of St John's, on the concrete patio that had once been a rose garden.

'I'm going to London and I'm not coming back.'

'You're certain about that?'

'I saw his friend in Norwich. He wouldn't tell me at first, he's in antiques too . . . then he said, "I think you should know . . ." It's been going on for some time, apparently.'

'You won't forgive him?'

'No. You see he did this before, and I was the secretary . . . it'll go on . . . ' She drank her coffee unsteadily.

'I'm divorced,' said Tessa.

'Are you?' Mirabelle stared.

'Twice.' She had never actually married Murray but sometimes it had felt like she had.

'And is it . . . awful?'

'It could be worse.' She laughed. 'The last one married a younger woman. They're blissfully happy and they've got a baby. You know, I think I'm better off being single.' A dragonfly skimmed past and they watched it as it flew towards the moat. A tiny streak of shimmering blue. 'The freedom's fine, if you can stand the loneliness,' she said.

Mirabelle shuddered. She looked into the dregs of her coffee as if they contained her fortune. 'Well . . . well . . . divorced people never get invited to dinner parties.'

Mirabelle left. She had four matching suitcases already packed. She handed Tessa a cheque and a card with a solicitor's address on it.

'Send the pictures to me there, I still want them.'

Tessa examined the cheque. It was for more than they had agreed. 'That's trusting of you,' she said.

'Is it wrong to be trusting?' Her voice shook, but she did not wait for an answer.

Tessa went to the great hall and reclined on the Hallivands' enormous sofa. There was a certain luxury in knowing Mirabelle would not be back. It was as if St John's were actually hers. 'Yes, thank you, I'll buy it all,' she said to an imaginary Bernard. She had a mental picture of him, fifties, greying, suave. Rather like Murray and with Murray's elegant way of discarding people he didn't need any more. But Murray's weakness was that he did need people, like mirrors to reflect his importance. On his own he was nobody.

She wondered if Bernard was like that.

It would be hard for a third Mrs Hallivand to live at St John's when the previous two had fled its history. And Bernard wouldn't live here on his own. He'll probably sell the place, she thought, looking at the tapestries and the rugs.

The great hall à la Hallivands was not homely but austere, despite their wealth. Tessa perused each artefact carefully as if indeed she were a buyer. Music was propped up on the piano, a nocturne by Chopin. She played a few notes with one finger.

I've got to draw all this, she thought, reaching for her sketchpad. Outside, a hot sunny morning. The martins were flying high, the sky was almost cloudless. The windows were huge but the hall was only warm at sunset when light fell in obliquely and the room became golden. Now, in the morning, the sun could rage and burn but it never seemed to shine in there.

She sat on the window seat at the furthest end of the hall. She could see the whole length of it, the massive fireplace and the brass lantern hanging from the rafters; the pinky cream-coloured stone of the floor and the vast church windows, two in the decorated style and two perpendicular, pinched from some nunnery after the Reformation, the decorated ones all leaves and curls and carved mullions, the others right-angled and unadorned. A long-ago owner of St John's trying to make his home more grand but instead producing an effect that was odd and almost amusing.

Hot outside, and the window panes were hot. Inside, the stones of the great hall were quite cold, the air smelled of damp and woodsmoke . . .

* * *

111

The long, long hot summer of '76. Nobody who lived through it could forget it. 'Do you remember that summer when . . . ' When it didn't rain for weeks and the news was all drought and water shortages, when the grass shrivelled up like it does in the South of France, when people got Greek tans from sitting in gardens in Pudsey, when an entire nation suffered an identity crisis because Torquay was hotter than Torremolinos and Southsea was as dry as Sardinia.

At St John's the atmosphere was like a carnival and just as hectic. Previously unknown friends of Jack's arrived 'on their way to Barsham' and stayed for weeks. Several in vans camped until September. But these people kept to themselves; they made their own meals, their own amusements, they wandered in and out of the Hall sporadically. Tessa couldn't even remember their names; 'Jack's friends'. Like him they played folk music, expressed an interest in all things natural and didn't have children.

Helen was not managing Beauty any better, but now Beauty was outside from dawn till dusk doing exactly what she pleased, wearing her grubby nightdress which she wouldn't take off, and everybody ignored her. Helen worried constantly. Beauty was never there, at mealtimes or any other time, and everybody ignored Helen. She couldn't cook, she couldn't garden, she couldn't clean. Helen was hopeless.

Dee-Dee, usually sympathetic, was half in Norwich and too preoccupied to listen to another of Helen's mishaps. 'Yes, Helen, oh dear, what a shame . . .' Don, although feeling responsible, had not time to deal with her either; he was much too busy finding new contracts and more and more of his life was spent in Norwich too. Jack had nothing to say to Helen whatsoever and this was also Tessa's position.

The continuing drought heralded major panic in the gardens. Jack devised all sorts of ingenious watering devices but the one that was most effective was filling up buckets from the moat. The guests were roped in to help. 'Don't just slosh it, sprinkle it, you'll damage the crops,' shouted Jack. 'Couldn't you manage a full bucket, couldn't you manage two?'

'Can I help?' It was Helen, looking hot in an Indian dress.

'What? No! Go away! Make some lunch!' And Helen would pad off sadly to pull up lettuces.

They ate salad every day and every meal was outside, from just Tessa and Dee-Dee having early breakfast in the rose garden, quiet on the dew-wet grass, to twenty or so on a folk-music evening drinking pints of home-brew and eating bowls and bowls of lettuces under the stars in the orchard, drunk and stoned, propped up against the apple trees.

'It won't rain till late August.' Jack was certain.

'They're rationing water in the West Country.'

'Who are you? I haven't seen you before?'

'I'm Tessa, I live here.'

'Dee-Dee. I can't find Beauty, she was in her bed and now she isn't, I'm ever so worried . . .' Then across the courtyard, white in the moonlight, in nightdress and gumboots, they could see her running.

'Beauty, come back, you naughty girl, come here, come here at once!'

The water in the moat became a thick green sludge and smelled like the bottom of a fish tank. Never in anyone's living memory had the moat at St John's dried up, and now it looked in danger of doing so locals came from as far as St Lawrence to have a look.

'Them fish'll all be dead, and when them fish die . . .'

'It's bad, I never seen 'im this bad.' And they stood on the far side in the wheatfield and proclaimed doom.

Dee-Dee topless under the apple trees, and across the water several men in rolled-up shirts and braces.

'Nice ones you got there.'

'What?' She blushed all over.

113

'Nice pink ones. Plump ones. Apples. Nice apples on yer tree!'
They thought it was funny.

Tessa was scooping up sludge in buckets. 'Clear off, can't you, we're busy.'

'That moat, I never seen 'im so low.'

'Can't be good.'

Tessa scooped up the fourth bucket. Sweat was running down her face and into her eyes.

'Hey, miss, don't you drink that!'

The dry days: sweat and dust and slimy water on the vegetables; everybody at St John's irritable and hot, and the black storm-flies stuck on their arms and there never seemed to be enough lemonade or elderflower fizz, and if only they had a fridge they could have ice, and the thought of ice was enough to make them weak. Tessa working in the garden in a bikini and Jack in walking boots and swimming trunks. There was plenty to look at at St John's. Jack's friends too, half naked, and nobody cared any more, and Beauty's nightdress got dirtier and dirtier until it was impossible to tell what she was wearing and her hair matted up with leaves and old daisy chains, and Helen left damp footsteps on the stone floors and Don found a straw hat in a jumble, and if Jack wasn't looking they might have a hosepipe fight and the cold clean water collapsed them in soaking giggles.

St John's was never peaceful. Behind every door was somebody and it was usually Beauty, who, when she wasn't outside, hovered within earshot. Jack's friends would walk in when Tessa was in bed, or Tessa would walk in and find them in bed, anybody's, it didn't matter, and St John's was a madhouse, there was no quiet anywhere. The furthest part of the garden: somebody sunbathing nude; her own room: Beauty using up her paints; the great hall: Don reciting poetry and God knows how many others on the floor – 'Hey, wow, fantastic.' The only peace was work because nobody wanted to do that, but the soil was dry and needed more and more water, insatiably, like a greedy baby.

Towards August, when the harvest was imminent, Tessa's father became ill with heart trouble. Her mother began writing begging letters. They had communicated only sporadically over the last five years. 'Come home, he won't last long now . . . it's all right for you wasting your life away but some of us have to think about the future . . . Come home, see your daddy . . .' And Tessa went. She hitched to London in the dusty heat and by the time she got there her father seemed better and her mother was accusatory and by the time she got back her father was worse and the letters started again. For the rest of the summer she was up and down the London road looking so fierce and dishevelled. Lifts took hours and it was always bored lorry drivers who wanted to tell of their sexploits in Amsterdam, which lasted from Barton Mills to Baldock. But Tessa didn't listen and watched instead the parched countryside and the flat fields of Cambridgeshire where the combines churned up dust.

Tessa in a west London suburb, in a tree-lined road that was quieter than St John's hamlet, but deathly quiet. The road was surprisingly unchanged, in fact everything was unchanged, and she could have been six or seven walking back from school.

Her mother opened the door wearing a blue nylon housecoat.

'Tessa, you're filthy!'

'I've been hitching.'

Her mother's face became more tense and worried than usual. 'Whatever for? Can't you get a bus like everybody else? The state of you!'

Tessa was still on the doorstep. From inside the house came a familiar smell, lavender air-freshener. 'Can I come in? I got stuck near Royston.'

'Take your shoes off . . . if you call them shoes.'

Tessa in her parents' house, unchanged since she was a little girl. The mantelpiece clock, the books in the same place, the same colour on the walls, tan, and the doors, chocolate brown, and the bowl of plastic flowers on the coffee table. Everything clean, scrubbed clean, but worn and the curtains had faded. Her mother upstairs tending to her father and she wasn't to see him yet, not until she had a bath. The house felt as if nobody had ever opened a window. Smells were suffocated by artificial lavender, cabbage boiled in the kitchen. Tessa opened the door into the garden; a square of lawn needing cutting, an apple tree. It used to seem so tall. Father's dahlias untended and drooping, and her mother calling down the stairs, 'Theresa, Theresa, are you having this bath or not . . . ?'

In the evening, and her father snored in bed. They had eaten cabbage and pork chops for supper. The food stuck in Tessa's innards. She was clean, dressed in something found in a drawer which she used to wear when she was fourteen, a mini dress with swirling patterns. She felt uncomfortably bloated. Her mother always made far too much food and they were now in the sitting room eating chocolates and upstairs her father coughed and her mother tutted and continued knitting, a yellow nylon baby's cardigan. But there were no babies.

Her mother was watching *Upstairs Downstairs* and knitting, knitting. The television set was new and big and turned up too loud.

'Well, it's nice to have you home,' said her mother, turning a row and not looking at her.

'But this isn't my home,' said Tessa.

'Well, it's nice to have you home, anyway.' And her mother turned another row and Tessa said nothing but closed her eyes. Into her head came a picture of St John's, not as it was with Jack's friends and Helen and Beauty and the muddle and the heat, but how she wanted it. Silent, with just the wind in the chimney and the solemnity of the great hall. She longed to be in her panelled room and painting. And mentally she smoothed out a sheet of thick watercolour paper and dipped her brushes in the water . . .

116

'Well, I wonder what that Mrs Bridges is up to?' said her mother, helping herself to another chocolate mint, and upstairs her father wheezed erratically and downstairs the mantelpiece clock ticked.

CHAPTER THIRTEEN

Tessa's father didn't die and her visits became less frequent. The summer ended with a downpour at Barsham Fair, which seemed fitting – they had been doing rain-dances since June. They rolled in the mud and painted mud pictures on their bodies. Barsham was crowded, reminding Tessa of the Isle of Wight and the mud of 'desolation row' where she spent two days stoned stupid under a blanket. Everybody then had said, 'It's got too big.' Big was bad, commercial, capitalist, heavy. This was the last Barsham Fair. Next year there would be four smaller ones, 'The Albions'.

Tessa felt a sense of loss, but the long-haired men with flared jeans flapping – why were they now ridiculous? And she and Dee-Dee unwashed, and Jack having the same conversations with the same people, and Don eager as always – 'But the Albions will be better than Barsham, the whole of East Anglia bringing everybody together . . . I can see it . . . Theatre groups, music, a common theme . . . it's exciting, Tessa, it's happening.' But Tessa felt nothing was happening.

Sue and Wally, Trish and Herbie, Sandy and Ted, her and Don, everywhere were couples. She had heard of communes splitting up because of people becoming territorial. Every woman she met these days was pregnant.

Under leaky canvas at Barsham, Don and Tessa were still awake.

'The Mill Farm lot are going.'

'They couldn't get anything together, they were too stoned.' Don was reading *Small is Beautiful* by torchlight.

'And the ones from Stiffkey.'

'Well, there were too many people, what did you expect?'

118

'Don, what about us?'

'Us?'

Tessa sighed. Outside she could hear Jack explaining goat husbandry. There were still no animals at St John's; it was too expensive to feed them.

'I wouldn't worry,' said Don after some time; 'of course, at the beginning people swarmed out here. It's a drop-out rate.'

'Oh Don, how can drop-outs drop-out?'

'Perhaps they'll drop back in.' He was deadly serious. He turned a few more pages. 'We're organised at St John's, we know what we're doing, we plan and budget. Look how much we've learned, we'll show the way ahead. St John's is a unit, a productive unit. Come on, Tess, when you first came to Suffolk you couldn't even use a spade.'

These were echoes of Jack and it made Tessa depressed. They were all becoming that, echoes of Jack.

That winter was slow. It seemed to drag on for ever. It snowed and Tessa was shut inside with Helen, Beauty and Jack. Dee-Dee and Don stayed in Norwich. Helen cooked inedible food. Beauty wailed because she was so cold. Jack was irritable. He spread out plans for a new greenhouse on the table. 'What do you think, then?'

Tessa forced herself away from the Aga. 'Oh . . . I don't know . . .'

'Come on. I need better than that, I've spent days on this. Look, it takes up half the length of the walled garden. We can double our production of tomatoes. I'm working on a rudimentary heating system . . .'

'It's a pity you can't do that in here.'

Jack glowered. 'I get no feedback, I have to do everything.'

'It's probably brilliant.'

He slammed his hand on the table. 'You sarcastic bitch.'

'Yesterday I was a lazy cow.'

He made guttural noises. Sometimes he was most inarticulate.

119

'What's this?' He picked up a cup of liquid Helen had set next to him.

'I think it's coffee, Jack.'

'Coffee? It's like mud!' Beauty wailed louder. 'Can't you shut her up, she's driving me mad.'

'It's just she's so cold, and all the other rooms are even colder . . .'

Tessa couldn't decide who was the more repulsive, red-faced Jack or cringing Helen. Beauty was holding her breath in between sobs. Helen tried to pacify her.

'She's spoiled, she's totally spoiled, what that child needs is control.'

'You know all about it then?' said Tessa.

'Well, I know more than her.' He pointed at Helen. 'I never met anyone so useless. Anyway, they've only got until March.'

Helen burst into tears.

'Jack, for God's sake, leave them alone.' Helen's crying was almost as loud as Beauty's.

'Social parasites. The child's a nuisance and the mother's a moron.'

'Shut up!' yelled Tessa.

'I'll make sure they're out by March.' He thumped the table again, this time knocking the coffee all over his plans.

'I'll wipe it up, I'll wipe it up,' sobbed Helen, dabbing ineptly at the mess with a dirty cloth. Beauty clung to her skirt.

Jack left, slamming doors right through the house. His absence was more oppressive than his presence. Helen's mopping smeared the coffee further. She glanced at Tessa apologetically, but Tessa felt she would only defend them from Jack; they didn't have her sympathy. Helen's tearful face was distorted and ugly, Beauty, still clinging, looked like something demented.

'Leave it,' said Tessa, and she left too, to the preferable iciness of her own room.

The snow thawed and Don and Dee-Dee reappeared. Dee had a

genuine excuse to stay away, after all she had to get to work and St John's was twenty-five miles from Norwich. Don's excuses were thinner; he would never admit it but he hated winters. It was after a winter that he had enticed Tessa and Dee to live with him, and just before one when he had found Jack. The cold, the mud, the isolation and bad tempers; Don loved stacks of people enjoying themselves.

'Well, we're all glum.' The inhabitants of St John's were around the breakfast-room table after their evening meal. For a treat Dee had cooked it and she had kept up a cheerful monologue about the happenings in the Sunshine Café. She was now quiet and cleaning up the plates. Don looked from one sour face to another. Nobody spoke. Helen began to help Dee-Dee, Jack giving her acid looks as she fumbled and clattered. Beauty was asleep with her head in a plate of mashed potato. From the kitchen came a loud crash.

'Helen!'

'They just slipped! I'll clean it up. Are they all broken?'

Beauty woke with a shriek.

'God,' said Jack.

'I'll go to bed now,' said Tessa.

Don leant back in his chair thoughtfully. 'What we all need is a party.'

If it had been June fifty people might have turned up. Don spent weeks organising it, but even he only found four; Sue and Wally and Jude and Tony from the café. St John's was not popular in the winter.

Late February. The snow had gone and the drive was a rutted mire, navigable only by trucks and Land Rovers. Ordinary cars sunk to their axles. The wind was bitter and drove rain in blinding sheets. Walking was impossible. The milkman wouldn't deliver, the postman wouldn't deliver. St John's was abandoned to a stone-age way of life. Eat, sleep, keep warm. And Don wanted a dinner party. He was not to be discouraged. 'An evening of

121

friends,' he called it, even though Jack had not spoken a decent word to Helen since August and Tessa had hardly spoken to her at all, and Jude and Sue, according to Dee-Dee, 'found each other very difficult', and Tony was a committed Buddhist into macrobiotics and self-discipline and Wally was an old waster.

'It's going to be awful,' said Tessa sitting on Don's bed, which she hardly ever did now. But Don smiled confidently: 'It'll be interesting.'

He looked warm in woollen pyjamas and Geoffrey's threadbare dressing gown. He had four blankets and two quilts. Tessa, sitting on the end of the big carved bed, was cold, and her room she knew was colder still – the heat from the Aga warmed the solar.

'Don?' began Tessa, but she didn't know how to put it. She wanted him to know that just because she slept on her own at the moment it didn't mean she always wanted to sleep on her own.

He picked up his book and started to read. After a while he looked up and she was still sitting there.

'Your room cold, is it?' He rummaged under the quilt. 'Go on, have my hot-water bottle.' And he gave it to her with a big smile.

She took it and went to her own bed and lay there for some time holding it close to her. It felt somehow that he understood.

Don's 'party' started badly. Helen and Dee-Dee had a row in the kitchen.

'It's quite all right, Helen, I don't need any help.'

'I just thought I could be useful, perhaps . . .'

'It's quite all right.'

'Perhaps I could peel potatoes?'

'We're having rice, Helen, it's a curry . . . Helen, you're in my way.' Dee was rushing to and fro from the breakfast room. The Aga was playing up.

'The wood's damp,' said Tessa, poking the fire.

'What wood did you use?' asked Jack coming in from the dairy.

'I stacked some in the corridor, did you take it from the right or the left of the pile?'

'Helen took it,' said Tessa.

'Oh, I'm not really sure, does it matter?'

'You mustn't put damp wood on the Aga,' said Dee, trying to be patient. She dashed back to the kitchen. 'Oh, Helen, must you get in the way?'

'I was just trying to help.'

They heard Beauty coming down the stairs. Helen had put her to bed an hour ago. 'I want Mummy.'

'Go to bed, darling . . .' Helen, agitated, glanced at Jack.

'I don't want to.'

'You must, darling, we're all very busy here.'

Beauty squinted in the light. 'What you doing?' She looked wide awake. She grabbed Helen's skirt and stayed there defiantly.

'Can't she stay up for a little bit?' Helen's voice was high-pitched and wavering. 'She'll be very good.'

Jack snorted.

'Sue's children aren't coming,' said Dee pointedly; 'they're all in bed, even Willow. The lady next door is looking after them. I bet they're asleep now.'

'I don't want to go sleep,' said Beauty.

'The fire's hotter,' called Tessa.

Dee-Dee squeezed past Helen with a pot of vegetables. She examined the curry and the boiling rice.

'It'll be a late meal,' she sighed. Bending over the Aga she and Tessa exchanged glances. Jack was being aggressively silent.

From the windy blackness of the night they heard the familiar chug-chug of Don's truck. He had gone to collect Sue and Wally; their ambulance would never make it up the drive. Jack stood up.

'I want do drawing,' said Beauty loudly. The truck rumbled into the courtyard.

'Why can't I do drawing?'

'Because we're having a party,' said Dee-Dee firmly. Jack left.

123

Helen was too scared to speak. She kept patting Beauty, 'Shh, shh, shhh.'

'Take her to bed,' said Dee-Dee, 'please.'

Helen ushered Beauty out of the room; she was beginning to cry. Outside, Don, Sue and Wally were laughing.

'Jack, great to see you, man.' They crashed into the breakfast room, bringing with them the smell of the cold night and dope. Wally heaved a crate of wine onto the table and grinned, showing all his black teeth.

'It's good plonk,' said Don, examining a bottle; 'I say, St Émilion.'

He was quite stoned. Tessa threw him a frown.

'Couldn't resist it, Afghani black . . .' He steadied himself on the wall. From the lane a car was honking. 'That's Jude and Tony, I bet they're stuck. We'll go and fetch them.' And he and Jack went back into the night.

Wally laughed and hugged Sue, who was bouncing Sky, the youngest, on her hip; a cherubic one-year-old with round pink cheeks, used to much cossetting. Upstairs, Beauty was screaming.

'Whatever's that?' asked Sue.

'The ghost of St John's, man,' laughed Wally.

'Actually it's Beauty, Helen's putting her to bed.'

Sky giggled and clapped his hands. He was remarkably similar to Wally.

Then the others came back. Jack was carrying Jude – she had forgotten her boots and Tony had mud splashed all up his jeans.

'We'll get the car out later,' said Don, still extremely amiable. 'It's always happening, we'll get some planks and a torch . . . Jack, where is the torch?'

Wally opened a bottle. 'Cheers, here's to the mud!'

'Glasses, glasses!' said Don. 'Wally, this is Tony, Sue, this is Jude . . .'

'We've met,' said Jude.

'And the baby Sky. The winter sky, the summer sky. Well, here we all are then. Dee, when do we eat? Now?'

Dee went pink. 'It won't be till late.'

In an hour Wally had got everybody drunk, everybody except Jude and Tony, who never drank and sat disapprovingly at the end of the table, and Helen, who was still upstairs with Beauty.

'. . . Jack, do you remember Mike Barton at the George when his goat got out and ate Nelson's roses . . . ?'

Wally was rolling joints. 'Afghani appetisers? Where's the nosh?'

'It'll soon be ready, I'm sure.' Dee-Dee was hot and exasperated by the Aga.

'Well, Jude, how are you?' asked Tessa. Tony was trying to clean the mud off his jeans.

'I've joined a women's group in Norwich, I'm finding it very searching, I think women have to redefine their position on this planet.'

Wally slapped Sue on the bottom which made her and Sky giggle raucously. 'You love it, lady.'

'More drink?' said Don' 'Wally, where did you get it?'

'I'm not saying, but backs of lorries might be near it.'

'Tony, none for you?'

'No thanks, Don. Actually, I'd better tell you now. I'm changing my name to Pranyananda—'

'Wow, that's a big one,' laughed Wally.

'—to fit in with my Buddhist beliefs.'

'I'd love to hear about Buddhism,' said Dee, still at the Aga; 'I mean, is it like church and all that?'

'It's a bit difficult to define in a few sentences,' began Tony. At this point a tearful Helen came in followed by Beauty.

'Ah, La Belle Helen and the beautiful Beauty!' laughed Wally.

'She won't go to bed,' said Helen hopelessly. Beauty's face was angry and sullen.

'I want some food!'

'So do we all. Come on, lady, feed your men!'

'It's nearly ready,' said Dee-Dee carrying in plates. Helen sat nervously at the table, holding Beauty close to her. Beauty scowled.

'She's nearly as big as Tansy now,' said Sue. 'Oh look, Sky wants to say hello.' Sky reached out to pat Beauty, but Beauty screwed up her face.

'He's just a baby,' said Helen.

'I hate babies . . .'

Dee-Dee started dishing up.

'At last, Dee. It smells delicious, you are wonderful.'

Dee-Dee blushed. 'More rice, Don?'

Tony surveyed the food. 'Is it organic rice? I think I'll just have some vegetables.' He was thin and angular and had a monk's ascetic face.

'Dee, you must come circle dancing,' said Jude quickly; 'I think women should be finding ways of sharing their experiences in unthreatening environments.'

'Do you mean without men?' asked Don. 'Do you really think I'm threatening?' His mouth was full of carrot curry.

'Don is never serious,' said Dee fondly; 'he wouldn't know a feminist if one—'

'Bit his balls off!' laughed Wally. 'I'm all for liberation!'

'Helen, some for you?'

'Oh, a little, yes, not too much.' She always asked for tiny portions but by the time she had eaten hers and Beauty's and nibbled at leftovers she ate more than anybody. It was a habit irritating to Jack. Every time she put something in her mouth he stared at her. Beauty mixed her food up with a spoon and flicked it across the table. A portion of aubergine bhaji hit Tony in the eye.

'Ow!'

'Darling, darling, don't do that. Are you hurt? I'm so sorry.'

'No.' He wiped his face stoically.

Beauty flicked some more.

'Why don't you eat it?' said Tessa.

126

'It's hot.'

'Blow on it.'

'Willow never ate a thing, not until she was two, did she Wal, only milk, but Josh and Jesse and Sky, they're hungry all the time.' Sky was demonstrating his unusual appetite and laughing as he did so.

'It's horrible,' said Beauty.

'Shh, shh, shh.' Helen patted her.

'Get off, you're horrible.' Beauty tipped her food on the floor and ran into the kitchen. She stayed there for some time, banging the door.

'There's a book I'd like to lend you, Dee,' said Jude. Everybody was trying to ignore Beauty. 'By Germaine Greer. You might find it interesting.'

'Oh, I'll give it to Tess and she can tell me all about it, it takes me ages to read a book.'

'You like feminist literature then?' asked Jude.

'Sometimes.' Tessa didn't feel conversational. Beauty was still slamming the door.

'Tell her to stop it,' hissed Jack.

'Er . . . darling, darling, please stop doing that, we're all trying to have our supper and you might frighten the baby . . .'

Jack snorted and rubbed his beard.

'Jack,' said Don, helping himself to seconds, 'tell them all about the new greenhouse.'

'So we can grow more tomatoes so Don can sell them,' said Dee-Dee helpfully. Bang went the door.

'She'll break the hinges . . . The basic idea is for a twenty-foot structure along the south-facing garden wall, wood and glass, with a rudimentary heating system for the colder months . . .'

Wally and Sue were squeezing each other. Jude eyed them judgementally. Tony picked at his plate of vegetables. Helen ate her way through the leftovers. Slam went the door.

*

127

Jack outlined the next season's growing schedule, frequently interrupted by Beauty, who gave up slamming doors and was now dancing round the table. 'Oh dear,' sighed Dee-Dee. Beauty was getting more manic and Helen was getting more distraught. When Beauty danced near her she tried to grab her. Her antics at least amused Sky. Beauty stopped and looked at him.

'He's horrible.'

'That's not a nice thing to say.' Sue could not bear her children to be insulted.

'He's got a fat face.' She poked him with her finger. 'Fatty.'

'Don't,' said Sue, brushing Beauty away. She moved nearer to Wally but he was too far gone to notice what was happening.

'. . . There may be a market for organic vegetables at the Sunshine,' said Tony, who had been following all that Jack said.

'Well, that's something we must discuss further,' said Don. He looked across the table at Sky. 'Isn't he a picture!' and Sky giggled.

'Wally, that son of yours is amazing.'

'Far out,' said Wally, lost. Everybody laughed and Dee kissed Sky.

'He's a fatty, he's a horrible fatty,' shouted Beauty. She ran up and poked him again. 'Horrible, horrible!'

'Don't do that!' and Sue slapped her. It was a tap, really, but Beauty shrieked. Helen jumped up.

'I'm sorry,' said Sue, all defensive; 'she was hurting him.'

Beauty pulled his hair.

'Get her to bed!' ordered Jack above the noise.

'Darling, please come with Mummy.' Helen tugged her arm.

'I won't! I won't!'

'This happens all the time,' said Tessa to Jude.

Beauty made another grab at Sky. 'Oh, she's mad!' exclaimed Sue, hoisting him into the air. 'Look at her face, she's evil!' Beauty, screaming and clawing at Sue, did seem to fit that description. Dee-Dee rushed to rescue her.

'Naughty girl, go to bed. Poor Sky, poor Sue.'

128

'Man, this is heavy,' said Wally.

'Ugly, ugly baby,' shrieked Beauty, knocking several plates on the floor.

Jack stood up. 'I can't stand it! Get that bloody child out of here!'

His shouting threw Beauty into hysteria. Helen tried to catch her but she was kicking and scratching anybody she could reach. She slipped Helen's grasp and ran round and round the table.

'For God's sake get her out!'

'I'm trying, I'm trying,' puffed Helen. Beauty ran into the kitchen. Helen followed and hauled her out, but now Helen was crying.

'Christ, useless, fucking useless.' Jack pushed Helen away and grabbed Beauty himself. For a moment it looked as if he would beat her to a pulp. Beauty was terrified. 'Stop crying!' yelled Jack, and then louder, 'Stop bloody crying.' Beauty shut her mouth and stared at him, gulping. 'Go to bed!' She ran out of the room with Jack following.

A long time passed before anybody spoke. Helen was in the corner sobbing uncontrollably. Upstairs there was silence.

'Wow,' said Wally. 'Party's over, Don.'

'Yes, I suppose it is . . . Well, um, thanks for coming everybody . . . Oh gosh, Tony, your car's still in the mud . . .'

Then in strode Jack. 'Going?' he asked. They all looked at him. 'We'll have to get that car out, I've got the torch.' Nobody moved. 'Don, you take Wally and Sue back. You . . .' he pointed to Tessa and Dee, 'clean up, and you,' he made a dismissive gesture towards Helen, 'get out, and leave that wretched daughter of yours alone.'

'Yes, Jack. Yes, Jack,' and she scuttled away.

'What have you done to Beauty?' asked Don.

'Done?' he smiled arrogantly. 'Done? Nothing, she's asleep.'

Chapter Fourteen

Jack became Beauty's tamer, and what could Helen do? However heavy-handed he was, one thing was certain, it was having an effect.

Beauty got nothing to eat unless she sat down quietly and Jack sent her to bed at seven. Life at St John's began to be calmer. Beauty may have been afraid of Jack, she never screwed her face up at him, but she was also fascinated. She stared at him as if he were an angry wolf, amazed he hadn't gobbled her up.

'Sit still! Stop kicking the table!' Instant silence. 'And eat with your mouth shut, then go to bed!'

Jack loved it. Every time a little hurdle was crossed, like getting her not to chuck food everywhere, a self-satisfied grin stuck to him for hours. He even managed to get her in the bath, which was something Helen had never done. Tessa watched the whole business suspiciously. Jack even told bed-time stories which usually began, 'Did I ever tell you about the time when I . . .' It could have been a touching scene, the little girl staring in wonder at the grown-up man, if he wasn't so appallingly smug.

The sleets of February became the rains of March. Beauty and Jack became inseparable. He treated her with the same detachment as one might treat a house-trained puppy. Helen, as far as Beauty was concerned, existed only as a minor irritation.

'Darling, darling, shall I make you a drink?'

Beauty was sitting with her nose pressed to the breakfast-room window watching Jack in the garden.

'I could make you hot chocolate, or banana milkshake.'

Beauty turned her head; she looked at her mother blankly.

130

'Or anything you liked, a sandwich, or a cake?'

'Before supper?' Jack forbade snacks between meals.

'Oh . . .' Helen blushed and glanced at Tessa, who was on the sofa reading *The Female Eunuch*. 'But if you didn't want, perhaps we could do drawing, or . . .'

But Beauty was fixed to the window again. Suddenly, she got up and dashed to the back door. 'I'm here, wait for me, I'm here.' Jack was calling.

'Where are they going?' asked Helen hopelessly.

'I think he's going to show her how to plant carrots.'

Helen, without Beauty to fuss over, had nothing to do. She hovered in the kitchen nibbling guiltily. Jack's emotional abduction of her daughter was obviously painful, but she was unsupported. Beauty's current behaviour was more preferable. Nobody could stand being with Helen, even Dee-Dee who was generally tolerant, even Don.

'Oh . . . Helen, I didn't see you, making supper are you?'

'Dee-Dee's making supper, I was just getting a little snack, I didn't have any lunch, you see, well I did, but it was only an apple and . . .'

'Have you seen Jack?'

'He's in the walled garden, I think he is, but he could be upstairs or . . . anywhere really . . . Do you want a sandwich? I could make you one, supper won't be for at least an hour.'

'Um, no, thanks . . .'

'Were you in Norwich today? Dee-Dee was saying there's quite a—'

But Don had already left.

Beauty and Helen's future at St John's was supposed to be decided by March. It was March now. They waited for Jack to call a house meeting, but he didn't; he was busy with the spring planting and the new greenhouse. For Tessa, everybody was reluctant because there was only one option: Helen and Beauty had to go. She and

131

Dee-Dee discussed it all in the floral comfort of Dee-Dee's room. 'It's not that I don't like her, Tessy . . .'

'I don't like her, she's a fat bore.'

'Oh, Tessy, you are hard sometimes . . . she is a pain, but she's unhappy, and she has improved a lot . . .'

'Has she?'

'Well, she is a bit calmer.'

'She's fatter.'

'Oh, Tessy, and what about Beauty, we can't send her back to an awful bedsit?' But despite such emotive issues, Dee-Dee had to finally admit: 'This isn't the right place for them, really. They can't contribute much and St John's is all about contributing, isn't it?'

Don, preoccupied with finding outlets for his vegetables, thought about the problem for nearly five seconds. 'Helen? Beauty? Of course, they'll have to go. The whole thing's an absolute disaster. We did our best, didn't we?'

Jack, since turning Beauty into his pet dog, had expressed no views on the subject. Tessa assumed he would be glad to see the back of them. She attempted to talk to him in the vegetable garden.

'Jack, we ought to have a house meeting about Helen and Beauty.'

'Hmm. Oi, careful with that hoe, I've seeded there.'

'I am being careful . . . if they're going to go, they ought to know soon.'

'Yes, yes.' He rubbed his beard.

'When then, this week?'

'What? No, not this week . . . I'm worried about those cabbages, there's a frost on the way.'

'Next week, then?'

'No, absolutely not, Tony's coming to see what we've got. I don't want to be faffed by irrelevancies.'

Tessa hoed silently. She was annoyed. Beauty came up with a flask of soup. Jack took it off her without looking at her. 'Thanks,' said Tessa, feeling suddenly sorry for her. Beauty was gazing at Jack expectantly.

'Off you go then.' He waved her away like a fly. Tessa watched her run all the way back to the house. Jack poured himself more soup. 'Hmm, lukewarm.' He handed the cup to Tessa. 'End of March,' he said, 'definitely.'

The week before the end of March Tessa was on her own at St John's. The others were in Norwich. She was in the vegetable garden by the orchard, but there was little she could do there, the ground was waterlogged. She carried her tools back to the porch; she might as well paint for the rest of the day. Her latest picture was the big field behind the Hall, with a misty sunrise, the Hall and the trees silhouetted against it, 'Early Morning at St John's'. As she worked on the soft colours of the picture she felt strangely emotional. The image was very different from her daily experience, yet it was what she wanted St John's to be, shadowy and magical. She leant back in her chair.

A car was honking up the lane. Shit, thought Tessa, and watched the courtyard through the window. The honking persisted until a Range Rover drew up in front of the house. Two people got out. Tessa had never seen them before, a middle-aged couple in green quilted anoraks. The woman wore a headscarf, the man a cap. She presumed they were farmers, but not the sort with twenty acres and some tumbledown barns. The man knocked loudly on the porch. Tessa had no intention of letting them in; she thoroughly disliked this breed of people. Whatever they wanted they were impatient. They were now pacing up and down and peering in through windows. The man went back to the Range Rover and started honking the horn again.

'Christ!' Tessa tore down the stairs and threw open the porch door.

It was the woman who approached her. 'Well, so somebody's

in . . .' She looked Tessa up and down disapprovingly. She was tall, taller than Tessa, with haughty heavy features.

'Yes?' said Tessa insolently.

'What is this place?'

'It's St John's Hall.'

'Yes, I know that, but who lives here?'

'I do.'

'Just you?'

Tessa said nothing.

'There's other people here, aren't there, we've heard all about it.' The man joined her; he had a reddish face obscured by jowls. 'We're looking for someone,' he said.

'I'm sure they're not here.'

'It's taken us several weeks . . .'

'I'm sorry to hear that.'

'The man in the pub told us . . .'

'In the George?' Tessa laughed. 'What did they tell you?'

'About you lot,' said the man, getting redder. They stared at each other critically.

'Look,' said Tessa, 'we're a bunch of people living together, we're not maniacs, we're not criminals, we grow vegetables and sell them, and despite what you hear in the George we don't have orgies.' The couple stiffened. 'If you're looking for the person who nicked your pheasants or whatever, they're not here.' Tessa felt quite blameless; Jack had not gone poaching for months.

'Who does live here?' asked the woman sharply.

'It's none of your bloody business.'

'We're looking for our daughter,' said the man.

'Run away, has she? I'm not surprised. Sorry, but we've got no runaways here.' She was about to close the door.

'We were told she's been here, she's called Helen.'

'What?' Her hesitancy made the woman pounce.

'She is here, isn't she? Where is she? And Jennifer, where is Jennifer? We know they're here, we'll get the police if you don't tell us. Where are they? We'll search the house . . . Bill, search the house!'

Tessa barred their way. 'What is this?'

The woman composed herself and grabbed the man's arm. 'I'm Marjorie Marsh-Warren and this is my husband, William. We're looking for our daughter Helen who has a child called Jennifer.'

'You've been misled,' said Tessa; 'Helen does live here but she's not called Marsh-Whatsit and her daughter's called Beauty.'

At this name the woman made a disgusted snort. 'Stupid girl!' These were indeed Helen's parents.

Tessa felt suddenly dizzy. She wanted nothing more to do with these people. 'She calls herself Helen Clarke.'

'Of course, of course, it's typical, absurd . . .'

'We've come to take her home,' said Bill.

'Great,' said Tessa, leaning on the doorpost.

'And Jennifer. Beauty? Whoever heard of such a name?'

'It's pretty daft.'

'Well, where are they, then?' Marjorie walked back to the Range Rover.

'They're out. They'll be back later. I don't know when.'

'We can wait,' said Bill.

'You could come in, get her things, you know.'

'Absolutely not, it's probably all rubbish,' and Marjorie sat in the car.

An hour or so passed. Tessa had a ridiculous conversation with Bill about 'the appalling state of the country and damned socialists'.

She decided he had the sensitivity of a pile of manure and was just as obnoxious.

'. . . Nice place you've got here, bit of smarting up, could be worth something . . . Land?'

'About two acres.'

'Can't do much with that . . . Thousand hectares, now, that's what I call a bit of ground.'

'Do you.' Tessa could hear the truck coming, winding round the crazy lanes.

135

'. . . Dig up the hedges, nice big fields, get some return for your money . . .'

'They'll be here soon.'

'Eh, what?'

The truck bumped up the drive; Bill and Marjorie waited for their errant daughter.

Don and Dee were in the back of the truck; it was Don who leapt out first. 'Tessa, we did amazingly well in Norwich, Tony's agreed to take us on for a year . . . oh, visitors.'

'There's a problem,' said Tessa, feeling completely defeated.

'Can I help?' asked Don' 'Did you want to buy potatoes?'

Marjorie pushed forward. 'I'm Marjorie Marsh-Warren and this is my husband, William.'

'Oh, wow, I'm Donald Bell and . . . I own St John's Hall.'

From inside the truck Tessa could see the white scared face of Helen. Bill and Marjorie approached her purposefully.

'They're Helen's parents,' explained Tessa.

Dee-Dee was helping Helen and Beauty out of the truck. 'Helen, what is it? Just jump, honestly you don't have to be so . . .' Helen jumped and landed in an untidy bundle at her parents' feet. Shakily she stood up, then ran towards the Hall. At the door Tessa grabbed her arm.

'Don't be so stupid.'

'I just don't want to see them,' she blubbered.

'None of your tricks, young lady,' shouted Marjorie rushing over. Tessa held on to Helen. Don ran up too, as did Dee-Dee carrying Beauty.

'Jennifer! Bill, look at the state of her, it's your grandma, Jennifer.' Beauty screwed up her face. 'She doesn't recognise me. It's your granny and grandpa, don't you remember, Fudge the pony and your cousins Sarah and William?'

Beauty looked around. 'Where's Jack?' He was unloading the truck.

'Jack, who's Jack?' Marjorie shook Helen. 'Look what you've

done to Jennifer, and the state of you, we've been at our wits' end . . .'

'We've been most upset,' said Bill.

'I'd like an explanation, you even changed your name, why should you be ashamed of us? We're decent, respectable, responsible, Helen, and you . . . filthy, living in a hovel with unsuitable people.'

'Now wait a minute,' said Don, 'St John's is one of the finest examples of medieval architecture, well, for miles . . .'

'And I'm not unsuitable, how dare you,' said Dee-Dee.

'St John's a hovel? It's unique, the oldest bit is twelfth century, didn't you even notice the windows in the great hall?'

'It's really unfair. We may not look like you, but we rescued Helen. We've looked after her, and Beauty, haven't we? We gave them a home when they had nowhere, and all for nothing. Helen, why don't you say something?'

Helen was still white and quivering.

'She did have a home . . . with us,' screeched Marjorie.

'We didn't know that!' And everybody stared accusingly at Helen.

Tessa let go of her.

'You didn't say you had parents.' Dee-Dee sounded quite poisonous.

'It's just that—' began Helen in a tiny voice '—I just didn't want to see them any more.'

'Well, that's understandable,' said Tessa.

'I want Jack.' Beauty was still being held by Dee-Dee. 'I want Jack!'

Marjorie pushed some strands of hair back inside her headscarf and straightened her anorak. 'And who is Jack?'

Jack strode over with a sack of flour across his shoulders. For once Tessa was glad he was big and strong. He dropped the sack with a thump. 'What the fuck is going on?'

'This is Jack,' announced Dee-Dee.

'So, you're in charge?' said Bill.

137

Jack smirked. 'Well, you could say that.'

'They're Helen's parents, she didn't tell them where she was or anything.' Dee was still angry.

'They've come to take her away,' said Don.

Marjorie studied Jack carefully. 'You're Helen's boyfriend, then?'

'God no.' He was disgusted. There was a moment's silence. Jack folded his arms and stared at Marjorie.

'We'd better go, then. Come on Helen, be quick now.'

'You'll be better off at home,' said Bill.

'She can't go, we have to have a house meeting about it.' Jack stood as near to Helen as he could bear. 'We're democratic.'

'A meeting? When? We haven't got all day.'

'Shut up!' shouted Jack and Marjorie flinched. 'We'll have the meeting now. Don?'

'Well . . .' he looked around at everybody. What they were going to decide was obvious. 'Well, I think . . . it hasn't worked out, has it . . . sorry Helen.'

'Dee?'

'The same, it's nobody's fault really . . .' Helen was starting to cry.

'Tess?'

'She has to go.'

'Quite right, and I think so too,' said Jack.

Marjorie looked triumphant. 'Come along, Helen, don't worry about your things, I'm sure you won't need them with us. Go and fetch Jennifer.'

'Who's Jennifer?' said Jack.

'Beauty is Jennifer,' said Tessa.

'Go and fetch Jennifer and do stop crying, Helen, it's for the best.'

'Beauty's not going,' said Jack.

'What?' Marjorie stared at him, as did everybody else.

'We made a decision about Helen, not about Beauty.'

'This is ridiculous.' Bill's jowls wobbled.

'Helen is an imbecile, but Beauty has proved herself quite useful. I think with some attention she could be almost competent.' He glared at Marjorie. 'But I am totally opposed to Beauty leaving with people who are as imbecilic as her mother.'

'Jack,' remonstrated Don. The Marsh-Warrens were so insulted they couldn't speak.

'Totally opposed, that's my final position.' He went back to the truck to get another sack of flour.

'I can't leave Beauty, I can't,' wailed Helen.

Jack dropped the sack of flour dangerously close to her. 'That's your problem.'

'This is mad. We can't send Helen away and keep Beauty.'

'Tessa's right, she is her mother.' Don didn't often argue with Jack.

'I would have thought it obvious. Helen is an unsuitable parent.' Jack's voice was sliced with sarcasm. 'We are responsible for her daughter.' And to prove it he picked Beauty up.

She beamed radiantly.

'I like Jack.'

'Yes, Jack, but—'

'OK, let it be a majority vote. Does Beauty stay here with us or does she go to be corrupted by these privileged land grabbers?' he sneered.

'I'll get my solicitors,' shouted Bill.

'Sod you, Jack, you're bloody right, aren't you?' And Tessa knew what the consequences would be.

'Beauty stays, then, it's agreed.' Jack smiled arrogantly.

'It's agreed,' sighed Don, speaking for Dee-Dee as well as himself.

Marjorie started up the Range Rover. 'I just don't believe it.'

'I'll drag you through every court from here to John O'Groats,' shouted Bill.

'Come along, Bill, come along, Helen, we can't stay for more insults. They'll change their tune after a court order. I've never met such people. Helen, Helen, come along, there's nothing you can do.'

'I'm not going, I'm not, I can't leave Beauty.' She was desperate.

Beauty, held by Jack, had her arms round his neck. 'Where's Mummy going?'

'Beauty, darling, my baby, my own darling, I can't leave you.'

'I thought this might happen,' said Jack.

'Helen, will you come. Now.'

'We can't let her go, it's terrible,' and Dee-Dee started crying.

'I'll do anything,' wailed Helen, 'I'll do all the work, please let me stay, Beauty's all I've got. Please don't make me leave her.'

'Oh Christ,' and Don held his head in his hands; 'Helen has to stay, Jack, we can't do this to her.'

'Is Mummy going now?' asked Beauty, and Helen dissolved into inarticulate moans.

Jack put Beauty down and Helen flung her arms around her. Beauty screwed up her face, 'You're squashing me,' and because Helen was crying so loudly she began too. Marjorie and Bill watched the scene.

'She'd better stay, then,' said Jack, rubbing his beard.

Don ran up to Marjorie and Bill. 'Look, they're staying with us. If you want to change that get the law, now clear off or we'll wreck your fucking car!' he was nearly in tears too.

The Marsh-Warrens disappeared up the lane shouting recriminations.

Dee-Dee helped Helen and Beauty into the house. 'It's all right, Helen, it's all right now.'

'I'll do anything, I'll do all the washing . . .'

'It's all right, it's all right.'

'Shit,' said Tessa.

'I think I'm going to have a walk . . . by myself,' said Don, still overcome. Jack was carrying the sacks of flour into the house as if nothing had happened. Tessa watched him, and Don striding off towards the fields, and Dee and Helen as they shut the door behind them, and the stone front of St John's becoming golden in the afternoon light, and the future they had just chosen for themselves.

Chapter Fifteen

Marjorie and Bill did not come back, but Helen's sister did. It was supposed to be a friendly visit, but Susan's husband was a solicitor.

They arrived with their two children on a Sunday afternoon. Jack and Don were out, which was fortunate; they might not have been so welcoming.

They all sat in the great hall. Dee brought in cakes and tea. Rain dribbled in through the broken windows.

Susan and Charles Goodland sat uncomfortably; most of the sofa's stuffing was coming out. Susan was made in much the same mould as her mother. Charles was long and bespectacled, with curly hair brushed flat. The two children were extremely quiet and remarkably clean.

'Mummy's terribly upset, you know,' said Susan, sipping tea from a cracked cup. All the cups at St John's were cracked.

Helen shuffled her feet and looked at the floor. She was holding Beauty protectively. Beauty was wriggling. Dee handed round fruit cake. Beauty took a piece and stuffed the lot in her mouth. It was lucky Jack wasn't there. The Goodlands ate theirs carefully, balancing plates on their knees.

'Do you want to play?' said Beauty with a mouth full of cake. Sarah and William looked as if they didn't know how to play.

'I got a den in the garden.' Beauty pulled something out of her hair and looked at it. Susan grimaced.

'It's raining, dear,' she said.

'I like rain.'

Charles inspected his tea. 'Helen—' he paused. 'As you know, Marjorie and Bill are ever so worried about you and . . . Beauty.'

'I'm fine.' Helen scowled and for a moment looked exactly like her daughter.

'Helen wants to be here, don't you?' said Dee-Dee. 'We're not keeping her, you know.'

'Of course.' Susan wiped her mouth. 'But there did seem to be some confusion when my parents visited. They left with the impression you wouldn't—' She glanced at Charles.

'You wouldn't let them take Beauty away,' said Charles.

'Oh, honestly,' said Dee-Dee; 'this is all so stupid. Tell them, Helen, what you said to me yesterday.'

Helen coughed. 'It's just . . . I like it here.' She attempted a smile. 'It's better for Beauty to be here than with Mummy, I'm sure.'

'How can you say that? Mummy and Daddy could provide everything for her, it's obvious here you haven't . . . well, adequate resources.'

Dee-Dee was getting very pink. 'Helen wants to stay and we say she can and Beauty's going to stay with her and it's nonsense to say we haven't resources.'

Susan and Charles looked critically at the crumbling interior of the great hall.

'There's nothing you can do. Helen can do what she wants. We all look after Beauty. You should have seen her when she first came here. Helen doesn't want to live with her parents, do you? Say something, Helen.'

'No, I don't,' mumbled Helen.

'You see, there's nothing legal you can do at all, nothing at all. Jack checked up.'

'Ah, Jack,' said Charles; 'Mr Marsh-Warren mentioned him, and the other one, Don, wasn't it? Now, who are they?'

'We wouldn't all be here if it wasn't for Jack, and Don is the kindest person in the whole world,' and Dee-Dee blushed scarlet.

'Don owns the Hall. He could kick us out if he wanted to, but he doesn't,' said Tessa.

'He paid Helen's rent and it was nearly two hundred pounds,' said Dee-Dee.

142

Charles and Susan raised their eyebrows. Helen looked at the floor again.

'I don't want Mummy and Daddy to be upset, but every time they see me they get so cross. I couldn't live with them again, I just couldn't.'

Beauty wriggled free of Helen and sat on Dee-Dee's lap. 'Shall we make bread?'

'Later perhaps.' Dee smoothed her hair affectionately. Sarah and William had finished their cake and were now silently working through puzzle books.

'We all love Beauty,' said Dee-Dee defensively.

'They help me look after her, they've been very helpful.' Helen's voice was barely audible.

There was a long silence punctuated by the rustle of puzzle books.

'It's a pity you can't bring yourself to see your parents sometimes. Tessa does and she can't stand hers,' said Dee-Dee. 'We didn't approve of Helen not contacting them, you know, we thought they didn't care.' She glared at Helen. Since the incident with the Marsh-Warrens Helen was not the most popular person at St John's.

'We don't want them to be upset, do we, Tessy.'

Tessa shook her head.

'We could take her to see them and bring her back, perhaps one weekend a month, that would be all right, wouldn't it?'

Helen's face proclaimed a definite No, but she was not going to argue with Dee-Dee.

Charles and Susan conferred in whispers. 'Mummy was most worried about losing contact with Jennifer,' Susan said at last.

'It could be a satisfactory arrangement,' said Charles.

Dee smiled lovingly. 'There. Everybody's happy! Don said it was a good idea.'

'When?' Tessa had not heard it discussed before.

'Oh, last night, very late,' and Dee was suddenly flustered; 'we

143

were talking and you and Helen had gone to bed and Jack came back from the George and he said it was a good idea.'

'I see.' Tessa knew if Jack wanted it then it would happen.

'Well, I'm glad you've decided to be responsible,' said Susan.

'I—' began Helen.

'We won't keep you, it's been good of you,' and she handed the cracked cup to Dee-Dee.

The children picked up their books. 'Thank you for having us,' they said.

Dee, Tessa and Helen stayed in the great hall. Beauty sat on the floor balancing one cup on top of another. Helen had a nervous baffled expression on her face.

'Why don't you wash up?' said Dee-Dee suddenly.

'Yes, yes.' Helen jumped and collected the cups and plates. 'Beauty can help you, won't you, Beauty?'

'I like being helpful,' said Beauty.

'I thought Jack was totally opposed to the Marsh-Warrens,' said Tessa after Helen had gone.

'He is, but one stay a month, it's nothing really. He said Beauty can't be influenced by one weekend a month, especially if Helen's there.'

Dee-Dee sat on the sofa and poked some stuffing back inside the cover. 'I ought to make a new cover, really,' she frowned; 'it could look quite nice. I might be able to get some material in the market.'

'I wish you would tell me when things have been decided.'

'I meant to,' said Dee-Dee, still poking.

Tessa sighed deeply. Outside they could hear Beauty giggling in the rain and Helen, 'Come in, come in, you'll get soaked.'

'I'm not angry, but I feel set up,' said Tessa, and they were both silent because it was obvious the only person who was set up was Helen.

*

That summer. Bad feelings were easy to disperse. There was prolonged fine weather, fairs to visit, people to see, continued work in the gardens, Jack's friends, though not so many of them, and Dee-Dee still made bread and she and Tessa rose early and ate breakfast in the rose garden and Don was selling produce to Tony, and Jack was busy with the fairs that summer, but Tessa felt they were all crystallising, remote and uninvolved with each other and Helen was the cause of it.

In the beginning, Don, Dee-Dee, Jack and herself, they had started in a big muddle, formed roles for themselves, but now these roles were definite, unchanging. Tessa felt herself slipping, as if off an edge, away from the breakfast-room discussions and the late-night discussions and laughing people, into a tangled part of herself that needed so much digging and weeding it was difficult to concentrate on anything except real digging and real weeding.

'Oh, that's Tessa, she likes to be by herself,' said Dee-Dee to one of Jack's friends, and she didn't think to contradict her.

The landscape around St John's was changing too. A tree felled here, a field widened there, and that summer Tessa stood in the middle of the big field behind the house and realised she could see all the way to St Lawrence. She knew then how drastic the change was. There'll be no hedges soon, she thought. She stood in the field with the stalks tickling her legs, and the Suffolk sky so wide and huge it made her feel tiny, and the breeze blowing from Russia rippling the wheat and the cloud shadows rushing towards her. She looked towards St John's which was still in a tangle of green as it always had been, elder bushes, hawthorn bushes, the high elms, and she knew the old Suffolk, which lasted until Geoffrey, was going, going. They had watched trucks carrying away knotty remnants of hedgerows, trucks carrying concrete pipes coming back. Trucks with hewn lumps of elm trees.

Dutch Elm disease had arrived. At first this meant Jack arranged enough firewood to last them well over the winter, but then it meant trees they knew, they walked past every day, were coming down. Four big elms behind the Hall, six in St John's hamlet, three on the way to St Margaret's. The skyline began to look gap-toothed, for in the Saints the trees were planted at equal distances.

Then one morning they woke up to find the hedges on either side of the lane were being dug up. Don rushed out in his pyjamas and dressing gown. 'You can't do that, you can't do that!' There were six men, two lorries and a bulldozer. The young farmer was absent. The men shrugged their shoulders. Dee-Dee and Tessa ran up too.

'Don, Don, you must stop them, there might be birds, there might be rabbits!'

The bulldozer turned up a great section of hedge.

Don accosted one of the men. 'It's got to stop, that hedge is ancient, it's medieval. You can't, you can't. I mean, we pick our blackberries here.'

The man had a farm-worker's face, wrinkled and leathery. 'Him been 'ere a long time, that hedge. Them blackberries be the best.' But he was not moved.

'Then why dig them up? Why?'

'Guv'nor can't get his combines up.'

'I'm not surprised, they're too bloody big!' But Don's desperation only caused amusement. Tessa and Dee-Dee in their night-wear also caused amusement. Jack arrived.

'They're digging up our hedges!' pleaded Dee-Dee. 'Do something!'

Jack snorted. 'They're not our hedges, it's not our land.'

'Is there nothing we can do?' Tessa was ready to jump into the ditch to stop the bulldozer.

'Nothing useful.' One of the men waved at him. Jack waved back. Dee-Dee stared as if he were a traitor.

'They're being paid for it,' said Jack.

Don was still in shock. 'The blackberries would have been ready, they could have waited for the blackberries . . .'

*

146

Then the young farmer drove up in his Land Rover. He knew he had done something controversial because he didn't get out.

'Morning. Fine one, too.' Unlike his father his accent had been public-schooled out of him. 'Be finished by tomorrow.' A tractor hauled away a hawtorn stump.

'It's carnage.' Don banged the door of the Land Rover. 'It's disgraceful, it's rape, it's rape, I tell you.'

'Had to, sorry, had terrible trouble with the combines,' and he drove off rapidly.

They watched the men. Jack was right, there was nothing they could do. Helen joined them. 'What are they doing? Widening the road? Perhaps it won't be so bumpy, aren't you all freezing? I've made some tea and I'm just making toast.'

'You've left it under the grill? Oh Helen, it'll burn!' And they ran back to rescue Beauty from a smoke-filled kitchen.

'Helen, you're so stupid, you're so stupid!' Dee-Dee flung open the windows.

By early October they had almost got used to the de-hedged land. The young farmer had the worst potholes filled, tractors rumbled to the fields with greater ease. From the gardens Tessa could hear the seagulls following the plough, reeling and squawking. She was carrying a wheelbarrow of leaves to the compost bins, thinking about storing the last of the apples, and collecting fallen twigs and branches for winter kindling. Nothing at St John's was ever wasted. She had been alone all day, but she felt quite happy about this. It was approaching dusk. The lights in the kitchen meant that Helen was making supper.

She walked past the back of the house and into the walled garden, through the arch, making a mental note she must cut the raspberry canes. She began to shovel the leaves into the compost bins.

'What you doing?' It was Beauty. She had leaves in her hair and mud over her dress. Despite Jack's efforts she would never be clean.

'Making compost. It all rots down and then I put it on the garden.'

'Why?'

'It makes things grow better.' Tessa didn't stop shovelling.

Beauty stood on one leg and picked her nose. 'Why?'

'Look, let me do this, I'm busy.' Beauty watched her. 'Where's Jack? Perhaps he needs some help.' Tessa and Beauty spent very little time together.

'He's gone out.'

Tessa emptied the wheelbarrow. Beauty was now hopping from one foot to the other.

'Why don't you go and play?'

'I got a den.'

'I know you got a den. Why don't you go and play in your den?'

Beauty hopped towards her. 'My den's secret.'

'I know your den's secret.'

Beauty frowned. 'How do you know, you've never seen my den.'

Tessa laughed. 'How can I if it's secret?'

This completely baffled Beauty. Tessa picked up the barrow and wheeled it towards the arch.

'You can see my den if you like,' said Beauty in a whisper as Tessa passed her.

Tessa put down the barrow. Beauty was as serious as only a child can be. 'Yes, I would like.'

Beauty's den was in an uncultivated part of the garden behind the barns. She led Tessa underneath an elder bush and into a mat of brambles.

'Is this it?'

'Shh, you have to be quiet because it's secret.'

There was just enough room for Tessa to sit curled up; under the brambles was a natural hollow, but there was ample space for Beauty. Her den was damp and smelled foxy. On the ground were things like jam labels, broken toys, rusty tins, defunct batteries

148

and scraps of material. It looked like she was using the place as a rubbish tip.

'Look,' said Beauty and picked up some jam labels and laid them carefully on her skirt. 'These are my best ones.'

Tessa looked.

'I washed them off carefully and they didn't get torn.' Balkan Extra Raspberry Jam. 'And look . . .' She picked up two batteries and rubbed them clean. 'These are Jack's.' Her voice was full of awe. She showed Tessa her entire collection. Each article, even a safety pin, had a history. 'I used to have it on nappies when I was a baby, and this—' a scrap of material '—is a bit of Dee-Dee's curtain.'

'Well, they're all really wonderful,' said Tessa, fascinated.

'They're treasures,' said Beauty.

They stayed in the den. Through the leaves Tessa could see glimpses of the field. Somebody walking past would never guess what was behind the brambles. Beauty was rearranging her treasures, humming to herself. Tessa recognised a paintbrush, a fine sable one. It had gone missing months ago. Now it was stuck in the ground with other sticks and pencils. She watched Beauty absorbed in her game and remembered watching Dee-Dee fussing over the dolls, and suddenly she felt sad, for what was happening was something that would never last. And she wanted to fix this moment in time and keep Beauty always as a grubby mud fairy so she wouldn't have to grow up.

'If I find things when I'm gardening would you like me to give them to you?'

'What?' She had almost forgotten Tessa was there.

'Sometimes I find bits of china and nails, would you like them? I think I've got some here.' She reached for her pockets, which was difficult to do in a cramped position. She handed the debris to Beauty, who eyed it like a connoisseur.

'I think the china's willow pattern,' said Tessa.

'Willow pattern,' repeated Beauty, turning it over.

It began to get late. Tessa and Beauty were still in the den. Tessa was getting cramp from being curled up and her hair was catching on the brambles. The den did not smell healthy. Beauty was chattering and humming, telling herself a long story. Every time Tessa moved she said, 'Shh, we must be quiet.' Then suddenly she said 'Listen.' And Tessa listened but couldn't hear anything but the wind in the bushes and the lapwings and then, faint and distant, chug, chug, chug, the truck coming back.

They scrambled out of the den. Beauty shook leaves off herself and wiped her face, smearing the dirt further. They could hear the truck coming nearer.

'You won't tell.'

'I'll tell nobody.' And standing up Tessa realised how very much taller she was than Beauty, who now looked small and grubby and insignificant, and for the first time she felt protective towards her. Beauty was anxious and excited.

'I'd go and have a wash if I were you. Jack likes to see you clean.'

At his name Beauty looked critically at her filthy hands as if she hadn't realised they were dirty. 'I could put on a clean dress.'

They walked towards the house. There was a sharp edge to the air as if it might be frosty later. The sky was becoming indigo, the sun had already set. Leaves were falling off the chestnut in the courtyard. Beauty ran inside to transform herself and Tessa stopped for a moment to take in the last peaceful seconds of the day. A crow alighted on the roof of the Hall.

Then the truck rattled into the courtyard and everything was suddenly noisy, Dee and Don laughing as they always did when they came back from Norwich, Jack's loud voice. The breakfast-room door opened and there was Helen holding a saucepan and the light shone out from the windows.

But Tessa felt where she wanted to be was in a damp space under some brambles. The crow flew away and she too moved, towards the noise and activity that was St John's.

Chapter Sixteen

Tessa in the great hall with the morning light pouring everywhere but inside, and outside the creeping combines. She was angry. She was angry with Jack for manipulating them, she was angry with Dee for being so wet, with Helen for being cringingly useless and with Don for being noble and right-minded, but most of all she was angry with herself. Tessa in the great hall saw how she had slipped away to the tangle and brambles and the slippery mud. Ice and steel and stone, she had been none of these, but slippery wet mud, ankle deep. The great hall was lofty and spacious; the Hallivands made it as welcoming as a museum. It was here they had all met to celebrate, if that was the word, Christmas, Easter and St John's Day, but for Tessa the great hall was linked with dissent, somehow; all of them choosing to be together, instead of passing in transit, was too much.

* * *

It was their last Christmas, but they did not know it. Dee-Dee and Tessa had decorated the hall with holly and ivy. Big bunches hung in the corners of the room. Don 'found' a Christmas tree. It was a bit lopsided and an ugly shape but when covered in tinsel and paper chains it looked splendid. Candles shone all over the place. It was a wonder the Hall hadn't burnt to the ground. Christmas Day, and they were waiting for lunch. Dee-Dee and Helen had been cooking and arguing since the morning, Don and Jack were drunk and jovial, slapping each other on the back, and Tessa spent most of the time chopping wood. She was carrying basketfuls into the hall. Dee-Dee had given her a jumper with rainbow stripes and bits of bark and dirt were already stuck to it. Helen had given

Beauty a new dress, a frilly pink thing with bows, and she was wearing it on top of winter pyjamas.

'Look! I got a new dress. Look, Jack, I got a new dress. Look, Don.' She had been saying this since seven in the morning. 'Look, Tessa, look.'

'It's great. Do you want to help me make a fire?'

'I can't, I'll get my new dress dirty.' And she danced to the kitchen to pester Dee-Dee.

The men brought the table in from the breakfast room; it took a long time to get it through the door despite Jack's instructions. Eventually they stood it by the fire. Don got the best white cloth and the least cracked plates and began to set places.

'Why are you laying for eight?' asked Dee-Dee, coming in from the kitchen to check up on everything.

'Well, somebody might turn up.' Don had invited loads of people but over the years Christmases at St John's had become smaller.

'Oh Tessy.' Dee had just seen the state of Tessa's new jumper. Tessa by the fire shrugged her shoulders. Dee-Dee flounced back to the kitchen. Helen came in, tearful, banished from cooking. 'I got a new dress,' said Beauty, spinning round. Jack, on the sofa, was tinkering with his mandolin.

'Yes, yes, music,' said Don; 'that's the idea. "O, come all ye faithful", can you do that one? Or a dance, a medieval dance, where's my tambourine?'

Don was arranging sprigs of holly on the table; he and Jack began to sing 'Angelus ad virginum'.

Helen blew her nose on a dirty handkerchief.

'You should have gone to Marjorie's,' said Tessa. This was a sore point. The Marsh-Warrens had insisted Helen and Beauty stay with them for Christmas, but Helen had refused. Helen glowered.

'Come and dance,' called out Don; 'you can't just sit there. Helen, why aren't you helping Dee-Dee?'

'That fire's going out,' said Jack.

'No it isn't,' said Tessa.

'I got a new dress,' sang Beauty, dancing with Don round the table.

'It's ready, it's ready,' called Dee-Dee from the kitchen.

There were more roast potatoes that year and less turkey; the pudding was small and barely enough for all of them. In the damp great hall around the long table it was not exactly a party. Helen sniffed throughout; Dee-Dee was exhausted, with hardly enough energy to talk; Jack was furious because Helen took the last bit of Christmas pudding; at least Don and Beauty were cheerful.

'Beauty's got a new dress, did you see it?'

Beauty stood on her chair. Her dress now had gravy and custard down it, but she was as radiant and shining as the Christmas tree fairy.

'Isn't she a picture,' laughed Don; 'I propose a toast, here's to Beauty, may she always be as beautiful as she is today.'

Jack grimaced disapprovingly.

'Jack, it is Christmas,' said Don.

'She doesn't need spoiling. Anyway, it's a ridiculous dress, it's quite impractical.'

Beauty's sparkle disappeared instantly. 'Shall I take it off then?' She had the face of a tortured martyr. She sat down.

'That was really mean,' said Tessa.

Jack shrugged his shoulders.

'It's a party dress, it's not meant to be practical.' Beauty was looking at him with big sad eyes. Jack rubbed his beard and studied her. She would have melted the hardest heart, but Jack probably didn't have a heart. 'I suppose it's suitable for parties,' he said eventually.

Beauty beamed, it was what she wanted, Jack's approval. 'Can I go and play now?'

'Yes, go and play,' said Dee-Dee fondly. They watched her skip out of the door.

'She is a dear,' said Don; 'Helen, you must be proud of her.' But

153

Helen was looking miserable as only Helen could; she had not said a word the entire meal.

'Why can't you cheer up. Oh, honestly, it's Christmas, can't you make an effort?' Dee-Dee was not tolerant that day.

'It's just that—' but Helen didn't finish, she fiddled nervously with a spoon.

'Stop it, it's irritating,' snapped Jack.

'I think we should have some more music,' said Don.

Jack played the mandolin, Don the penny whistle and the tambourine. Dee sang, she had a clear, sweet voice. Tessa drummed on a log and Beauty came in and danced around. Only Helen didn't join in but sat glum and uncomfortable. 'Angelus ad virginum . . .'

Then the door opened and in came Tony and Jude carrying a box of presents.

'Wow, amazing!'

'We left our car down the lane.'

'Happy Christmas, happy Christmas!' Dee and Jude hugged each other and Dee-Dee was so ecstatic she hugged everybody else as well. 'Happy Christmas, happy Christmas.'

'Actually, we're celebrating the winter solstice.'

'There's no more food, but have some wine, oh, you don't drink, what about herb tea?'

'Jack, keep playing, don't stop,' and Don led Jude in a polka across the room.

'I got a new dress!'

'It's very . . . pink . . . isn't it?'

Tony solemnly handed round presents. He had brought his violin. He didn't play very often and only in select company. He seemed to be treating the whole occasion as a penance.

'Oh, *The Fundamentals of Buddhism*, what a big book,' said Dee-Dee, 'and it's got pictures in it.'

Tessa opened hers. It was *Of Woman Born* by Adrienne Rich.

'It's fascinating,' called out Jude from the other side of the room. Don had *The Complete Book of Self Sufficiency* and Jack was already disputing the contents. 'He's got that completely wrong, I wouldn't do it like that.' Jack had a collection of Irish folk songs. 'Some of them are most interesting,' said Tony, tuning his violin.

'The Rocky Road to Dublin!' called out Don; Jack picked up his mandolin. Don played a few notes on his whistle. Tony frowned. He was used to proficient musicians.

'What I need is a borran,' said Don.

'A sporran?'

'No, Tess, silly, a borran, an Irish drum, you get me one for my next birthday.' But for the moment the leather seat of a chair would do, banged with a wooden spoon. Dust flew everywhere. Tony coughed but kept playing.

The musical men were on one side of the room working through a repertoire of Irish songs. Fairy Beauty danced, lost in a dream world and the women sat by the fire. Dee and Jude swapped stories about the Sunshine Café. Helen flicked through her new book, a guide to Suffolk; she didn't look as though she found it interesting.

'What is up with you?' said Tessa, next to her, poking the fire. 'Is it Marjorie?'

'No, it's not.'

'Well?'

Helen shifted restlessly and moved close. She looked around quickly to see if Dee was listening. She was beginning to quiver and sweat, but then Helen always smelled sweaty.

'You can tell me,' said Tessa, poking the wood.

'I've been thinking, for some time really, before Mummy and Daddy came, in fact.'

She spoke in a whisper. 'And I've thought and thought about it but I didn't want to tell anyone in case they got angry and I wouldn't want that to happen and—'

'What is it?'

'I just don't want to live here any more,' she said in a rush.

Tessa stared at her. Helen couldn't look anybody in the eye for more than a few seconds. 'You just don't want to live here any more?' she repeated, quite loud enough for Dee-Dee to hear.

'What?' Dee-Dee turned.

'Helen just doesn't want to live here any more.' Tessa threw another log on the fire.

'How could you say such a thing, oh Helen, why don't you want to, why? I thought you liked it here?'

'It's just—' But Helen was lost for words.

'After all we've done, you're so ungrateful, you could still be in that awful bedsit. I didn't know you felt like that, and all those scenes with Marjorie. Oh, Helen.'

'I thought the point of a community was honesty,' said Jude, taking the subject very seriously. Helen was beginning to cry.

'Oh, Helen: you've been a wet blanket all day, all you ever do is cry. Tessy, what else did she say to you?'

'Nothing, she never does.'

'I think we should tell Jack. I wonder what he would have to say about it.'

'No. No, don't, I'm wrong, I know I'm wrong,' mumbled Helen, and they all looked at Jack and Don and Tony, who were far too preoccupied to notice the incident by the fire.

'You see, to live together successfully one has to be open,' Jude tried to comfort her.

'Not sneaky, not tell Tessy sneaky things when I'm not listening . . .'

'. . . In any relationship there has to be honesty and trust. I think perhaps you don't trust your friends here.'

Helen blew her nose loudly.

'Or we don't trust her,' said Tessa standing up. 'I'm going to get some more wood,' and she left the Christmas party for the icy wind and the squelchy earth-smelling ankle-deep mud.

Nearly Easter. A year after they had decided Helen and Beauty could stay for good. Jack and Tessa worked in different parts of the garden and Beauty ran errands. Don and Dee-Dee went off every day to Norwich and Helen now went with them. A community arts project had started up in one of the more run-down parts of the old city and Helen was 'helping'. What use she could possibly be was a mystery to Tessa. She mistrusted Helen. Everybody else at St John's was only too keen to discuss the direction of their lives, even Tessa, who could talk at length about the management of roses, but Helen kept silent. They still all met for the evening meal around the breakfast-room table. April rain fell in sheets outside but there was a new fresh smell in the air, blackbirds and thrushes warbled despite the wet. Inside there were candles, lentil soup and plenty of talk.

'Tony thinks we should up our soft fruit production, they sell well.'

'It's too risky, Don, a bad June and what do you get, mouldy strawberries.'

'I like strawberries.'

'Beauty, it's gone seven, off to bed.'

'Yes, Jack.'

'And don't forget to brush your teeth.'

'Yes, Jack.'

'Goodnight, darling,' said Dee; 'tell Helen to come and have her supper.'

'Oh, I forgot, she doesn't want any,' said Tessa from the shadows.

'Why ever not, I've made far too much now, why didn't she say?'

'She's on a diet.'

'She's always on a diet. Beauty, tell her to come down.'

'Yes, Dee-Dee.' Beauty went upstairs, and Dee-Dee sat at the table. She looked tired, her lips were pursed. Tessa did not often think Dee-Dee was hard, but she did that night.

'. . . Oh, strawberries, I love strawberries, Hetty used to grow them, you know, they were delicious, cream and sugar in

157

the June sun, perhaps we could have just a few, for us . . .'

Jack was sharpening a knife. 'There's going to be five Albions this year, it'll be a lot of planning, but I suspect we can cope. Advance organisation, that's what I told them at the meeting . . .'

'Where is Helen? Is she scared of us or something?'

Tessa thought, I'm not interested in any of this. She yawned; upstairs was her own quiet room. She stood up.

'Oh Tessy, tell Helen to come here, do.'

Tessy didn't often go into Helen's room; nor did anybody else. It was a jumbled mess of dirty clothes and Beauty's toys. She opened the door; Beauty was in bed whispering to an eyeless teddy. Helen was at the table writing. Lit by only a table lamp, she looked furtive. Tessa crept towards her. Beauty, nearly asleep, did not stir.

'Dee wants to see you.'

Helen jumped and quickly covered up what she was doing. 'Oh, does she? Oh, you gave me a fright.'

'Dee's angry because you didn't tell her about supper.'

'Oh, really?'

Tessa waited.

'I'll be down in a minute, I will—' She was flustered.

Tessa looked at her. There was nothing she liked about Helen and standing next to her she felt strong and powerful, but in a malignant way. Helen's shifty eyes were darting around the room like a trapped rabbit's.

'What's this?' Tessa whisked the piece of paper from under Helen's podgy fingers.

'Don't!'

It was a piece of white card; 'Single mother seeks nice home for herself and little girl. Can do cooking or cleaning or anything in return for rent.'

Tessa laughed. 'You are a stupid idiot, aren't you?'

'Please, please, don't show the others.' Helen was terrified. She glanced at Beauty, but she was now fast asleep.

158

'If you were a bare-faced liar, I could stand it, but you're not, you're a snivelling, cringing one.'

'I'm not a liar, I was going to tell you, I was.'

'You undermine us here,' said Tessa, no longer laughing but acid, and she left, with Helen following rapidly.

In the breakfast room Dee was still at the table, Don and Jack still talking monologues.

'We've got to have a house meeting, now!' announced Tessa, storming in like an icy wind.

They looked at her blankly and for a moment she thought, is it worth it? Then in blundered Helen, all tears and apologies. Tessa thumped the card on the table and they all read it.

'We don't want any more single mothers, do we?' said Don, misunderstanding.

'I knew it, I knew you were up to something,' and Dee looked as if she might start a fight.

'Oh, I see . . . Well, Helen, you could have discussed it,' said Don. Jack was silent.

'I'm sorry, I didn't mean it, it's just that . . .'

'Shut up!' yelled Tessa. 'Look at us, we're becoming separate, we're slipping away, we can't talk to each other, Helen's in the project, Dee's in the café, Don's God knows where, but here is what's important. Right here. Helen's a dope,' and she practically spat at her, 'but if she's not committed, then none of us are.'

'Hmmm, I think you have a point there.' Don looked thoughtful.

'We have to decide, is this what we want? St John's, here, all of us, is it? If it's not, then I'm going.' And by the way she said it they knew it wasn't an empty threat.

'Tessy, you can't go, who would do the vegetables?'

She shrugged her shoulders. 'It's up to you.'

Jack stood up. 'She's right. A house meeting, now, in the great hall.'

*

Three hours later they were still arguing. Tessa had moved from vitriolic to sulky and back to vitriolic again. Don, as usual, was unhelpful. 'Yes, Tess, of course, I understand what you're saying, but couldn't we settle it in the morning, after all, it's getting awfully late.'

'Now, it has to be now!' screamed Tessa.

'She's right, she's absolutely right.' Jack was determined to be calm.

'Don't be so bloody condescending,' and Tessa waved the poker at him.

'Oi, put that thing down.'

'Right on your head, Jack.'

'That's unnecessary, that's completely unnecessary.'

Dee-Dee and Helen had long passed the stage where they could make rational suggestions.

'Oh Tessy, please, I'm so tired, what's happening to all of us?'

'Listen!' shouted Tessa with the poker. 'How many times do I have to say it, we need commitment, dedication, not excuses and ego trips.'

'The only one on an ego trip is you!' shouted Jack.

'Shut up, shut up!'

There was a lull. Don paced up and down. Helen and Dee sobbed on the sofa by a dead fire; Jack and Tessa scowled at each other.

'OK, OK,' said Don, 'commitment . . . yes, we do need it. Dedication? To what?'

'To us,' said Tessa desperately.

'Us? All of us, all of us together?'

'Remember the beginning, we were going to be a light to the world.' She sounded bitter.

'The beginning . . . you and me and Dee, in paradise . . .'

'Oh, Don . . .' wept Dee-Dee.

'Yes, we had lots of ideas, didn't we, and plans and then there was Jack, and he helped us and we got it together.' Don slapped him on the back. 'We needed you, Jack.'

'Thanks.' Jack was beginning to look smug.

Don caught Tessa's eye; she was waving the poker again.

'I'm committed,' said Don; 'this is my place, and I want it to be wonderful. Perhaps we have lost track a bit, life takes over, doesn't it?'

'And I'm committed,' said Dee-Dee through tears; 'I know I'm in Norwich and it may not look like it, Tessy, but I wouldn't live anywhere else, I really wouldn't, and I know I'm working and it makes me tired and you're here all the time, but I'm working for all of us. Well, that's what it feels like . . .'

'Admirable,' exclaimed Don and Dee-Dee blushed.

'Of course I'm committed to this project. I've been invited to join all sorts of other ventures, but I've stayed here, I think that about sums it up.' Jack yawned.

'This is my life, this is my home, you're my friends, you're my family, if you like. It's important to me, and I'll fight if I think it's being threatened . . .' and Tessa glared at Helen, who, after all, was the cause of this evening's debate. 'You've heard what we've all said, now it's your turn.' Helen didn't look like she was capable of speaking.

'We won't judge you, you were the last one here, perhaps you don't feel committed,' and Don sat next to her and patted her hand. 'If you find things difficult then you must tell us, we're your friends,' and Don looked so friendly and welcoming Helen nodded and blew her nose.

'I'm sorry,' she said; 'I'll try harder, I will, I won't look for anywhere else, I'll try really hard.'

'You mustn't be afraid of arguments, we can sort things out,' said Dee, holding her other hand. They made a beautiful picture.

'I'll go to bed now, if you don't mind,' said Helen, getting up unsteadily. They heard her in the room above them, walking about.

'Thank God that's sorted out,' said Jack, and Don and Dee looked warily at Tessa.

Tessa was grave and solemn like a dark angel. 'I hope so,' she said, and Helen above them was still sleepless. Tessa felt they had forced Helen to stay because her leaving would be to admit the unthinkable. St John's was a failure.

CHAPTER SEVENTEEN

St John's Day, their day, and it had been hot. It was Helen and Beauty's third summer at the Hall. Sue and Wally came, so did Tony and Jude, and Woody and Herbie and dozens of others. Jack's friends, Don's friends, Dee's friends. Elderflower fizz and long dresses, strawberries and straw hats, old roses in the garden and folk music in the orchard.

Now it was late and Tessa was alone. The last people were leaving, predictably Sue and Wally, gathering up noisy children. Tessa watched through the cracked glass of the great hall. Then all the guests were gone and Jack was ordering Beauty to bed. Don came running into the courtyard. 'I forgot the bonfire! We never had a bonfire, it's St John's Day, we must have a bonfire.'

'Oh Don, it's nearly one o'clock.' That was Dee-Dee.

'Perhaps we could just have a small one.' That was Helen.

'No, it has to be huge, enormous, it has to burn until daybreak. Where's Jack, where's Tessa?'

Jack called down from an upstairs window, 'What about the bonfire?'

Tessa left her window seat and joined them in the courtyard. 'Come on, get some kindling and logs, it won't take long.'

In the orchard they waited. Whatever could be said about Tessa, she could get a fire going.

'Get some petrol,' said Don.

'Get some more logs,' said Jack.

'No, it'll smother it, wait.'

They stood around the bonfire with the light on their faces, Dee looking as if she were gazing at a magic lantern, Helen wincing every time the flames leapt, Don excited. 'Yes, yes, it's marvellous, it's right.'

Jack with folded arms, 'Hmm, not bad,' and next to him Tessa, concentrating and frowning.

'We must hold hands,' said Don and they did, which was difficult because the fire was so hot.

'This bonfire,' said Don, 'is for St John, the real one. Now, what did he do?'

'He wrote a gospel,' said Dee-Dee.

'St John the Baptist,' said Helen.

'Well, whatever, I'm sure he was a pretty good bloke and the Hall is named after him. Our Hall. This bonfire is for us, and for the spirit of the Hall. So, here's to us.'

'To us.'

'And here's to St John's.'

'Yes, yes!' Don was jumping up and down. 'I can see it, every year, meeting like this, confirming our dedication . . . midsummer . . . We are the people of the longest day, we are the bringers of light, we are light and inspiration.'

'Oh Don.'

'Let's dance,' and slowly, still holding hands, they moved round the bonfire.

'We are the people of midsummer,' chanted Don, slightly off-key.

'And we are the bringers of light.' Dee joined in and Jack also and the thing became a beautiful song as they moved round the fire, Don holding Tessa's hand, and Tessa Jack's and Jack Helen's and Helen Dee-Dee's and Dee-Dee, crying because it was all so wonderful, holding Don's. And as they turned Tessa could see the Hall behind them, a vast squatting shape black against the sky, unlit and looming over those who waited for sunrise.

Don, Dee-Dee and Helen going to Norwich in the truck, Tessa and Jack in the gardens, Beauty somewhere, the long summer

164

days. French beans, lettuces, radishes, beetroots, honeysuckle growing up trellises in the walled garden, red clover in the grass, buttercups and self-heal. The old roses finished blooming, but the Zépherine Drouhin was still glorious on the wall.

Greenfly and blackfly and the gaps in the skyline where the elm trees used to be. Wheat and barley in the fields going golden but still with patches of green, and poppies only by the hedgerows, where the weedkiller couldn't get them.

Dee and Helen made supper, bread and cheese and lettuce, but fresh strong-tasting lettuce, crunchy and delicious, and tomatoes from the greenhouse which tasted so different from shop ones, and smell so different, pungent. All of them around the breakfast-room table.

'Jude says Tony wants to get into outside catering, you know, for parties and things.'

'Wholefood weddings,' said Don.

'I might have to work more, at weekends, you know.'

'Oh, what a shame,' said Don.

'But only sometimes, only some weekends,' and Dee-Dee was going pink.

'I went to the arts project with Helen today,' and Don helped himself to more lettuce; 'it's interesting, it's a good idea, it's a pity I didn't think of it myself . . .'

Tessa watched him and so did Dee-Dee. They smiled secretly at each other.

'Yes, that's it, the barns.'

Dee-Dee giggled.

'We could convert the barns and have workshops for craftsmen, pottery in the sheds, weaving in the stable, and all sorts. Jack, this is interesting, are you listening?'

'Money, Don, money.'

'Yes, of course, it'll cost money. Draw me some plans, I'm sure I know a builder.'

'Planning permission, Don.'

'That . . . I'm sure I know someone in the council.'

Jack rubbed his beard. 'We'll think about it.' He looked at Beauty, who was drawing a picture. 'It's seven o'clock.'

'Is it my bedtime?' she smiled sweetly and tidied up her pencils. 'Goodnight, everybody and goodnight, Jack.'

'Helen's going to read to you tonight.'

'Oh?'

'Jack's got an urgent appointment at the George,' said Tessa. Jack glared.

Beauty went upstairs. 'You must read me "Beauty and the Beast," ' she called to Helen, 'because it's my favourite and it's all about me.'

'How old is that child?' asked Jack.

'She'll be six in November.'

'Six? My God, why isn't she at school?'

'Helen's not keen on schools,' said Dee-Dee trying to be helpful; 'she thinks it'll be too rough, Beauty doesn't see many other children.'

'She never will if she stays here, she has to go to school, absolutely.'

'Sue and Wally educate their children at home . . .'

'Huh. Their children are hooligans. Anyway, Helen couldn't educate anything. I would if I had the time . . Don, what do you think?'

'What? The barns? Could have it on two floors . . .'

'Christ! I see I'll have to do it myself. Where is the school?'

'It's in St Lawrence,' said Tessa.

'That's three miles. She couldn't walk and we need the truck for work . . . I'll get a bike and take her myself.' And so it was settled.

Helen protested but Jack had made up his mind. He went to see the headmistress and Beauty was booked to start in September. He brought back a list of all the things she would need. A lunch box, a shoe bag, a navy-blue cardigan. Beauty, playing in the orchard with flowers in her hair talking to herself.

166

'I'm going to start school and make lots of friends and learn to read,' said Beauty.

'You have to sit down when you're told to and stand in a line and be quiet all the time.' Tessa thought she ought to know the truth.

'But I'll make lots of friends and learn to read.' Jack had convinced her entirely.

A hot day near the end of July. Helen brought Jack and Tessa cool lemonade in the orchard. She had stayed at home to do the washing and it was now flapping on lines tied from tree to tree. Beauty was running in and out of the sheets laughing.

'Be careful, don't get them dirty,' called out Helen. 'Are you going to work all day?' she asked.

Jack wiped the sweat off his face with his hand. 'Yes, there's a lot of weeding to do.'

'I might just go to Bungay, then.' Helen finished Beauty's lemonade. 'We're out of cheese.'

Jack frowned; Helen was always nibbling cheese like a rat.

'Get some blue Cheshire, I love it,' said Tessa.

'And don't eat it on the way back,' said Jack.

'I'll take Beauty.' Helen eyed them. 'If you don't mind.'

'We don't mind,' said Tessa.

'You see, I don't see too much of her and now she's going to school after the summer I thought wouldn't it be nice if I spent a bit more time with her and do nice things like . . .'

'How are the raspberries?' asked Jack.

'Oh, they're fine, should be ready quite soon. The gooseberries are nearly finished,' said Tessa.

'Well, we'll go now,' said Helen.

'Bye then,' said Tessa.

Helen looked around nervously for Beauty. 'Come along, Mummy's going to take you out.'

Beauty appeared from behind a pair of Don's trousers. 'I want to stay here.'

167

'Oh . . . but we're going to Bungay.'

'Walking?'

'It's not that far really, and we might get a lift, and when we get there we could go to the Gaytime and have a little lunch.'

'I want to stay here with Jack and Tessa.'

Helen coaxed her away, promising chocolates, ice creams, crisps, Coca-Cola.

'She'll be sick,' said Jack.

Past midday. Tessa and Jack didn't stop for lunch but kept working; they were weeding the vegetable garden in the orchard. They had done this only a few weeks ago but weeds seemed to grow alarmingly at that time of year. Jack took off his shirt. He was wearing shorts and was deeply tanned. His torso was muscled and hairy; so were his legs. Tessa, in a bikini and gumboots, her usual summer garb, was also brown and muscled but not quite as hairy. Sweat ran down her face and into her eyes, her hair stuck to her shoulders and she kept flicking it away. 'Should cut the damn stuff off.' Jack, sensibly, had his in a ponytail.

He looked at his watch. 'Twenty past two.' He straightened up and stretched himself. 'Time for a break.' They flopped on the grass in the shade of the apple trees. Tessa flung off her boots. She felt quite dizzy from the heat.

'What's it like to be cold? I can't remember.' She rolled onto her stomach and watched the martins flying low over the moat. The water, although green and murky, looked cool. 'I'm going to have a swim.' She said.

Jack sat up and wiped his face. He watched her walk to the moat. She put one foot in. 'God, it's freezing.' The bank of the moat was squelchy. A nettle rasped her leg and she jumped. Her splash disturbed the flies and they buzzed angrily. She was up to her waist in the water, her toes sinking in the river mud.

'God, it's so cold!' She splashed herself. She didn't care if the water was green and strong smelling, it felt as refreshing as a mountain stream. 'Come on, Jack, it's wonderful.' Jack stood up. 'Come and have a swim.'

He walked towards the moat. On the edge he paused and took off his shorts and took off his pants. Tessa stopped splashing. 'Well, why not?' said Jack, grinning hugely, slipping into the water.

Tessa stared. 'Well, why not?' And she took off her bikini and flung it into the nettles. Jack looked her up and down sharply. They swam into the middle of the moat where the water was deepest. Tessa's feet brushed through pondweed, a dragonfly skimmed past her eyes. Jack was ahead of her treading water.

'I've never seen you swim before,' said Tessa.

'I'm not much good at swimming,' said Jack.

'I've never heard you say you're not good at anything before,' said Tessa. Jack laughed, white teeth against a black beard.

They stayed there for a while, floating, the patches of sun-warmed water mixing with the colder water underneath, and the manic flies.

'We have to get back to work soon,' said Jack.

'I suppose so,' said Tessa.

They swam towards the shallows. Tessa stood up, and the water came up to her crotch. Jack was looking at her with interest, and he stood up too, grinning. He was sexually excited, it was obvious. Tessa was confused, not only by Jack, but by herself, for she was aroused too. The sun shining on her body increased it. Her desire was so strong she felt it might knock her over.

'I don't even like you,' she said in disbelief.

Jack laughed; this was evidently not a problem.

Somehow Tessa scrambled out of the water and onto the grass. She lay on her back, bewildered, staring at the clouds. Jack over her, still grinning, still arrogant, still excited. He smelled of sweat and moat water. His beard rubbed her cheek. She held her breath as he pushed into her.

*

169

'What are you doing?' It was Beauty.

'Christ!' Jack leapt up. 'When did you get back? Where's Helen?'

'She's in Bungay' She looked at him curiously.

'What?'

'I didn't go . . . why haven't you got any clothes on . . . ?'

'Why didn't you go, where have you been?'

'I've been here.'

'We haven't got any clothes on because we've been swimming,' said Tessa standing up, suddenly clear-headed. She took a shirt off the line.

Jack rubbed his beard. 'We were very hot,' he said.

'And then we were sunbathing,' said Tessa, looking at Jack.

'It looked very silly,' said Beauty.

'Grown-ups are silly,' said Tessa, putting on the shirt.

'I'm going to play in my den now,' and she skipped away.

Tessa and Jack faced each other in the orchard. Jack was still naked. Tessa was wearing one of his big shirts.

'Well?' asked Tessa.

'Well what?' he sneered, and went to find his shorts.

CHAPTER EIGHTEEN

Tessa didn't tell Dee-Dee, or Don, because nothing happened, she told herself, nothing, nothing at all. Except she had been turned on by Jack. She detested him even more. She avoided being alone with him. She didn't speak to him unless to criticise and Jack continued as if they had merely had a cup of tea together.

He was busy with the Albions and spent most evenings in the George. It was August and hot and there was talk of another drought. Sunday morning, and Tessa and Dee were in the rose garden having breakfast. Dee-Dee was lying on the grass, her golden hair spread out, and Tessa wished she could talk to her about Jack but she knew what Dee-Dee felt about him. The house martins chattered above them. Helen came padding across the grass to join them. It was an unwritten rule that nobody ever disturbed Tessa and Dee's breakfast.

'Oh, it's you,' said Dee-Dee, sitting up.

'I was just wondering,' said Helen, 'what you were all doing today.'

'Nothing, I'm absolutely exhausted,' said Dee-Dee.

'Oh . . . that is a shame, because I was wondering, because it's such a lovely day and all that . . .'

'What do you want?' said Tessa.

Helen glanced around furtively. 'I thought perhaps we could go to the beach.'

'Don won't drive you,' said Dee-Dee; 'he's far too tired, it wouldn't even be fair to ask him, though if you did I'm sure he would because he's so kind . . .'

'Ask Jack,' said Tessa, but this was like saying 'Ask God'. Helen was too scared to ask Jack anything.

Then Beauty came bounding out in her nightdress. 'We're going to the seaside, we're going to the seaside!'

Dee-Dee and Tessa looked at Helen.

'I'm going to build a great big sandcastle and go swimming and—'

'We don't know who's going to take you yet,' said Tessa.

'Jack is,' said Beauty; 'I just woke him up.' It was another unwritten rule – nobody woke Jack up, ever.

He was standing in the doorway. 'Who the bloody hell said I was going to the beach?' Helen shook with fear. He looked at her, then at the sky. 'Hmm, might stay fair . . . Five minutes, then we're off.' Helen ran to get ready, followed by Beauty.

'You'd better go with them,' said Dee-Dee; 'I foresee trouble.'

Tessa groaned.

'Go on, I'll make you a picnic, it'll be ever so boring here. Don won't get out of bed until lunchtime and I'm going to do nothing. Oh, Tessa, you might have a nice time.'

'Might I?' But Dee-Dee was already hurrying to the kitchen.

In the truck, all squashed together on the front seat. Beauty on Helen's lap.

'Where are we going, then?' asked Jack, driving down the Halesworth road. He was in a good mood.

'I don't care,' said Tessa, who wasn't.

'Perhaps Southwold, it's got nice shops and tea rooms!' suggested Helen.

'It's full of tourists, absolutely not.'

Tessa turned the map around. 'I prefer the North Norfolk beaches. Winterton?'

'We can't possibly go there, we've left it too late, we haven't got enough petrol, besides—'

'Jack, where do you want to go then?' asked Tessa.

'Covehithe, it's empty.'

Covehithe was empty. There was a ruined church, then the road stopped because the rest of it had fallen down a cliff. There were no snack bars, ice creams, loos or bathing huts, but a long stretch of pebbly, wind-battered beach.

On a headland was a group of twisted Scotch pines, which looked as if they were in agony. They scrambled down the sandy cliff and walked towards these. Jack had brought binoculars to go bird-watching. 'Look at that, now that's a sight.'

Tess could see a black blob on a tree.

'Can we make sandcastles now?' asked Beauty.

'There's too many pebbles,' said Tessa.

'Is it much further?' Helen was carrying the picnic. They passed the pines and kept walking. The wind blew sand in their hair. Beauty was flagging.

'Well, here we are then,' said Jack, taking off his backpack. A bleak stretch of beach, in front of them the dark North Sea and behind a reed-filled lake. 'This is Benacre Broad.'

Tessa and Helen sat down; Beauty put on her swimsuit and ran squealing to the water. It was a hot day but the wind was enough to put Tessa off swimming. She took her socks off. Helen fidgeted with the lunch bag. 'What time is it?'

'Eleven o'clock.'

Jack went bird-watching.

Later they had lunch; Jack ate three sandwiches in four seconds.

'You going swimming?' he asked Tessa with a grin.

'I don't think so.'

He stripped to his trunks. Helen made a sandcastle with Beauty; this proved disappointing as there wasn't much sand.

'I don't want it like that, I want it really big.'

'Yes, darling, I'm trying.'

Tessa and Jack sat silently. He scanned her from under his eyebrows. She said nothing. How could you talk about feelings

173

with Jack? She picked up a handful of pebbles and threw them down the beach. Click, click, click.

Jack stood up and yawned. 'Well, I want a swim.' He called to Beauty, who ran after him like a puppy. Tessa watched them. Jack took her out quite deep; she could see their heads bobbing above the waves. Helen sat down next to her and ate the rest of the lunch, but as far as Tessa was concerned Helen could have been invisible.

Beauty ran up the beach, soaking wet and laughing. 'I couldn't touch the bottom, Jack couldn't touch the bottom. Now,' she said, taking off her swimsuit, 'I'm going to go sunbathing.' And, naked, she lay down on a towel and started wiggling around.

'Darling, darling, what are you doing?' Helen covered her up quickly.

Beauty was puzzled. 'But I thought—'

'You wear your swimsuit to sunbathe,' said Helen.

'Except when it's really hot,' said Tessa, and Helen looked at her.

Jack strode out of the water, pebbles crunching under his feet.

'There's quite a swell out there,' and he seemed almost nervous.

Beauty, wrapped up, was still puzzled.

'I think it's time to go home,' said Tessa.

A few days later Tessa cut her hair. When Dee-Dee saw her she nearly dropped her bowl of muesli.

'Oh, Tessy, what have you done?'

'I've cut my hair.'

'But it's so short.'

Don, yawning in pyjamas, came downstairs. 'My God . . .'

Jack walked past. He said nothing, but then she didn't expect he would.

'I shouldn't have given you all those feminist books. Oh, Tessy!'

'It'll be better for gardening,' said Tessa.

'It's too butch.' Don helped himself to breakfast.

'I think I'm going to like being butch,' and Tessa smiled.

*

174

With short hair, dungarees and boots, Tessa went to Rougham Tree Fair, a packet of Gauloises in her top pocket and a scowl on her face. They camped with the travellers under the avenue of huge oaks. Dee-Dee in thirties chintz, Helen in an Indian dress, Don with his straw hat and Jack in shorts. The Albions were not much different from Barsham, but perhaps better organised. Hippies and lurchers, long skirts and loons, wild children and chick-pea curry, but here was another group in a huddle by the Hare Krishna tent, black eye make-up, and music blaring, '. . . No future, no future'. They were laughing loudly at everything.

Tessa felt suddenly outdated. These people were young, like dressed-up children. 'They're punks,' said Dee-Dee; 'they come in the café sometimes.' She wasn't at all bothered, but Tessa felt isolated. There was a whole world happening outside St John's; Vietnam, Watergate, punks, in London and in Norwich, the whole of the patchy, nostalgic seventies and she had missed it, stuck down a lane in a medieval field.

Bank Holiday Monday, and everybody had gone to the beach at Waxham. Except Tessa. She loved Norfolk beaches, with stinging sand and the wind and seagulls, but not with Don being daft, Dee-Dee peeling in the sun, Helen fussing about food and Jack staring at her. Today she wanted to be by herself. She was in the great hall painting, a picture of the walled garden, trellises of honeysuckle and roses, flowering herbs, and, through the archway, the Hall itself like a giant peering through a keyhole. Tessa with her new short hair had everything she wanted: her paintings, the garden, solitude.

'I wish it could always be like this,' she said to the damp and quiet of St John's.

* * *

175

Another Bank Holiday Monday and Tessa was still alone. She had the house to herself, the gardens, and her drawings on her lap, but now she felt so sad she was nearly crying. Now, a truck full of sticky people wouldn't bump into the courtyard to disturb her.

Chapter Nineteen

She was distracted by the noise of harvesting; she opened a window and looked out over the moat. On the other side the combine churned past pouring grain into a truck. The last field. It was the end of summer.

* * *

It was early September; Beauty was due to go to school on Wednesday. She had a navy-blue uniform, a satchel and new shiny shoes. She dressed up to show everybody at dinner.

'Beauty, aren't you smart? Isn't she smart, Helen?'

Helen looked more upset than proud about the progress of her daughter. 'I hope they won't be too rough.'

'Now I'm going to have lots of friends and learn to read.'

'Jack, what do you think?' asked Don.

'Hmm, she'll have to plait her hair, can't have it all over the place at school. Helen, did you sew the name tags on?'

'Oh!' Helen had forgotten.

'Then you'll have to do it tomorrow. Those clothes were expensive; I don't want her losing them. Go and take them off, Beauty, you're not to touch them until Wednesday.'

Saturday morning and it was a clear fine day. Jack, Beauty, Don and Dee-Dee were going to the beach. Helen wasn't; she was sewing on name-tags, doing the washing and it was her turn to make supper. Tessa wasn't going either; she wanted to tidy up the flower garden. It was before nine o'clock. Don was loading the truck with all sorts of useful things – straw hat, blankets, books, frisbee – and Dee had made enough picnic for nine people.

Beauty was running around. 'Jack's going to teach me how to swim, Jack's going to teach me how to swim!' Whatever she would look like on Wednesday, she now looked her usual self, breakfast down her front, a dress too small for her, odd socks and her hair a dark tangled mat with several ribbons in it. 'Can I take teddy, and dolly and bunny?'

'Just one, dear.' Dee was excited too; she hadn't been to the coast as often as the others.

Jack strode out with his binoculars and walking boots.

'Where are you going?' Tessa asked Don.

'To Winterton, to play in the sand dunes. Wish you were coming? Why don't you weed tomorrow?'

Jack was sifting through the contents of Don's bags. 'We don't need that. What's that for?'

'No thanks,' said Tessa and took her hoe to the orchard.

She was hoeing the bed alongside the moat wall and she heard the truck go down the lane. She watched it turn into the road and wind towards St Margaret's. The sky was blue with wisps of cirrus clouds. Martins gathered on the electricity lines, twittering. The fields were all harvested.

A peaceful day. She weeded the beds and took the barrow to and from the compost bins. A quiet day. A wren hopped from out of a hedge, a squirrel ran up the chestnut tree in the courtyard, the walls of St John's were pale gold in the sun. Helen brought her sandwiches.

'Thanks,' said Tessa and kept working.

A long day. The afternoon seemed to stretch on for ever. Apples were nearly ready to pick, so were the pears. Another barrow of weeds. The sun was sinking in a red sky behind tall trees.

Helen came into the garden. 'They're not back yet, it's gone eight. Jack always brings Beauty back for her bedtime.'

'Perhaps they forgot what the time was,' said Tessa, yawning and stretching herself.

'I've made supper,' said Helen.

178

'I'll have mine now then. Is there enough water for a bath?'

She had a deep hot bath. When she came down to eat it was well past nine. Helen had made a stew. It was tolerable and Tessa was hungry.

'They're still not back,' Helen fidgeted nervously.

Tessa wasn't the least bit bothered. 'Winterton's miles away, perhaps they got in a jam in Norwich.'

'I hope the truck hasn't broken down.'

'They'd hitch. Any bread?'

After supper Tessa went to her room. Helen's nervousness was irritating. It was possible the truck had broken down; it had been making odd noises recently . . . She lay in her bed in the panelled room and listened to the silence . . .

There was a commotion in the breakfast room, doors were slamming, people running, and Helen crying. 'Where is she, where is she?'

Tessa came downstairs groggy from sleep. Dee was in floods of tears being comforted by Don and Helen was outside.

'What's happened?' asked Tessa. Helen came in, her face sickly white. She was trembling. She sat at the table and stared at nothing.

'What on earth's happened? Where's Jack and Beauty?'

'We don't know!' wailed Dee-Dee.

'Oh my God, is that all! You've lost them at the beach?' And she started to go back to bed.

'I think it's a bit more serious than that,' said Don. He looked at Dee-Dee then at Helen and pulled Tessa aside. 'They were swimming,' he said in a whisper, 'and when we went to look for them they weren't there.' He sounded quite desperate. 'We went up and down the beach dozens of times.'

'I'm sure there's a simple explanation,' said Tessa, and as she did she remembered the flags at Winterton, the warning signs, and

179

Jack saying he wasn't much good at swimming . . .

'They'll turn up.'

'It's all my fault. I'll never forgive myself,' sobbed Dee-Dee, clutching Beauty's teddy.

'How can it possibly be your fault!' snapped Tessa. Helen was still staring into space.

'Because we were . . . we were . . .'

'We were on the other side of the sand dunes,' said Don, putting his hand on her shoulder, 'out of the wind and we fell asleep. If it's your fault, Dee-Dee, then it's mine too,' he continued uneasily. 'They might have been picked up by a fishing boat . . . or they might not have been in the water at all, they might have gone for a walk.'

Dee-Dee looked at Helen.

'I didn't pack a jumper for her, she'll be cold.' Her face was expressionless.

'It's shock,' said Don; 'I think we should get her to bed.'

'And a warm drink,' said Dee, standing up and rubbing her eyes; 'I'll make everybody one.'

'I sewed all the name tags on,' said Helen.

'Oh good . . . wonderful,' Don looked anxiously at her. 'All ready for Wednesday, then?'

'I hope she doesn't get too cold, I don't want her to get ill.'

'Of course you don't.' Don's face was twitching. 'I think I'll help Dee-Dee in the kitchen.'

Helen and Tessa sat at the table. Helen now looked baffled, as if she were trying to work something out but couldn't. 'I put name tags on the socks, Jack said I had to . . . they'll be awfully hungry, I hope he's got her something to eat . . . perhaps they'll sleep under a bush, like the gypsies, he is a gypsy, isn't he . . . I just hope she isn't too cold.'

Dee brought in the cocoa. Don had been crying. They drank it silently. Tessa thought of Jack and Beauty in the waves. 'I couldn't touch the bottom, Jack couldn't touch the bottom.'

180

'What shall we do?' she said.

'I'll go to St Margaret's and phone the coastguard again,' said Don.

He seemed to take ages. Dee-Dee washed the cups up, Helen talked about all the things she had to do before Wednesday, then the truck came up the lane. They heard Don running and Dee-Dee and Tessa didn't dare breathe for a second. He threw open the back door. He looked wild. 'A body's been washed up.'

'Oh Jack,' and Dee-Dee burst into tears.

'No, no, a child's body . . .' Nobody spoke.

Tessa felt as if a wind were rushing through her, freezing and angry.

'Poor thing,' said Helen suddenly.

'Christ, Helen, you don't understand, do you?' Tessa shook her. 'It's Beauty, Beauty is dead.'

'It's not certain, they want me to identify . . . it.'

'Oh, Tessy, don't shout at her.'

'Of course it's certain, Beauty is dead, she's dead, you dope!' Helen looked more bewildered and confused.

'We'll have to get a doctor.' Don ran his hands through his hair distractedly. 'I'll call for a doctor on the way. I have to go back, I have to identify . . . it.'

'Do you want me to come with you?' asked Tessa.

'It's all my fault.'

'Stop saying that. Of course it's not your fault. If it's anybody's it's Jack's.' They were in Dee-Dee's room lit by a fading candle.

'Do you think Jack's dead as well?'

'I don't know, if he isn't he's going to feel damn guilty.'

Dee-Dee sighed. 'I think I'll sleep now, Tessy.'

'Do you want me to stay?'

'No, I'm fine, I am.' And in the candlelight Dee's face again looked strangely hard.

*

Towards daybreak Don appeared. He sat in the breakfast room with his head in his hands.

'Was it awful?' asked Tessa, sitting next to him.

'She looked a bit pale and wet and she had sand in her hair . . . she looked like a little mermaid . . .'

Tessa put her arm around him but he didn't hug her back. 'And Jack?'

'Nothing . . . It could take days. Heavier, you see . . . But there's still a chance, he could still be all right.'

'He wasn't much good at swimming.'

'Jack?'

'He told me.'

'When?'

'Does it matter? He told me he wasn't any good at swimming.'

'He's dead, then, isn't he?'

'I think he must be, Don.'

And Don broke down and wept, 'He was a real friend, you know, he was unique, he was splendid . . .'

'He was unique,' Tessa agreed.

'Perhaps he'll just walk in through the door, you know, the way he always did, perhaps he'll walk in tomorrow . . .'

'Perhaps he will.'

'. . . And poor little Beauty, our little fairy.'

'Don, do you think we ought to go to bed, it's nearly dawn.'

'Tess, you're so sensible.' He wiped his eyes and smiled. 'How's Dee?'

'Smitten with guilt.'

'It wasn't her fault, Tess, it really wasn't.' And he hesitated as if he were going to say something else.

'It was nobody's fault,' said Tessa, but she still felt she couldn't forgive Jack for drowning himself.

'And Helen?'

'I don't know, the doctor said she'll sleep for hours.'

'We must help her.'

'Yes, I suppose we must.'

182

They sat there for some time and the early morning light began to fill the room. Don yawned. He was absolutely shattered. Tessa wanted him to say something, to do something comforting like pat her hand or squeeze her knee, but he looked tired and sad and preoccupied and completely separate from her. Never before had she wanted so much for him to hold her but never before had she felt so unable to ask him. He stood up.

'You go to bed, Tess, I'm going for a little stroll. I'll see you tomorrow.'

'It is tomorrow,' said Tessa.

Up in her room she could see him walking towards the big field. She threw herself on her bed but she didn't feel at all like crying.

They somehow got through the next few days; everybody kept bursting into tears at irregular moments, except Tessa. Friends brought flowers, homemade cakes and sympathy.

'She's gone to the spirit world to await her next reincarnation,' said Jude.

'She's at one with Nature, now, with the trees and the flowers,' said Sue.

'She's dead,' said Tessa.

At the end of the week, Marjorie came screeching up the lane. She had read about it in the local paper. Nobody had even thought to tell her. She hurled abuse at them, then burst into hysterical sobbing.

'I knew you couldn't look after her, I knew it.'

'It was an accident,' said Tessa.

'And Helen, where were you, why weren't you with your little girl?'

'I was sewing on name tags.' It didn't sound like a satisfactory excuse.

'You let her go off with that man.'

'I don't think you should say any more, Jack was a fine person,' said Don.

Dee-Dee led her back to her car. 'We're all very upset,' she said gently; 'Helen's taking it very badly.'

'And so she should,' and Marjorie slammed the car door.

There was a funeral in the tiny church at St John's. Marjorie and Bill were there, so were Susan and Charles. Helen was so distraught she could barely walk, her face red and blotchy from crying. The Marsh-Warrens and Goodlands were in their best sombre clothes. Don, much to their disgust, wore his dressing gown. The rest of them were in whatever came to hand; washing clothes had not been a priority recently. Of Jack there was still no sign.

After the service they grouped round the grave to watch Beauty's pathetically small coffin lowered into it. Lapwings screamed in the fields, a fresh wind blowing from the sea disarrayed finery. Don read a large extract from *Sylvie and Bruno*. He seemed to find it meaningful. The Marsh-Warrens and Goodlands laid sumptuous wreaths and the residents of St John's bunches of wild flowers and late roses. The vicar said a few prayers for 'those whose ultimate fate remains unknown'. Don started crying and Dee-Dee led him away. Helen, looking like a wrecked ship, hovered near the grave with her parents.

'Dee-Dee says I should invite you all for a cup of tea,' said Tessa.

'No thank you,' said Marjorie.

'It is indeed a terrible pity,' said Bill solemnly. These were the only words he had said all day. Charles looked at his watch.

'You're going to stay with these ... people, then,' said Marjorie, making 'people' sound like 'murderers'.

'I think so,' whispered Helen.

'What? I can't hear you?'

'She said yes, dammit,' said Tessa.

'Well then, we probably won't see too much of you.'

'It's for the best,' said Susan.

'. . . Indeed, a terrible pity . . .' said Bill.

*

184

Jack's body was never found and stories began to circulate of his whereabouts. He was seen with some travellers in Wales, hitching on the A9 near Inverness, working on a vineyard in France, and in a monastery in Ladakh. Don and Dee-Dee listened avidly. Neither of them could really believe he was dead.

'It would be just like him, wouldn't it, to up and away. He must have thought, well, that's it, I've done enough of that.' Don smiled. They were in the great hall by the fire, the evenings were getting colder. 'And perhaps because something terrible happened with Beauty, he decided not to come back, because he adored Beauty, didn't he, he was like her father, wasn't he?'

'Perhaps he went on a spiritual quest to sort out his karma,' and Dee-Dee looked into the flames.

'Yes, yes, if there was an accident, he could have lost his memory, it happens, doesn't it? A tragedy can make you forget everything; I had an uncle who, when his dog died, couldn't remember where he'd put his pipe . . . Well, that's not quite the same, is it, but perhaps Jack forgot all about us.'

Tessa put more wood on the fire. It occurred to her they would have to sort out fuel for the winter; Jack had usually done that. She felt annoyed. Jack had done a lot of things. She was sure he was dead, dead as wet Beauty on a cold slab, as a hedgehog squashed on the road, as a tree riddled with Dutch Elm, and he had died trying to save Beauty. It didn't matter that nobody had seen this happen, that Don and Dee-Dee had been sleeping off the picnic. In dying, Jack was an undisputed hero.

Don and Dee-Dee were telling their favourite Jack stories. In the month after the incident this was a nightly pastime. Listening to them one would never believe he was arrogant and selfish.

Jack went as he had come, out of thin air. No relations turned up, no grieving parents, brothers or sisters, nothing. They didn't even know his surname. Jack who knew everybody from Cornwall to Caithness left no clues, no passport, no National Insurance number. His clothes brought back from the beach had in them a bird-watcher's handbook and a tin of tobacco.

Tessa curled up in a dark corner. In the room above them she could near Helen padding about restlessly. She didn't sleep well these days. For her there was no hope Beauty might come skipping in through the door.

Chapter Twenty

Damp misty mornings, wet leaves on the grass, conkers falling off the chestnut tree, leaves falling and the wind blowing through the cracks at St John's. The sadness of autumn. Hawthorn berries, rowanberries, elderberries, blackberries, but Dee-Dee was too busy to make jam any more, and so was Tessa, working, working in the gardens from frostbitten dawn to bonfire-smoke evenings. Too much work, everything Jack had done, then suppertime round the table for a meal Helen may or may not have cooked, Tessa so tired the room seemed hazy, and Dee tired too, yawning, and Don trying to cheer them all up. But the sight of Helen's puffy sad face, and how she always laid too many plates . . . the conversation kept stopping and everybody listened – to what? To the silence.

Early October and rain fell. There seemed to be leaks everywhere. Water plopped into buckets in the great hall, on the stairs, in the bathroom. Jack had always fixed the roof. Don knew somebody who knew somebody who knew somebody who could help, but they didn't turn up. Tessa and Helen at St John's. Tessa in her room watching the rain in the courtyard, thinking of the leaky greenhouse and the walled garden and the spring planting and where would they get the money from; and Helen in her room, still a mess and nobody else had been in there for weeks. Beauty's things were still there. Helen pacing up and down; what was she thinking? But Tessa didn't want to know. Helen more bumbling and untidy and fatter and unwashed and they were supposed to be helping her, but nobody wanted to talk about Beauty. Tessa would rather be with the cabbages and slugs, and Don and Dee-Dee came back later every day.

Mid-October. Thick mist settled round the house at night blanketing it. They couldn't even see the lights of St John's hamlet. Don went to the George to find out about fuel. Dee and Tessa waited up for him, both of them remembering only too well another evening.

'I hope he's all right, Tessy, the fog is terribly thick.'

But Tessa couldn't give reassurances. Nothing seemed certain any more. When he did come back it was gone one.

'Oh, Don, we were so worried, did you get lost?'

Don laughed. 'I met this chap called Barney. Well, we got talking and went back to Redlesham, you see, he used to know Jack in Wales and he was saying that only last week . . .'

Dee-Dee's eyes widened. '*Yes*? Yes?'

'Did you find out anything about wood for the winter?' said Tessa.

'Oh my God, I quite forgot.'

Then Helen came in, red-eyed and confused. 'I just thought I heard something . . .'

'It's only Don,' said Tessa. Dee-Dee went back upstairs with her. Tessa frowned. 'We must sort out about wood.'

'Yes, yes, of course.' Don yawned loudly. 'Tomorrow, yes, I'll do it tomorrow . . . perhaps I'll go and see Barney tomorrow, too . . .'

Early morning at St John's and Tessa was awake. Perhaps a mouse scratching behind the panelling or a robin had woken her. A grey morning, and cold; she could see her breath. She pulled the blankets over her head to shut out the day, to pretend it was still night, it wasn't time to get up.

Fix the greenhouse roof, check the gutters, they were full of dead leaves, barrows of dead leaves, brown rotting dead leaves.

Pick the last apples, rake the dead leaves . . . Downstairs a door opened and shut. Dee making porridge? She heard someone walking across the courtyard, couldn't be Don, it was too early for Don, somebody running across the courtyard. The rooks, startled, began squawking.

'Come here, come here at once, you naughty girl, come inside at once. Where are you? Come inside, stop hiding, where are you?'

Tessa had heard it so many times it was unremarkable.

'Come here, you naughty girl, stop hiding from your mummy.'

There's something wrong, thought Tessa, and sat up. Then Don burst into her room, and she remembered.

'What's happening?' They stared at each other.

Helen outside was becoming more frantic, her voice shrill and nervous. 'Stop hiding, I know you're there.'

Neither of them wanted to look out of the window, but they did and caught a glimpse of her running towards the barns.

'We'll have to get her,' said Tessa, throwing on a jumper. Don in Godfrey's dressing gown looked positively terrified. Then Dee-Dee came in, tearful.

'I thought I was dreaming, but I wasn't. Oh, what shall we do?'

Don put his arm around her; they weren't going to do anything. Tessa dashed down the stairs and outside into the damp morning. 'Helen! Helen!' She ran across the courtyard towards the barns. A pheasant screeched in the grass. The rooks were going berserk. She looked in all the barns. The crumbling barns with nettles growing thickly and wood pigeons cooing on the rafters. The old stables with light shining in squares through the missing slates, and rat's eyes peering in the gloom.

'Helen, where the fuck are you?' Nettles were stinging her legs and her pyjama trousers were soaked with dew. Dewdrops on spiders' webs, blotchy fat spiders poised in the middle, but no Helen. And this was the end of their land, the big clump of brambles that used to be Beauty's den; but, God help her, she wasn't going in there.

189

'Helen, Helen!' The rooks were flying in manic circles. She listened. She heard the wind in the tall trees, water dripping off a roof and a pheasant clucking in the field. Helen could have run into the fields. And then something went splash in the moat. The far end of the moat, the dark end, the deep end.

'Shit!' Tessa ran like fury, leaping over nettles and brambles, pushing herself through the bushes, and there was Helen, one leg in the water, shaking with fear, hanging onto a branch, the bank giving way underneath her.

'You stupid clot!' yelled Tessa, grabbing hold of her, but Helen was too scared to be helpful. Tessa thought they would both fall in the water. She tugged harder. Clothes ripped. She put both arms around her and heaved.

Tessa fell backwards with Helen on top of her and another section of the bank gave way, slopping into the water, but they were on firm ground. She pushed Helen off her and stood up. In the dark water she could see an even darker shape. Two-foot long and slow moving. It came to the surface momentarily and snapped. A pike.

Helen on the ground whimpered.

'Get up, you idiot,' said Tessa and Helen did. Tessa pushed her from under the trees into the open.

'I saw her, I looked out of my window and I just saw her . . .' mumbled Helen.

'Who?' But Tessa already knew.

'Beauty, I saw Beauty, she was there, outside, she was there. I thought she would get cold, she was in her nightie, she ran to the moat, I thought she might fall in, I went to save her . . .'

'Beauty is dead,' said Tessa, shaking her like one shakes somebody who is having a nightmare. 'She's dead, you clot, she's completely dead.'

But Helen looked more bewildered and crazed. 'She might fall in, it's dangerous to play by the moat, I'm always telling her, I wouldn't want her to hurt herself, I wouldn't want my baby to get hurt.'

'Oh, shut up!' Tessa pulled her back towards the house. Helen began sobbing.

Don and Dee-Dee ran out to meet them.

'A fat lot of use you were,' said Tessa.

'Is she all right?' asked Don.

'She tried to chuck herself in the moat and appears to have lost all her marbles, but apart from that she's fine.'

Dee-Dee tried to comfort her. 'Helen, Helen, it's me, it's Dee-Dee, it's all right, now, everything's going to be all right.'

'Why doesn't she come when I call her? She's so naughty, she always runs away, she won't listen to me.'

Don looked despairingly at Tessa, who shrugged her shoulders. He ran his hands through his hair. 'What on earth do we do?'

'God knows,' said Tessa.

They managed to get Helen inside and up to her room. There was Beauty's bed as if she'd just bounced out of it, the new school clothes waiting on a chair, the toys she had been playing with; it was eerie and horrible. Tessa wanted to run away. Dee helped Helen back to bed. 'Go to sleep, Helen, try to rest.'

'I'm so worried about Beauty, she might hurt herself, I'm so worried.'

'We'll look after Beauty, won't we, Don, won't we, Tessy?'

'Oh, of course.' Don tried to sound cheerful.

'We're your friends, Helen, you're safe with us, try to rest now.'

'. . . But I'm so worried . . .'

Eventually Helen sank into a sort of stupor. They left her and sat in the breakfast room. This was much worse than the accident, or Jack not being found, or anything.

'I've got to go to work today,' said Dee-Dee hopelessly.

'Don't you dare leave me with her,' said Tessa.

'It's lack of sleep, that's what it is, lack of sleep,' said Don.

They sat there for a long time; upstairs there was no noise.

'I suppose,' said Don, 'that we'll have to call the doctor.'

'I suppose we will,' said Tessa.

'And we'll have to tell Marjorie, too,' said Dee-Dee. 'Yes, we'll have to do that too.'

A few days later Marjorie came. She strode across the courtyard and knocked loudly on the porch door.

'Well, is she ready?' Marjorie looked older and harsher than when Tessa had last seen her. Susan was with her.

'We've packed all her things.' Dee-Dee pointed to a pile of boxes.

'She won't need them, not where she's going.'

'Shall we keep them?'

'Do what you like with them, burn them.'

'But there's Beauty's things too.'

Marjorie didn't answer.

'Hello, Mummy,' said Helen in a flat voice.

'Hurry up, we mustn't waste time,' said Marjorie.

Susan looked at her uneasily. 'Come along, Helen.'

'Where am I going?' asked Helen.

'Oh, we told you,' said Dee, trying not to cry. 'A nice place where you can have a rest and be quiet for a little bit.'

Helen padded to the Range Rover like a sleepwalker; Susan sat next to her.

'We'll come and see her,' said Don. 'Hmm, perhaps you could tell us where it is?'

Marjorie regarded the remaining occupants of St John's with disgust. 'I don't think you have any right to know.'

Then there were three. Don, Tessa and Dee-Dee, back to the beginning. But it wasn't like the beginning. There was no hope, no fun, no optimism. Helen's boxes still waited in the corridor. Don tried to contact Marjorie several times, he even went round there, but the Marsh-Warrens wouldn't tell him where Helen was.

'What shall we do?' asked Don at supper, but this was asked too

192

often to warrant an answer. What shall we do about Helen's things, about the truck needing money spent on it, about the leaky roof, wood for the winter, Tessa working flat out and barely coping, about them all feeling so sad.

'What shall we do?' Don stirred his soup, vegetable soup for three days running.

A week after Helen had gone. Four weeks. Soup, stale bread and cheap cheese. Helen's room empty, her things in the corridor. November was wet and cold and foggy. In the day, Don and Dee were in Norwich. Don was looking for work now, half-heartedly, but he was looking, and Tessa was struggling in the gardens. At night the wind boomed down the chimneys.

Don in the solar in the big carved bed. Through one door was Tessa alone in her room and through another door was Dee-Dee.

Then on a Sunday, on the week of the first frosts, all of them up late because it was warmer to be in bed, sipping porridge in the breakfast room, Dee-Dee said, 'I can't stand it.'

'Try more honey,' said Don.

'No, I mean here, it's so empty. I hate it.'

'We won't find more people in the winter,' said Don.

'Everywhere echoes.' It was true, footsteps could be heard right through the house.

'It's all right,' said Tessa.

'Oh, Tessy,' Dee-Dee was quiet for a while. Somewhere in the house a door creaked. Don ate more porridge.

'I'm going to move into Helen's room,' said Dee-Dee suddenly.

'What if she comes back?' said Tessa.

'She won't, I know she won't, you don't think so either . . . It's a big room, and it's warmer than above the dairy, it's got a big fireplace, and you could have my room, Tessa, and do your paintings.'

Tessa was thoughtful. 'Helen won't come back, Marjorie won't let her.' And they were silent again.

'It would be nice to have all the house . . . used,' said Don. Nobody had been near Helen's room since she left.

'I'd like a studio,' said Tessa; 'I'd still sleep in my room, though . . . I could do a large painting . . .'

'You could all come and have tea with me,' said Dee.

'Yes, yes, this is excellent!' said Don. 'We don't need anybody else, we managed before, we can do it again, spread ourselves out, quite right.'

'And I could put comfy chairs up there, and a nice carpet and do sewing and knitting.'

'I could paint a mural,' said Tessa.

And they rushed over to Helen's room to discuss it all, bookshelves, cupboards, wallpaper, and they were so excited they didn't want to remember they had no time or money to do any of these things.

'We could have music evenings, soirées,' said Don; 'Miss Deirdre Stallard requests the pleasure of your company,' and Dee-Dee laughed and so did Tessa and they laughed louder and louder, and there was Helen's empty bed and Beauty's . . .

'Let's go out,' said Don; 'let's go to the pub and have lunch, all of us, let's go now.' And they ran down the stairs like children. At the bottom in the corridor was a pile of Helen's things.

'What shall we do about them?' said Don, exasperated.

'Burn them,' shouted Tessa.

'Oh, Tessy, we can't.'

'We can.' And they did.

They put the boxes in the courtyard and Don poured over a jerrycan of petrol, lit a match and it went woomph. They watched for a while, giggling. The heat was terrifying. 'Let's go now,' said Tessa.

When they came back, full up with lunch and slightly drunk, there was a soggy black heap in the courtyard. They stood in the drizzle and stared at the remains; a charred shoe, Beauty's, a sleeve of a jumper, Helen's, a melted clock, half a book, smouldering.

194

They weren't excited any more.

'It's horrible,' said Dee-Dee and burst into tears.

'What's done is done,' said Don.

'I'll get rid of it,' said Tessa and went to find the wheelbarrow.

Chapter Twenty-one

Tessa in the great hall stood up and stretched herself. It was midday; the help would come at two. I could go now, she thought, out of the door, down the lane, down the road, away. But not this time. She picked up her sketchpad and left the great hall. A last glance at the church windows and the shadows on the stone floor and the brightness of the day outside. Then the door shut.

Across the house, right across it to the breakfast room and up the other stairs, the winding ones, to the guest-room, Dee-Dee's room, her studio. This room was at right angles to the rest of the house. She could see the courtyard and the porch and at night the light from the windows fell onto the courtyard.

It was never really a studio, she never had enough time, but sometimes she would come in and lean on the window-sills, as she was doing now, and look along the length of the house. She did start a large picture, supposed to be the Hall in afternoon light, all glowing and golden, but it became formless and darker, and darker still, black and red like sunset in storm clouds or coals in the fire, burst open and bleeding.

* * *

Cold November, colder December, thick frosts and the loo froze. Wearing coats all day, and jumpers and long johns, but never warm, not even hugging the Aga. Tessa alone at St John's. It would be warmer in the gardens, but there was little to do; the ground was as solid as steel. Thin vegetable soup and week-old bread – Don got it free from a baker's in Norwich – and the sack of rice was nearly empty and all the wood was damp and rotten.

Tessa was going to see her parents, a pre-Christmas duty visit.

'How long are you going for?' asked Dee-Dee at breakfast. Tessa was stuffing clothes into her rucksack.

'Oh, about a week.' Her father was an invalid now and her mother liked to use Tessa's visits to explain how miserable her life was.

'Give them my love,' said Dee. 'And mine,' said Don.

They had all been invited to George and Hetty's for Christmas. It would be the first Christmas away for six years but it would save money.

Tessa walked down the lane. Everything was white and icy. Looking back, as the road turned towards Bungay, the Hall wasn't made of stone but was a sugar house on a cake, delicately frosted and impermanent.

After the second day in London she woke in the frilly nylon bedroom. Downstairs her mother was frying bacon for Tessa; she didn't understand the meaning of the word 'vegetarian'. Tessa had been dreaming about Beauty in her den and the wind on the beach and something important she had to say to Jack but she couldn't remember what it was.

'You're up very late,' said her mother as Tessa sat down; 'it's all right for some who have nothing to do, but others have, plenty to do, especially when there's an invalid in the house.'

Upstairs her father was taking his morning walk to the bathroom; it took him about ten minutes.

'Here,' she handed Tessa a plate of bacon, eggs, kidneys, bread and tomatoes, all fried. Tessa grimaced. 'It's good food, and it costs money, some of us have standards we like to keep up.' Her father shuffled along the corridor.

Tessa nibbled the fried bread; her mother poured a cup of strong orange-coloured tea. At St John's, Dee-Dee would be making porridge and whole-wheat toast. The red sun in a frosty sky. The lapwings in the fields. Her father shut the bathroom door.

197

'So . . . you're sponging off the Bells for Christmas.'

'They invited us.' Tessa ate half a tomato.

'When you and that husband of yours sort yourselves out, chance'll be a fine thing, and that Deirdre . . . live in a decent place like decent folk . . . and I didn't tell you Mrs Doyle's coming today for coffee so you'd better smarten yourself up.'

Tessa wiped her hands on her jeans. Upstairs her father was coughing in the bathroom.

'There's no need,' said Tessa, 'I'm going.'

Her father's parting speech about duty and responsibility, delivered in a hoarse voice, left Tessa in a black mood. It took her nearly all day to hitch to Suffolk. By the time she reached St John's it was already nightfall. The Hall was dark and empty; the Aga was down to a few embers. Don had Dee-Dee must have been out all day. Tessa built up the fire and stayed by it, trying to warm herself. The frosty weather had changed to drizzle and a gathering wind started to blow down the chimney. She was tired; she went upstairs to the studio and lay on the bed there. She was glad to be at St John's. She wondered when Don and Dee-Dee would be back.

At some point in her half sleep she heard the truck from across the fields. Good, she thought, and rolled over.

She woke up and it was about half-past eleven at night. She looked out of the window. The only light was shining from Dee's room. Don must have gone to bed. She opened the door into the solar. 'You awake?' she asked, but Don was not there. Tessa, in socks, walked the length of the house to the room above the hall.

The door was ajar. She pushed it open. Don and Dee-Dee were in bed together.

If she had caught them making love it would have been awful but they were lit by the bedside lamp, in nightclothes. Dee was knitting and Don was reading. Somehow the fact that they looked comfortable and blissfully domestic was even more painful.

Tessa walked closer and they started.

'Oh, Tessa, gosh.' Don was so embarrassed it was all he could say. Dee-Dee's face was going all shades of pink and scarlet. Tessa said nothing; she stood at the foot of the bed.

'I thought you weren't coming back for a week,' said Dee-Dee feebly.

'Is that supposed to make me feel better?' said Tessa.

'Oh, gosh, oh.' Don ran his fingers through his hair. They were scared of her when she was angry and she knew it. However, she didn't feel like shouting. What she felt was far more clear.

'Why didn't you tell me?' she said.

Don and Dee looked at each other. Don put his arm round Dee-Dee, who was in danger of bursting into tears. 'Oh Tess,' he said.

'No, don't give me that, you should have told me, I had a right to know. Anyway, how long has this been going on?'

Don stood up and wrapped his dressing gown around him. 'It's my fault, blame me, Tess, not Dee-Dee, anyway . . .'

'Shut up!' yelled Tessa with a force that silenced everybody. 'Just tell me,' she said softly now, but like a knife cutting, 'tell me how long, one day, two, weeks, what?'

It was Dee-Dee who spoke. 'Since Winterton.'

Don looked round at her quickly.

'She has to know, Don, we have to tell her.' Dee-Dee was quite firm about it.

'Oh, I get it,' and Tessa laughed sarcastically; 'sleeping after the picnic, was it, so fast asleep in the sand dunes, was it, sex in the sand dunes . . .'

'Tessa, don't,' said Don.

'Why not? You were fucking in the sand dunes . . .'

'Don't, please,' and Don was close to tears. Dee's had already started.

'Tessa, please, we've done something wrong, let's talk about it sensibly.'

'Sensibly? It was sensible of you to have secret screwing

sessions.' Her voice became menacing. 'You killed your best friend, Don, how does that feel, and Beauty, little fairy Beauty, was that sensible?'

'Stop it!' shouted Dee-Dee. 'It was an accident, you know it was, Tessa,' and she held onto Don who was visibly hurt. 'Don't you think we've been through enough?' she said.

'Oh, it's "we" now, is it? I thought I married him.'

Don wept, 'Tess, I'm so sorry,' but Tessa stood like a punishing angel. 'I'm glad you're sorry,' she said.

'Tessy, you're horrible, leave him alone, it wasn't his fault.' Dee-Dee looked brave enough to challenge her. 'You never paid him any attention, you ignored him, night after night, you didn't care about him . . .'

'How do you know?' And Tessa turned on her oldest friend.

'It was obvious, anybody could see it, all you wanted was your bloody garden. He was lonely, Tessa, he's so kind and nice and you never cared.'

Don wiped his face with the sleeve of his dressing gown. 'Tess, I'm sorry, but it did seem a bit like that.'

She almost softened. 'You should have told me, I hate underhand things, I hate deceptions.'

'That's a lie!' shouted Dee-Dee suddenly. 'I would never have started anything with Don if you hadn't had an affair with Jack.'

'What?'

'When I knew, I felt so sorry for Don and he never knew, well not until after Jack . . . went.' Dee was speaking rapidly now. 'I told him and you know what he said, he said "I'm not surprised, Jack was a splendid person," no recriminations, that's the sort of person he is.'

'I don't believe this,' said Tessa.

'Why lie about it now?'

'I couldn't stand him, I never had an affair with him . . .'

'Tessy stop lying, Beauty saw you in the garden.'

'She did,' said Don.

'What did she see?'

200

'She said she saw you with no clothes on.' Dee-Dee was blushing.

'We were sunbathing.'

'She said something else too, she said when Jack stood up he had a big willy.'

'Shut up!' screamed Tessa. 'What did Beauty know, she was a child, it was nothing, absolutely nothing. I hated Jack, you were the ones who thought he was bloody marvellous.'

'We loved him,' said Don simply.

Tessa stared at him and at Dee-Dee. She was burning with a cold fire.

'Let's try and sort this out,' said Don gently, but Tessa remained silent. She was breathing slow and hard.

'Tessy, don't stare like that, it's frightening!'

'Let's forgive each other, we've all been wrong,' said Don.

'Never,' said Tessa and left. She walked right across the house to her studio and locked herself in. Don and Dee-Dee followed her and banged on the door.

'Don't be like that, don't shut us out, talk to us.'

'Please, Tessy, please.'

But Tessa lay on the bed ignoring them as if they were buzzing flies.

'Oh, what shall we do?'

'We'll come back in the morning, we'll sort it out.'

They went away. Tessa lay in the dark. The wind and the rain rattled the windows. She was cold and tired but she couldn't sleep. She felt herself becoming colder until it seemed there was not a warm place inside her. Now, she was pure marble and ice and steel, sharp and clean and decided.

What was clear to her now was that Dee-Dee was right. She had ignored Don. She had locked herself away and been solitary and aloof and the next thought could have made her cry if she wasn't feeling so much like stone. She always thought Don would be there. She always thought she would just have to turn round and say 'Come on, then,' and he would be bouncing and smiling as usual. She hadn't realised just how far up a rutted track she had walked.

None of these thoughts softened her. Don and Dee-Dee being lovey and cosily domestic, she couldn't stand it. The more she thought about it the further away from them she felt. She knew she would never forgive them for being happier than herself.

At some point when the windy night became dawn she got up. She looked towards the hall but there were no lights on. Don and Dee-Dee were together. They were asleep, probably, waiting for her to come to them. She got dressed, Tessa quietly unlocked her door and went downstairs. They were waiting for her forgiveness, but she was pure ice, pure steel, she had no such quality left.

She opened the back door and stepped into the wet morning. Down the rutted lane the rain slashed her, but she hardly felt it, and onto the Bungay road, she didn't look back, and the road turned and turned again, and the Hall was gone.

CHAPTER TWENTY-TWO

Tessa at St John's walked across the house to the room above the hall. She opened the door. It was a pretty sitting room with pink furniture and pale pink walls. Of Helen's pain, of Don and Dee-Dee's and her own, there was nothing.

She went downstairs and outside to her car. She put her sketches on the back seat, but she wasn't leaving, not yet. Tessa, as she had done nineteen years ago, walked down the lane, but this time she wasn't icy and clear, she was confused.

The hot dusty day and the noisy combines and in the sky the white hanging clouds. She walked towards the church.

The hamlet of St John's was still tiny; one farm and two cottages in the shadow of the church tower. But in the field next to it was a modern house. A shiny copy of an old-fashioned one. It was brand new. The garden hadn't been planted yet. It was so ugly Tessa stopped to look. In the drive was a Lotus and a young smart couple on their way out. The man called out to the woman in a voice as flat as an Essex housing estate, 'Aw, come on, hurry up!'

Tessa watched them climb into their incongruous vehicle and speed up the lanes towards St James.

Watching them she felt the full weight of the years that separated her from this generation of shiny modern people where the countryside was an investment and history was something you found in a heritage centre. It made her feel sadder than ever.

But the church was as she remembered. Wallflowers grew on the church tower and in the graveyard the grass was uncut, speckled with willow herb and St John's wort. She waded through, past the grave of Molly's Charlie, and Molly, the

Hoskins, Becks and Palmers; and there it was, hiding in the long grass, a small white marble angel, in loving memory of Jennifer Marsh-Warren.

There was a bunch of dead flowers. Beauty, with daisies in her hair and juice down her front, whispering to something that could be called a doll, in the orchard at St John's.

'Oh shit,' said Tessa and began to cry, for after all Beauty had been her little girl as well. She went into the church and sat down. The church was musty and used only once a month. It smelt of bats, but Tessa was crying too much to notice. 'Oh Christ!' she said irreligiously. She had never believed in God. Tessa wept. They were all gone, everyone she had ever loved. Don, Dee-Dee, and all those muddled naïve people, for she had been so stern and proud and rigid, like St John's, and so cold. And Tessa felt herself slide over the edge, but she didn't care any more, and right down, beneath the brambles and the mud, to the deepest roots, and for a while she felt as warm as the earth itself. The earth where Beauty was asleep with her dark lashes on her cheeks holding a bunch of wild flowers.

The sun shone through the fragments of medieval glass in the dusty church and she went outside towards it. There was a man in the graveyard. She only noticed him because he was putting flowers on Beauty's grave. She went closer. He was small and shabby with faded scanty grey hair. He wore an old raincoat. He saw Tessa and smiled. 'Lovely day.' He had thick spectacles and a sunken face.

'Isn't it,' she said, not caring if he could see she had been crying.

'I come here every year, you know.' He squinted at her. He had a Lancashire accent.

'Do you?'

'Pay my respects every August Bank Holiday. I stay in a nice place in Beccles and come for the day.'

'Well, that's nice.' Tessa edged away. He looked like he hadn't spoken to anyone for weeks.

'You see, my son hasn't got his own grave, so I put my flowers here, you see, they never found my son.'

'Your son?'

'Colin. Drowned, he did, trying to save that little girl,' and he pointed to Beauty's angel.

'Colin?'

'Took me a long time, left home at fourteen, he did, and when Maureen died, my wife, I thought, I'll find him if it's the last thing I do, then three years ago I came to this very spot. Popular, he was, round here they called him Jack.'

'Jack?'

'Knew him, did you?' The man's eyes lightened behind his glasses. Tessa thought he was going to leap over and hug her.

'Sort of.'

'And wasn't he a fine person, left home at fourteen, he did, and we never saw him again, but he was too good for us, he was always the clever one. Quiet, he was, never said a word, but I thought, that one, he'll do well.'

'Where are you from?' asked Tessa, staring at him.

'Barrow in Furness. I worked for Her Majesty's post, you see.'

'Yes, I see,' said Tessa. 'Have you been up there?' She pointed to the Hall just visible between the trees. 'He used to live up there, you know.'

'Oh, I'm not going to bother them, they wouldn't want me to bother them up there.'

'He lived with a group of people,' Tessa said cautiously.

'So I hear, but they've gone too. I wouldn't want to bother them up there; I don't want to bother anyone. I leave my flowers and then I go to the pub. It's a nice place in St James. They serve a decent meal of an evening.'

'The George?' And Tessa couldn't help smiling.

'The George and Dragon. A real old-fashioned pub. The couple who run it come from Canvey Island.' He rearranged the flowers on the grave. Chrysanthemums. They would be dead in a few days. 'He was our only child, I always knew he would do well for himself.'

'I have to go,' said Tessa.

He shook her hand. 'Ted Fogget. Nice to have met somebody who knew our Colin.'

Walking back to the Hall, Tessa was laughing now. Jack, mysterious gypsy Jack, the invisible man, was really Colin Fogget, son of a postie from Barrow. She wanted to hug him.

As she crossed the moat, she paused as the sun glinted on the upstairs windows. But Jack was dead. Arrogant Jack, created by himself, Jack the hero, pretending to everybody until at last, with the waves and sucking currents and a frightened child round his neck, he couldn't pretend any longer.

In the courtyard was another car, and a young plump woman in a lilac tracksuit was locking the doors.

'You must be the help,' said Tessa.

'So there you are.' She had a round pleasant face and curly brown hair. 'Have you finished?'

'Yes, everything's finished,' said Tessa.

The help looked at her oddly. 'Did it go well?'

'Yes, it's fine,' and Tessa smiled.

'When is Mrs Hallivand coming back, did she say?'

'She's not coming back.'

'Oh?' The help was evidently curious, but Tessa didn't feel like explanations.

'I suspect she'll contact you,' she said.

'And Mr Hallivand?'

'I don't think he's coming back either.'

'Oh dear . . . Well, I thought something like this might happen.' And they both looked up at the stone front of St John's, as golden as the wheatfields.

'It's a shame,' said the help; 'it should have a family in it. My Nan said that before the war the farmer's kids and her were always playing in the gardens. Mind you, I wouldn't live here, it gives me the creeps. I wonder what will happen to it now?'

'I don't think it cares any more,' said Tessa.

As she drove away, she stopped on the first bend. St John's was surrounded by its trees in a field of harvested wheat. Combines worked up and down the rows. St John's was alone and solid and empty waiting for the next person to live out their life there. Nights of bitter cold with the wind down the chimneys and the windows creaking and echoes through the house; they'd have to be strong. And warm days of roses and hollyhocks and lemon balm and wormwood; they'd have to be appreciative. And spring days of apple blossom and cowslips, and autumn days, ripe pears and hawthorn, convolvulus in the hedge, lapwings in the fields, and the sternness, the oldness of the place . . . She started up her car. There was one person she still had to see.

Just south of Norwich was a village that wasn't a village any more but a commuter suburb, but people who lived there called it 'the village'. There were a few old houses; the rest were modern with drives and patios and mown lawns, and there was a Georgian house, not large but well-proportioned and 'well-presented', as estate agents say, set in a largish garden, and a drive that curled towards the front door. Tessa drove up here. In the gravelled space outside the house were two cars and a Range Rover. She knocked on the door. A young man opened it.

'Does Marjorie still live here?'

'Who? Grandma? She's on the terrace. Who shall I say it is?'

'Don't say it's anybody,' said Tessa.

Marjorie and Susan were sitting on sun chairs on a paved area at the back of the house; flowers fell in profusion out of tubs and large earthenware pots. Marjorie was asleep; she looked very much older, thinner and ill. Her hair was streaky grey. Susan looked very like Marjorie used to look. 'She wants to see Grandma,' said the young man.

'I'm Tessa from St John's,' said Tessa.

207

'Good God!' said Susan.

'Shall I make some tea?' said the young man, baffled.

'No, William, you'd better leave us alone. What do you want?' hissed Susan, gesturing for Tessa to keep quiet, but Marjorie opened her eyes.

'Oh, it's you.' She stared at Tessa distastefully.

'I've come to see Helen,' said Tessa.

'She's not here.'

'It's all right, Mummy, I'll get rid of her,' said Susan. She took Tessa up the other end of the terrace.

'You won't ever find her.' Marjorie's voice was thin and venomous.

'Do you live here now?' Tessa asked Susan.

'Yes, since Daddy died, we moved in to look after Mummy.'

'She killed him, the whole business killed him.'

'She's not well,' Susan said in a whisper, and then louder, 'Well, you'd better go then, as you can see, Helen's not here.'

'Animals, you lot were. Filthy animals and she was the same. She got what she deserved.'

Susan led her through the house and back to her car.

'God, she's bitter,' said Tessa.

'Yes, I know,' said Susan with the voice of somebody who had to put up with it daily.

'How is Helen?' asked Tessa.

'She's fine, she doesn't know any better.'

'Where is she?'

Susan sighed. 'She's in Heyton Hospital on Waveney Ward. I won't tell Mummy I told you. You'd better go now.'

'Thanks.' Tessa got into her car.

'Don't expect too much,' said Susan.

Heyton Hospital was north of Norwich. It was red brick, Victorian and vast. It had pleasant enough grounds with cedar trees. Tessa didn't like hospitals. She walked down echoing corridors looking for Waveney Ward. It took some time because most of the place was closed. Waveney Ward was a fifties extension tacked on the end of the longest corridor. It was the long-term ward.

Tessa walked in. There was a large day room with the telly on and various people sitting around not particularly watching it and looking like they were waiting for a bus that had long been cancelled. None of them was Helen. There was a smaller room with another group of people and what distinguished them from the occupants of the day room were that they were chatting and laughing. Tessa opened the door. 'Where's Helen Marsh-Warren?' she said. The five or so people all looked at her. 'If it's a nice day she'll be outside, she usually is,' said somebody.

'She doesn't get many visitors,' said somebody else.

'Where outside?' said Tessa.

Nobody could answer that. 'Are you a relative?' asked a woman.

'Not at all,' said Tessa and left them. She crossed the day room past the telly and the lifeless occupants and pushed open the French doors to the garden.

Tessa searched the gardens. Nobody looked at all like Helen. Then she spotted a fat woman in a headscarf sitting on a bench looking away from the house towards the countryside. Tessa moved closer. The face had lost its features in fat but the resigned passive attitude was definitely Helen's. Tessa sat next to her. The Helen person wore a shapeless jumper, a flowery skirt and long socks. Her hands were resting on her lap. Puffy fat hands.

'Hello,' said Tessa.

Helen glanced round with the same nervous furtive glance Tessa recognised from years ago. 'Is it dinner?'

'No, it's not. I'm Tessa.'

'Tessa?' Helen frowned. She looked like somebody trying very hard to remember a vague dream.

'Tessa, Dee-Dee, Jack, St John's . . . we used to live together.'

'In the Hall? With my little girl?' and Helen stopped. 'She's not here, she'll be back later.'

'She's dead,' said Tessa. A look passed across Helen's face as if she had been found with a packet of biscuits in her hand. It was the nearest Tessa had got to the old Helen.

'She went away,' said Helen slowly; 'she went away . . .' Then all her hopelessness seemed to flood her. 'But she'll be back later, and we'll have tea.'

Tessa sat on the bench with Helen for a long time. Tessa looking at the view, the fields, the clouds and Helen just sitting.

'Is it dinner?' asked Helen.

'I was never very pleasant to you,' said Tessa. What did it matter what she said now. 'I'm very sorry about Beauty, and you, I'm really sorry, Helen.'

'Beauty's my little girl.'

'. . . she used to play in the orchard . . .'

'She's always hiding, she won't get dressed.'

'. . . in her gumboots . . .'

'She plays in her den, then I'll make some tea, then it'll be bedtime,' and Helen smiled. 'Is it dinner now?'

'Yes, it probably is. I'd better go.' Tessa stood up.

'Dee made bread,' said Helen as if she'd just remembered, 'and Tessa did the garden.'

'I'm Tessa,' said Tessa and Helen looked at her very hard.

'We went to the beach,' she said, 'and Jack took her swimming.' And she stopped and opened her mouth as if she didn't want to say the rest. She shut her mouth and frowned and put her hands on her lap. She gave Tessa one quick glance and in it was enough cunning and awareness to make Tessa wonder how mad Helen actually was.

'I'm going to go now,' said Tessa and Helen looked ashamed and hopeless. 'I don't blame you,' said Tessa; 'I suppose it's not that bad here.'

'I like it here,' said Helen in a whisper.

'I could come and see you again, would you like that?'

Helen nodded, slowly but she was agreeing to it.

210

'Goodbye then,' said Tessa.

'We could have dinner,' said Helen with a nervous smile.

Back in her hotel room in Bury she went to bed early. She was driving to Bristol tomorrow, but lying there in the bland hotel bedroom she felt something she hadn't felt for a long time. She felt almost happy.

Going home, across England, where every road seemed to be newly widened and every town had a by-pass. Roundabouts, lorries and car after car on the rolling road from the monoculture fields of the eastern counties to the greener fields of black and white cows and dumpy sheep.

She was thinking of Don and Dee-Dee. They didn't last much longer at St John's. It was impossible, they couldn't cope. Don had to sell Geoffrey's gift to him, his wonderful paradise. In that time of pain and despair he still managed to negotiate a handsome sum. They now ran a country-house hotel somewhere in Yorkshire, Dee-Dee cooking buns and pies and scones for cream teas, and Don a New-Age businessman. They were blissfully happy.

Tessa's Morris rattled towards Bristol. She wasn't bitter about them now. She didn't begrudge them their satisfied way of life or their three children. If she were to visit them they would run out and smother her with affection. Don and Dee-Dee, forever loving and generous, but she wasn't quite ready for that yet. She now knew the reason for her bitterness and jagged feelings. It was not losing Don that had been so hurtful, but losing Dee-Dee.

Tessa faced this as she approached the outskirts of Bristol on the M32, and she wasn't shocked or rebellious or angry but sad, really. She had held onto Dee-Dee for so long. Dee-Dee was a part of her, like a foot or a leg. Losing her was like losing a part of herself.

Now she could see her own house on the high hill in Totterdown, clinging onto the edge, and this sight comforted her. Here was her life. She turned into the street with scaffolding and skips outside several houses. This was an up and coming area. This pleased her too. She had refused all money from the sale of St John's. Her house was her achievement.

She opened the front door. The house was quiet and sparse and smelled faintly of linseed oil. She went straight to the kitchen and opened the door onto the garden. A tiny city patio garden but bursting with flowers and late roses up trellises. The early evening air blowing up from the city smelled of car fumes and diesel from the railway but underneath was the fresh growing smell of her garden. Her garden. Her house and her paintings.

She went upstairs to her studio. Black and red canvases stared at her from the wall. Oh, they were all right, but she didn't feel like that any more. She had an idea for a new picture, something golden like a sun-freckled face or a wheatfield, and blue and white like a June sky, and pink like someone lying on the grass in a rose garden. A new picture, and she would give it to Dee-Dee. After all these years it could be the first gesture of reconciliation.

Tessa took out all the sketches of the last two weeks and lined them round the studio. Fleming Hall, Hengrave, Kentwell Hall, Lavenham, Heveningham, St John's. She was pleased. Stone walls and great trees, beautiful gardens and topiary. A few days in August. A few moments of her life preserved. But nothing is permanent, she thought, and imagined a great wind, like the hurricane, hurling down the trees she had painted, flattening flowers, bursting glass in orangeries and even St John's, so solid and sturdy, could be damaged.

And in her studio, at the top of a house looking over Bristol, she felt this, the changing, ever changingness, of everything. Tessa looked out of her window at the city, at the setting sun glowing the sky deep red. Black rain clouds blew in from the west, falling in bands across the sky. The city buildings were dark silhouettes, black on red, jagged forms against crimson. She stayed by her window watching. Slowly the sky became more indigo, slowly the clouds gathered and the crimson faded and it was night.

Nothing is permanent, thought Tessa, taking in each moment; nothing except . . . and now lights were coming out over the city, red ones, green ones, yellow ones, but they weren't just lights, they were people lights, from houses and cars, shining out of people's lives. And then she saw it, the light on Cabot Tower. High, high above the city, like a signal, telling her of the warmth and strength of it, of the continuity of it, the permanence of human love.